SACRIFICE OF THE SEASON

DARYL PARKER

BALCONY BOOKS

This book is a work of fiction. References to real people, events, establishments, organizations, or locales are intended only to provide a sense of authenticity, and are used fictitiously. All other characters, and all incidents and dialogue, are drawn from author's imagination and are not to be construed as real.

DEDICATION

This book is dedicated to those friends and family who have guided, supported, and inspired me along the way. You know who you are, and if you don't, this probably doesn't apply to you. Seriously, this book would have never been completed without the love and support of my wonderful wife Jenn, my sister Laura, the encouragement of the world's best parents, Ray and Diane, and the inspiration of my five incredible kids, Justin, Amani, Kami, Allison, and Ashlyn.

PROLOGUE

Dust motes floated through the sunlight in front of John as he studied the picture on the wall. It was a black and white photograph of Grandpa Jack among the ruins of an Egyptian pyramid, wearing a khaki suit, tall boots, a handlebar mustache and a pith helmet. He was seated in the center of two other white men and a dozen native workers. Without a speck of dust on his highly polished boots and a pistol hanging from a Sam-Browne belt, Grandpa Jack seemed a hard man; much harder than John had ever known him to be. Studying the details in the photo it was easy to imagine the adventures of that time, mummies and camels plodding through the sand in his mind. John started out of his daydreams when a muffled cough drifted down from upstairs. Just outside the window his mother was hanging laundry on the clothesline. *She's looking tired*, John thought to himself, *tired and sad*. Sadness seemed an everyday part of their lives lately, he thought, turning toward the stairs.

He stepped softly across the wooden floor and up the creaking stairs. Making his way up and around the landing to the top, John turned down the hall to the second door on the right. He stopped in front of the door and listened for a moment. There was no noise from within, so he tapped lightly, turned the knob and eased the door open.

"Grandpa?" A small lamp on a bedside table was the only light in the room, illuminating the sleeping form of Grandpa Jack. John moved across the room as quietly as he could and standing next to the bed, stared down at his grandfather. He could still recognize the hard man in the picture downstairs, hidden beneath a fragile, aged façade. Grandpa's bald, wispy pate shone in the lamplight, but it was still surrounded on all sides by thick dark hair, combed back and curling at the ends. His salt-and-pepper handlebar mustache was growing a little wild and long, as were his eyebrows. His skin was permanently tanned and finely wrinkled, like old leather stretched thin over his bones.

Grandpa Jack's hands rested on the quilted coverlet, knobby knuckles standing out above gnarled fingers while his chest rose and fell in shallow breath. As he slept, John stared at the face of the man who had meant so much to him.

John was only six when his older brother Matthew drowned while swimming in a rock quarry. Matthew's death devastated his parents, but when his father also died two years later in a mining accident, his mother almost lost her senses. With her husband and firstborn child dead she was overwhelmed with grief and barely able to take care of herself, let alone young John. That was when Grandpa Jack came home from his long travels abroad. He saved them, becoming the rock they could both cling to and start healing. John went everywhere with his grandfather, and over time, Grandpa Jack filled the hole in his heart left by the loss of his father and brother. He smelled like fresh cotton shirts, pipe tobacco and cologne, and John loved him dearly. Now at age fifteen, the black despair he had almost forgotten came back into their lives; Grandpa Jack was dying. His health had been declining over the last few years and he was virtually bedridden these past three months. His condition was grave, and the tension in the house was almost unbearable, taking a toll on both John and his mother.

Grandpa Jack started, squinting his eyes open and trying to focus on John. With a faint smile he reached out and patted the bed, inviting John to sit down next to him.

"Hello there, boy," he said, "Where's Gigi?" That was what he called John's mother, short for Georgia.

"She's outside, hanging laundry. Can I get you something Grandpa?" John asked.

"No, no. I'm fine." Grandpa Jack paused, looking around the room. His brows furrowed, and he looked back at John with those piercing blue-grey eyes that seemed to see everything beneath the skin. "How are you doing, son?"

John looked down at the blanket, "I'm okay. I just wish you felt better." Grandpa Jack lifted his hand to pat John's leg, the silence stretching out for a few moments, before Grandpa Jack said, "John, we need to talk, just you and me. About time you knew a few things. Here," he said, stretching out his hand, "help me sit up."

3

John grasped his grandfather's hand and stood, easing the old man into an upright position. Still holding John's hand, he sat there a moment, wincing in pain and bringing his other hand up to rub his forehead.

"Okay, okay," he said, pushing a pillow behind his back, and releasing John's hand.

"Ah...ahhhhhh..." He groaned as he leaned back, letting out a long breath as he settled into his new position. Opening his eyes again he looked at John, who had sat back down on the bed.

"I'm dying John. There's nothing anyone can do about that now, every man has his time."

Johns' eyes suddenly blurred with tears, and he struggled to keep from breaking down, so he just bowed his head and nodded in mute understanding. As his vision swam Grandpa Jack continued, "Okay, stop that now, I need you to listen to me. There's something very important I want you to do for me."

John looked up, cuffing away an embarrassing tear which had appeared on his cheek.

"There are things I need to tell you first though, things about our family that even your mother doesn't know. Maybe I should have told you years ago, I don't know, but I was here to look out for you and I thought I would have more time..." Grandpa Jack's voice trailed off and his eyes were staring at a point somewhere else in time. After a long moment, he shook his head and resumed, "Well, that plan is out the window now though, isn't it?" He frowned and asked, "What do you remember of the day Matthew died?"

John was dumbstruck for a moment at the question, coming as it did out of nowhere.

"I… I don't know, it's been a long time," he said.

"I know, but think back on it now, it's important. Matthew was twelve years old and a strong swimmer. He was swimming in a rock quarry, so there was no current to sweep him away. What happened?"

John cast his thoughts back to that day trying to recall his brother's death. He retrieved the scene, surprised at how deeply it was buried. He hadn't been asked too many questions about that day, the adults not wanting to cause him additional distress, and so, he had only told parts of the story before now.

"We were lying on a shelf of rock, right at the water's edge. It was late afternoon, and we were going to leave soon to get home for dinner. Most of the other boys were jumping off some high rocks about twenty yards down the shore from us," he paused, eyes glazing as he told the story.

"Yes, and what were you and Matthew doing?" Grandpa Jack prompted.

"Well, I knew Matt wanted to go swimming with the other boys, but he was staying by me because I couldn't swim well, I was too small. We were lying on our bellies on the rock, trying to scoop minnows out of the water with our hands while our shorts dried."

"Was the water deep where you were? Could you see the bottom?" Grandpa asked.

"It was shallow right next to the rock, but it dropped off sharply, and that part was really deep." Something pinged in John's thoughts, something that made him anxious. He found himself suddenly breathing harder and his heart fluttered in his chest.

"Then what happened, what did you *see*?" Grandpa Jack asked.

John shook his head a little and said, "I'm not exactly sure. We were lying there one second, and the next, Matt just...fell in." His heart pounded now, "I wasn't scared at first, but then he came up and..." John wanted to stop, he didn't want to continue this, but Grandpa Jack held him there, "And what, John? Did you reach out to him, was he hurt?"

"I don't know, he was trying to say something, but he got a mouthful of water and started choking." Even as he spoke the words, the scene replayed itself in his mind, and he saw the terrified look on his brother's face once more. Matthew's eyes were wide open and straining, his face a mask of fear as he choked and slapped the water. John remembered looking into the water and seeing Matthew's right foot firmly planted on the small rock ledge, but something else was attached to him. A shadow under the water pulled on his left leg. John lay there with his mouth open only a few feet away, but as he reached out for his brother, a hand, long and dark, detached itself from Matthew's ankle and reached up to grab the waist of his shorts. The forearm descended into the murk beneath Matthew's struggling form. John's chest heaved, and he felt his grandfather's hand on his arm, but the scene played on. Matthew's foot slipped off the ledge and he went underwater again. John could see him sinking into the depths of the green water, his mouth open in a scream and his hands stretching toward the surface, terrified eyes begging John for help. John was stunned, and could only stand there until his brother's figure started to fade. Then he screamed. He screamed and screamed, and the other boys came then, leaping and splashing into the water around him, diving off the rocks and kicking into the depths to rescue Matthew.

"I screamed for help, but it was too late. They couldn't find him." Grandpa Jack stared at him with wide eyes, his face full of pity and sorrow.

"It wasn't your fault," he said, blinking his eyes and squeezing John's hand hard. "I know what happened that day." He stared at Grandpa Jack in confusion. He had nearly been able to forget that day, pushing it so far back in his mind that it seemed more like a dream than a real event. He had never spoken about the thing in the water, assuming it was imagined. As he got older it was even easier to believe in the heart-stopping terror of that moment his mind had created a bogeyman he could hold responsible for his brother's death.

"They found Matthew's body a few hours later, two hundred yards away from the rock you were on. He was lying on the rocks, right at the waterline." Grandpa Jack's brow furrowed, and his jaw pulsed with a smoldering anger.

"There's no tide in a rock quarry, so how he got there was a mystery; how could his body have come out of the water to lie on the rocks?" Grandpa Jack paused and fixed John with his stare, "Matthew's death was not an accident," he said, his voice sinking to a whisper, "but thank God he was too old."

"What? Grandpa, what are you saying?" John asked, completely confused now. Grandpa Jack gave him another strange look, and reached up to remove a leather cord from around his neck. Hanging from the cord was a brass key, which he handed to John.

"Open my trunk and bring me the long wooden box," he ordered John, pointing toward the foot of the bed.

In a daze, John stood and walked to the trunk on the floor at the foot of the bed. In one part of his mind he thought, *I've always wondered what was in here.* He used the key to remove the large padlock, lifted the lid and looked inside. Lying on top of a pile of blankets and clothing, was a long box, made of some heavy-grained reddish wood. It was intricately carved on all sides and inlaid with mother of pearl, ivory, and silver. It was beautiful. John carefully picked it up and walked back, putting the box on the bed. Grandpa Jack took it and laid it on his lap, softly running his hands over the top and sides of the box.

"John, I'm going to tell you something, something I hope you will believe and are old enough to understand. I've wanted to tell you for years, but there were plenty of reasons to keep it to myself. I'll explain, but for now let's look inside the box."

Grandpa Jack slid a small section aside at one end of the box and retrieved a key, which he inserted and turned with a small click.

"I showed this to your father many, many years ago. He was a few years younger than you, but he knew about my work. Your mother doesn't and I want to keep it that way."

That puzzled John, because as far as he knew Grandpa Jack had never worked. He didn't have to; John's great-grandfather had been Thomas Rutherford, a very wealthy businessman and landowner who had made his fortune during the Industrial Revolution.

"And now I'm showing it to you, because I need your help." With that, Grandpa Jack turned the box and pushed it toward John.

"Go ahead, open it..." He watched John's face as he reached down and lifted the lid. Inside the box John saw bones, long and slender. It was a skeletal hand and forearm, with desiccated, hairy flesh still clinging to the bones, long gray nails curving wickedly. The five-fingered structure was disturbingly human, but long-fingered like that of a raccoon. John instantly gasped and stood up, backing away from the bed. The scene seemed surreal; Grandpa Jack sitting in bed in a pool of yellow light with the box open on his lap, questioning him about his brother's death. He tried to control his breathing as Grandpa Jack stared at him, an intent look in his eyes.

"John, this is what I want to tell you about."

1

FAMILY ROOTS

"I PURCHASED IT BECAUSE it was simply too good a deal to pass up. Unfortunately I came to realize I'm not in a position to capitalize on my investment." Clay said into his glass of scotch, glancing at Thomas.

"It certainly sounds interesting Mr. Brenner. Four-hundred and fifty acres you say?" asked Thomas.

"Four-hundred and fifty acres of beautiful country in the hills of West Virginia, with a town already established and iron ore in virtually every stone. Look, here is the report from Mr. Phillips, a geologist who has surveyed the property as recently as June." He pulled a folded paper from his coat pocket and slid it across the table. Thomas picked it up, unfolded it and read,

"The indications of ore are very great upon the surface; large blocks lie promiscuously upon the top of the ground, and nearly everywhere the surface itself would make iron. Extending almost down to the river is an opening exposing the bed of ore in almost one continuous mass, being only a few feet from the

surface to depths not yet ascertained. Other sections of this tract
contain mass quantities, being either found in small masses,
closely compacted and easily taken out with the pick, or in large
blocks with many tons weight."

Thomas couldn't help but raise his eyebrows a little
as he considered the note. Written only a few months
earlier, if this report was correct Brenner may have
something worth considering.

"What did you say the town was called?"

"Cobbs. I'm sure you haven't heard of it, and no reason
you should have." Brenner adjusted his spectacles and
continued, "It's a typical mining town, but thus far it
hasn't been fully developed. A little out of the way, you
know."

"Yes, I understand." Thomas stroked his mustache
thoughtfully. Clearly there was more to the situation than
Brenner was telling, but Thomas hadn't succeeded by
being timid when opportunity knocked. "I'm not in the
habit of making purchases sight unseen Mr. Brenner, but
you say the land title has been properly filed with the state
of West Virginia?"

"Oh yes, all legal of course, and the gentleman who sold
it to me owned it for most of the past 30 years. The War
was hard on him though, what with our boys raiding the
foundries. You can be sure there'll be no other claims to
the property to contend with."

Seize the moment Thomas, he thought to himself, *Whatever*
Brenner's financial troubles, no need to embarrass the man with

11

too many questions. "When you wrote me with your proposition you were asking eighty-four dollars per acre, including the mining rights, correct? While I recognize the potential value of the property, paying over thirty-seven thousand dollars for an isolated, minimally equipped and undeveloped iron mine seems a bit more than I would care to wager." Thomas had already made his decision and was merely haggling at this point. He would have to cash out some of his ongoing business ventures and probably obtain a line of credit, but with the Industrial Revolution in full swing, a productive iron mine would be very lucrative.

It was 1882, and Thomas Rutherford was a prominent and wealthy businessman in Philadelphia. He and his wife Elizabeth and their two children, Jack and Abigail, lived in well-appointed apartments and enjoyed all the perks and conveniences of city life. It was the time of the inventor and the entrepreneur, and Thomas was both. Important people recognized him when he entered a drawing room or the opera house, and that was why Clay Brenner had arranged to meet with him today. Not because Clay Brenner was particularly important, but because he had a business proposition to discuss.

After another half-hour of bargaining, Thomas was very happy when they agreed on seventy-two dollars per acre. That left Brenner red-faced and frowning, not thrilled with the final number, but the two shook hands and parted.

At home, Thomas broke the news to Elizabeth. She was accustomed to his quick business decisions, so learning he had invested many thousands of dollars in an iron mine didn't greatly concern her. His instincts had always proven sound and she trusted his judgment implicitly. Still, she was not prepared for what he asked next.

"What do you think about moving the children out to West Virginia?" He saw the shock on her face and hurried to explain, "Not permanently of course, but just to see things off the ground. I think it would do the children a world of good to spend some time outdoors, don't you?"

Of course, that was the key to Elizabeth's heart, the children. Jack was twelve and his younger sister Abigail only five, and Elizabeth doted on them equally. She wanted the best for her children, so, while house servants tended to the cooking, cleaning and washing, she managed their education. She taught them music and literature, and arranged other tutors for the more academic disciplines of science and math. Most evenings the family went to one of the many theaters or opera houses. Thomas agreed these things were necessary for proper social upbringing, but he also wanted the children to be exposed to more active pursuits. From time to time he would take them to see the horse races, or a rowing contest. A few times he even took Jack to watch the boxing matches, cheering the bloody spectacle from front-row seats. He approved of Elizabeth's decisions concerning the children's education, but perhaps they were both becoming a bit pampered. Thomas was certain a trip out to the country to breathe the fresh air would do them good.

It took a lot of perfume to mask the smells of a large city such as Philadelphia. The offal of open-air meat and fish markets running in the gutters, horse manure in the streets, the muddy banks of the Schuylkill river flowing past and the unwashed masses of workers who kept the city running all contributed to a metropolitan stench which modern sanitation had not quite resolved. Truth be told, Thomas thought the fresh air might do him good as well.

"What of their studies, Thomas? When do you expect us to move?" Elizabeth asked, at this point just buying time to consider what Thomas was asking.

"Well, of course it will still take some time to get the finances arranged. I'll have to move some things around and talk to Mr. Mattinger at the bank. Then I'll have to get the land title confirmed and transferred. I'll go down ahead of you and the children to get operations at the mine moving and the household set up for your arrival. It will probably be six months or more before I'm ready for you to come. You and the children will be there by Spring. Can you manage here without me for that long?" Thomas smiled and kissed the back of Elizabeth's hand.

"I'm quite sure I'll manage," she said with a smile of her own.

"Good. That should be enough time to arrange tutors for the children's lessons," Thomas said.

They spent the rest of the evening making plans and discussing the move. As they talked, their excitement grew at the thought of a new adventure. They had lived in Philadelphia since they had been married, over fourteen years ago. Maybe it was time for a change.

* * * * *

The Ba'ath were ancient when Man uttered his first sound. They shadowed his lonely steps through dark empty forests, spear in hand. When he learned to hunt and grow food they were watching, just as they were watching when he began scratching symbols in the dirt. They witnessed his rise to domination of the earth.

Millenia passed as humans fought for survival in the savage dawn of time. Throughout these struggles Man was aided by the Ba'ath, who presented him with knowledge and power; the gift of fire, for example. Primitive and wary, Man eventually came to understand the Ba'ath were divine; special envoys from the Creator. Their charge was to teach, offering their wisdom and magic to help humans prosper and flourish against the harsh conditions of the world.

- From the Book of More

2

NIGHT TERRORS

A THREE-QUARTER MOON shone down on the forest, a crisp pale light in the autumn darkness. There were no clouds and the rainbow prism of the moon's corona pulsed like a heartbeat, overpowering the glittering background of stars. Filtered through the trees, only the occasional clearing allowed the moonlight to illuminate the forest floor. The lives of small animals were playing out tonight as they had for eons; the fox and the hare, the owl and the mouse. It was still warm enough for some insects to be out and the cricket's chirping added to the rustling leaves and creaking branches. One particular clearing had a game trail running through the center of it surrounded on both sides with tall grasses and scrub bushes. The wind blew in a sudden cold gust, and something changed. Every animal pricked its ears up and froze, listening. In the space of a few moments the entire forest held its breath; everything stood still and even the insect's noise died to silence.

Not complete silence though, because soft footfalls

could be heard moving down the game trail. Walking slowly, a small figure emerged from the eaves of the trees surrounding the clearing. It was a young girl dressed in a white nightgown covered by a blue, ankle-length robe and bare feet. Her curly auburn hair shone in the half-light as she walked toward the center of the clearing.

The little girl was named Catherine, and she smiled as she walked. In her mind, her eyes were filled with light, as if she were staring into the mid-day sun. She couldn't see, but her steps were confident and sure. She knew she wouldn't stumble or fall and even if she didn't know where she was, she was not afraid. She followed the music. It was so lovely, like a choir of angels in heavenly voice, growing faint when she dawdled, more breathtaking when she hurried. But now the music suddenly died to a whisper, even as she stepped along trying to catch it. She pushed on a few more steps before stumbling to a confused halt.

As though she were waking from a deep slumber, her senses began to register sounds, and smells. She recognized the hiss of the breeze through long grass and the moist scent of leaves and dirt. She shivered as a cool breeze blew on her skin. The light behind her eyes began to fade and her vision grew dimmer, until she could see it was dark, although the moon had risen. Clarity crashed into her like ice water, and she whimpered as she realized where she was; she was in the forest and it was dark. Catherine was only seven years old, but she knew about the dangers of the forest, especially at night. She heard frightening stories from playmates, they having heard them from their parents as well. Told amongst friends in the comfort of a barn full of farm animals and warm cheery lanterns it was wickedly thrilling, but this was something else altogether. How she had come to be here was a mystery, but all she wanted at this moment was to get back home.

She looked around trying to get her bearings, her heart racing and her palms sweating, despite the chill in the air. She was in a small clearing, tall grasses and shrubs thick around her. Trees surrounded the clearing, and the shadows under the boughs were thick and menacing. She had no idea which way home was, so she simply stood there shivering and terrified. Her quickened breath condensing in the air, Catherine felt horribly exposed with the glowing moon overhead, but she couldn't bring herself to move. Every shadow seemed to harbor some terror, just waiting for her to come closer. She wanted to call out for help, but her fear and instinct told her to be still and silent. She gave a little gasp at a scuffle of leaves in the trees to her right. She stared with wide eyes into the darkness. Just within the trees a pair of eyes stared back at her, shining with an eerie luminescence like that of a cat. *No, that's not a cat*, she thought, these eyes were pale blue. She ducked down into the grass, trembling and close to tears. Another scuffle, this time from a different direction, and she couldn't help the little whimper that escaped her throat. Tears welled up in her eyes.

Catherine had been raised to believe in the power of

prayer, that in times of trouble a person should ask God for help. She attended church with her family every Sunday and prayed before meals and bedtime. Reverend Fetch had once told her she was as pure and good as an angel. Catherine prayed now, fervently whispering the first thing that came to mind, *"Our Father who art in heaven, hallowed be Thy name..."*

There was a rustle of grass directly behind her and she squeaked as she whirled around, *"...Thy kingdom come, Thy will be done, on earth as it is in heaven..."* A figure stood in the grass looking at her. The prayer was forgotten as she stared at the grotesque creature. It was slightly shorter than she but obviously possessed of an animal strength. It had a thick-barreled body, while corded muscle ran the length of its abnormally long arms. With its legs bent akimbo and wispy black hair covering its dirty body, it looked very much like an odd monkey; except the face. Cloudy blue eyes, without iris or pupil, stared out of a stretched and grimacing gargoyle's face, projecting hatred and evil that Catherine, in the innocence of her childhood could never have imagined.

"No, no, no, please no..." she cried as she backed away. The creature stood still, but a leering smile broke upon its face, showing her a mouthful of widely spaced teeth, jagged and broken. The effect completely unnerved her and now she did scream; a loud, wailing cry of terror as she turned to run, coming face-to-face with the creature's twin. She shrieked even louder as it reached out for her. It enveloped her in its arms and she screamed hysterically, throwing her head back and trying to push away from that monster face.   Horribly fetid breath rolled over her, stinking of death and decay. Her hair was grabbed from behind and jerked violently as she was thrown to the ground.   From where she lay with her legs curled protectively, Catherine now saw four of the monsters. They were grinning and moved toward her making cackling sounds that reminded her of a crow. She realized they were laughing.

"No, no, NO, PLEASE!!" she screamed as they bent over to grab her limbs. She kicked and flailed, struggling with all her strength, terrified beyond the point of reason, but she could not resist them. Each of the creatures grabbed a limb and their strong, rough hands felt like leather over stone.   With their free hands they tore at her clothing, shredding her robe with long dirty nails and powerful fingers that ripped the cloth to pieces. In doing so, they scratched her many times and her body arced in pain as she continued to scream.

"HELP! Please, MOTHER! HELP ME!!" she sobbed and pleaded. They pulled her arms and legs until she was fully extended, and then pulled even harder. The pain was savage and Catherine cried, screaming without words. She had to stop for a second, panting, gathering her breath to scream again when something appeared above her face looking down at her. Through her tears and pain her wide eyes saw another creature, shaped like a man wreathed in smoke.   Roiling sooty-black clouds covered its' form, except nestled in the darkness where a face should have been were a pair of swirling blue eyes. She screamed again as loud and hard as her lungs would allow, but she couldn't take her eyes off the being as it leaned down toward her. The monkey-like creatures pulled on her body with renewed strength and she threw her head back, her scream becoming an animalistic shriek as her small arms were disjointed. The thing above her moved quickly and Catherine could no longer breathe as she felt its mouth clamp onto hers. Through the pain and the terror, her last thoughts were of her mother and heaven.

3

MOVING TIME

From THE WINDOW of the carriage, a profusion of
trees passed slowly by as the horses trotted down a well-
worn dirt road. It was past mid-day and the curtains had
been opened to allow the sweet June breeze to pass
through the coach. Lucille, his negro nanny, sat next to
Jack with his sister, Abigail, asleep in her arms. His
mother was slightly reclined in her seat, looking neat and
composed even as she tried to rest during the long trip.
Jack knew she was considered a beautiful woman and as
she sat there with her eyes closed, he thought she was very
beautiful indeed. He was told he favored his father with
his fair skin, blue-grey eyes and wavy dark brown hair
that almost reached his shoulders. Neither slim nor heavy,
Jack was an average boy of twelve.

It had been a little over eight months since Mother and
Father had announced the move to West Virginia. As
Father had explained in his letters, there were a few
unexpected delays in getting the mining operations
running smoothly, but now preparations for their arrival

were complete. Jack and Abigail were both thrilled at the prospect of moving out to the frontier, as they imagined Cobbs to be.

"Mother, how much longer before we arrive?" he asked. His mother opened her eyes, "Jack, please be patient and stop asking that question. I've never been there myself, but I'm sure it can't be much farther."

Jack knew he was pushing his luck, but they had been riding in the coach for over three hours after getting off the train in Mannington. John sat rocking back and forth, listening to the squeaking of the springs and the dull clip-clop of the horses' hooves on the dirt road. He longed to get out of the coach, so he risked testing her patience once more.

"Then could I please ride with the coachman Mother? I just want some air."

Elizabeth raised an eyebrow and pursed her lips slightly as she considered her son. It was warm inside the coach, so she conceded, "All right then, but mind you don't make yourself a nuisance, and we will not be stopping again until we arrive. I'm just as eager as you to see our new home." She lifted her hand and tugged on the bell rope, signaling the coachman to halt. Jack heard the coachman's command to the horses and the jangling of traces as he pulled back on the reins, stopping the matched team of four. The coachman clambered down and pulled open the coach door.

"Yes ma'am?" he asked.

"Sir, how much further to Cobbs?"

"Ma'am, we should be there in about two hours." Her brow furrowed momentarily in annoyance.

"In that case, may we take a short stop to refresh ourselves before continuing?"

"Of course, ma'am," he said, and reached down to unfold the steps. "I'll lay down a blanket and get the basket."

"Thank you," Elizabeth said as she motioned Jack out of the carriage. He didn't need a second prompting and jumped out of the coach without even touching the steps.

They had stopped on a long wide curve of road in a quiet little vale. To the east side, the hills rose quickly, blanketed in tall green trees swaying and creaking in the winds coming down the slope. The trees continued on the west side of the road where the terrain was almost flat, and by chance, surrounded a small clearing of short green grass. It was a beautiful setting and the shade provided by the surrounding trees kept the early-summer heat off. Elizabeth and Lucille climbed down from the coach and Abigail stirred herself awake. Blessed with natural curls, Abigail's golden ringlets framed her face as she rubbed at her eyes. Lucille put her down and the precocious five-year old yawned and stumbled over to Jack, automatically taking his hand.

"Mother, may we walk?" Jack asked.

Elizabeth nodded and waggled her finger at him, "Yes, but you are not to get your clothes dirty and do not wander out of my sight." She kissed them both on the forehead as they turned and raced toward the trees.

As they walked, Jack's senses were assailed by the many different sounds and smells of the woods. It was warm and fragrant with the pleasant sound of insects buzzing through the trees and the wind rustling the grasses. Jack had lived in the city his entire life, but he thoroughly enjoyed the new sensations of the outdoors. The air was fresh and wholesome here. In Philadelphia there were too many competing odors for the senses to separate and it was often unpleasant. Here, Jack breathed deeply, savoring the scents of unknown flowers and plants growing wild in the field.

"Jack, look!" exclaimed Abigail, pointing into the grass.

A large grasshopper gripped a hay stalk, big eyes looking at them. The grasshopper clearly knew they were there and merely waited to see what they would do next. He wondered at the armored construction of the insect and reached for it. The grasshopper instantly snapped into the air, legs straightened and wings unfolding to fly several yards away before once again landing in the long grass.

Abigail squealed with delight, "Catch it!" and they were off, chasing first one grasshopper then another around the field. Jack caught several and held them out to Abigail, who smiled and let him put them in her palm before the insects again snapped away into flight. There were also butterflies and dragonflies, and the children were both having a wonderful time. Jack spotted a large grasshopper at the very edge of the field, right at the tree line.

"Abby, look at that one, he's a giant! Come on, we'll show him to mother," he turned and winked wickedly at her, "and Lucille." Abigail smiled back and they crept toward the insect.

As Jack got nearer, the grasshopper took off, flying into the trees. Jack kept his eyes on the insect, following it as it came to rest on the trunk of an elm tree. It wasn't until he stalked closer that he heard the gurgling sound of running water and he looked out into the trees to see a small stream winding its way through the forest. In Philadelphia, the only significant bodies of water Jack had ever seen were the two rivers; the Delaware and the Schuylkill, which ran past the city in wide, muddy rushes, smelling of fish and the other leavings of a dense population. This was something completely different; a beautiful little stream, no more than thirty feet across with deep clear water. He heard Abigail walking through the grass behind him and he continued down to the water's edge.

As he stepped down onto the narrow pebble shingle of the stream bank, tiny little forms darted through the water, and off to his right there was a loud plop as something jumped into the stream. It was wonderful, beautiful and pure, teeming with life and soothing to the soul as it babbled. The water looked to be only waist deep at best, and he leaned over, staring into the depths to search for the creatures that lived there. In the shallower spots, tiny lobster-like creatures with armored tails and pincers, scooted backwards from rock to rock. Miniscule minnows schooled around, their heads all pointing in his direction, assuring him they could see him as well. Whenever he made a movement, the cloud of minnows would vaporize, then reform a second later to resume staring at him.

He squinted through the prism of running water, to discern the shadowy forms of rocks and branches resting on the bottom. The sunlight coming through the trees glinted off the water and created a mirror-like effect, and Jack studied his reflection. He found a long stick, intending to probe the bottom, and he pushed it into the mud, sending the minnows to the far side of the stream as he poked around. While he explored the bottom, his own face looked back at him out of the water. The current made him look odd and distorted, like a stranger. Even as the thought occurred to him, Jack looked up to see... something...standing next to the base of a tree on the far side of the stream. It was amazing he even noticed it, as it seemed to be covered in a profusion of leaves and grass, but perhaps the two light-green eyes drew his attention. He couldn't have said what kind of creature it was, because in the blink of an eye, it had vanished. He was still staring at the vacant spot, when a sudden piercing scream startled him.

Abigail stood a few yards away with her back to him, looking at the ground, and her high-pitched scream continued unbroken. Momentarily frozen, Jack heard a feverish rattling noise and saw his mother, the coachman and Lucille had already leapt to their feet and were rushing toward them. Realizing Abigail was in danger, he quickly jumped out of the streambed and ran to her side just in time to see a fat rattlesnake, it's dangerous viper's head raised and waving. At the same instant it struck, Jack grabbed Abigail by the shoulders and pulled her to him, then turned to hustle her out of the trees. They quickly moved toward the coach, even as he kept his eye on the snake making its escape into the brush.

"Abigail!" his mother cried as she flew across the clearing. She swept Abigail into her arms and began frantically looking her over. Jack noticed the coachman had pulled his revolver and stood ready. Abigail sobbed, while Lucille also inspected Abby's limbs, looking for telltale signs of damage.

"It was a snake, but I don't think it bit her." Jack said, hoping he was right.

"I'm all right, Mother," Abigail sniffed, "it frightened me, but Jack saved me."

The look his mother threw him made Jack feel like anything but a hero, and without another word, she stood with Abigail, walked back through the clearing and climbed into the coach. Lucille frowned at Jack, "You supposed to look after your little sister, Mister Jack. Get on up there now."

Jack climbed up onto the coachman's seat, feeling miserable. He was certain his father would take him to task when his mother told him what had happened. The coachman closed the coach door, folded the steps and climbed back into his seat. As he picked up the reins and chucked the horses into motion, Jack saw the revolver sitting in the holster at his side. It was a fitting reminder of the differences between life in the city, and where they were now; a place where it was still necessary to strap a pistol to your side for protection.

As the coach rolled off down the road, the Watcher opened its eyes, detaching itself from the side of the tree and breaking the magic of its camouflage. The wide green eyes followed the coach around the bend as it padded down to the stream and eased in, disappearing in the water like a snowflake.

4

HOMECOMING

AFTER THE EXCITEMENT of that afternoon, the rest
of the trip went quickly, and they rolled over a small
bridge and into the little town of Cobbs as the sun slipped
toward the horizon. Cobbs consisted of one main street
and three other roads running out of town. Besides the
general store their father had mentioned in his last letter,
Cobbs had a saloon, a smithy, a dry goods store, a few
other small shops, and the offices of his father's mining
company. Several homes stood just off the main road in
no particular order and others were built along the roads
branching out of town. As they rolled through the town
people stopped and stared at the shiny, black lacquered
coach with brass lamps and the unfamiliar boy sitting
beside the driver. Some of them politely looked away if
Jack saw them staring and some of them nodded or waved
in greeting. As the driver made a right turn at the end of
the main street, Jack could read the large letters painted on
an office window: Rutherford Mining Company. There
were curtains in the windows, but no lights were lit, so it

appeared vacant at this moment. The road they had turned onto ran straight for about a half mile, right into the entrance of a large Victorian style home. Jack knew they had reached their destination and he called down to the cab, "Mother, I see our house! It's beautiful!"

Elizabeth poked her head out of the coach window. She covered her mouth with her hand, drawing a surprised breath and smiling as she took in the sight of her new home. It was lovely, just as Jack had said. Much larger than their apartments in Philadelphia, it had a vast fenced yard with a gated arch. The lane ran through the arch and up to the front porch of the house. There were several large trees in the well-trimmed front yard, and the lane was lined with flagstones. The wide porch railing was decorated with curving, stylized ironworks, the trellises were painted white and scaled slate shingles covered the roof. Although it was not yet fully dark, lamps had been lit at the entrance gate and along the drive leading to the house.

As the coach drew nearer, Jack saw his father walk out onto the front porch and he waved to him. His father returned the wave and stood waiting as the coach approached. Other people also came out to stand with him on the front porch, until a half-dozen or more people stood waiting. Jack's father walked down the steps to meet the coach as it pulled to a halt, while the coachman jumped down to unfold the steps and open the door for Elizabeth. She emerged smiling, looking radiant as always, "Mr. Rutherford, I am so glad to have finally arrived. The house is lovely!"

"I am honored that it meets your approval Mrs. Rutherford, as it is yours to do with as you please," said his father, kissing her hand with a smile. Both Jack and Abigail hugged their father and the whole family turned to the small crowd assembled on the porch.

"Elizabeth, these are my two foremen, Mr. Dalby and Mr. French." both men smiled and nodded politely, "Good evening, ma'am." Jack's father continued, "These other good people are my surveyor, Mr. Davis, the local magistrate, Judge Cole, and his daughter, Ms. Celia." Pleasantries were exchanged, with Mrs. Rutherford taking an extra moment to clasp hands and warmly thank Ms. Celia for coming to welcome her home.

"The rest are the house staff, which I'm sure you will come to know very well, but of course you are tired from your journey, so let us retire to refreshments." he said, motioning to the warm yellow lights spilling out of the doorway as the twilight deepened around them.

As they made their way into the house the servants swarmed the carriage, pulling down the baggage and unhitching the horses. Jack stepped through the doorway into a beautiful wooden interior, both pleasing and impressive. Mother excused herself to go upstairs to freshen up a bit from her trip, but within minutes she was back to socialize and entertain her guests. Lucille took both he and Abigail to go find the kitchen, where she whipped up a respectable dinner for Jack and Abigail. After he had eaten Jack wandered around the house, staying out of the way of the adult company, but with a huge contented smile on his face; this was their new home.

5

HUNTER & PREY

THE FIGURE SAT CROSS-LEGGED in the darkness. Shifting his weight slightly, he leaned forward peering into the shadows surrounding his hiding place. The soft bed of pine needles muffled all sounds of his movements and the charcoal-dyed linen cloak-and-hood camouflaged him from anything passing his place of concealment.

The lone pine tree he sat under was nestled in a section of the forest made up of various types of trees, although hardwoods predominated, mostly oak and ash. The early June air was filled with the multitudinous chirping of crickets, while small animals rustled the leaves hunting for insects, roots and berries. He patiently tolerated the swarm of mosquitos whining in his ears and the occasional ant or beetle crawling over his skin.

He had been waiting and watching for several hours, but he was not tired or discouraged. He knew his patience would be rewarded soon.

The hoot of a nearby owl sounded loud and haunting, all the more so for the silence afterwards. Every tiny creature froze in its' tracks, ears twitching to evaluate the threat before returning to their present task. With a slight puff of air the owl pushed off its' perch, wings stretching out to glide like a vengeful ghost through the trees. The man turned his head slowly, following the flight of the owl, but stopped with a sudden jerk, straining his ears and inclining his head to the right.

"I know you're there," he said softly, "might as well come on out." As he spoke he turned his head to look over his shoulder, while his left hand reached into his lap to grasp the length of iron chain lying there, taking it up with a soft metallic clink.

He saw a patch of softly swirling black smoke, so dark nothing could be seen within until the being he addressed stepped forward. As it stepped into the natural darkness of the forest, the smoke dissipated within a heartbeat and the two eyed each other. The cloaked man started to unfold his legs to stand, but the visitor held up a hand, "No, stay, I would speak with you here." He walked around to face the man, then gracefully settled himself on the ground.

The man watched, wary and alert. A moment of silence stretched out between them as they stared at each other, weighing and measuring.

"You've been gone a long time. The years have not been kind, perhaps you should come back," said the visitor, hands resting lightly on his knees.

The man held the chain in front of him and shook it, "I claim sanctuary and you got to honor The Compact."

The being raised an open hand saying, "Peace, of course I will honor The Compact." He looked around, quietly inspecting their surroundings. "Is this how you plan to spend your days? Skulking in the forest at night? Are you an assassin now? Return to us and this will not be necessary."

"No, I ain't going with you. I can't trust you. What do you want with me anyhow?"

The creature shook his head, "You should know by now why you are important to us. We will care for you and protect you. It is not safe for you to be on your own at this time. Come, was your time amongst us so terrible?"

"Amongst you? I wasn't amongst you, you abandoned me. I saw you less than a dozen times in all the years you kept me," the man hissed, shaking the chain again.

"And yet, you were kept safe, were you not?"

"Yes, and I'd be there still if I hadn't escaped. That place ain't for me. I won't go back with you."

"You should reconsider. Time is slipping through your fingers. Another twenty or thirty years, a blink in time, may be all that's left to you and then you will be no more."

"I'm not going and that's final. Now leave me be." The man turned to look out into the forest. The being studied his face a moment, saw the set of his features and knew this wasn't the time to press the issue.

"Well then, if that's your final word, I'll take my leave of you." He stood easily, a supernatural fluidity to his movements. As the being turned to walk away he hesitated, then turned back toward the man and said, "The

Compact will not protect you forever. Not against those who want to see you dead. Good luck in your hunting." With that, the creature turned away again and within two steps had shrunk into a pinpoint of light floating in the air. The man watched as the would-be firefly floated off into the night, winding its way through the trees.

The man tried to slow his breathing, which seemed so loud in the relative quiet of the forest. His hands were shaking, and his heart still pounded in his chest. He returned to his vigil, feeling his muscles unclench as he calmed himself. He put the encounter out of his mind as he got back to the business he was there for.

The sounds of the forest quickly returned to full pitch, and he quietly watched and waited. His prey finally appeared, shuffling and grunting through the forest leaves. Silently, he raised himself to his feet, wrapping one end of the chain around his left hand and lowering the remainder to its' full length. He mouthed a quick prayer as he gripped the links in his hand and stepped toward his victim.

Using all his stealth he snuck within a few yards of his target and stopped behind a large tree. Raising his fist above his shoulder he waited for the creature to move past him before he struck, swinging the chain with all his might. A squeal of pain sounded through the forest as he whipped his arm back for another strike, and another and another. The creature rolled in the brush and leaves squealing and crying in pain, flailing its arms in an effort to ward off the attack. After several more hard blows it lay on the ground, whimpering. The man quickly knelt on the creature's chest and threw a loop of chain around its neck. The beast went limp and the man threw on another loop before dropping the end of the chain into the leaves.

* * * * *

As the tribes of men grew more numerous they fell into direct competition with one another. The urge to dominate was critical to their survival, but it was also the black seed of all that has befallen them since.

First it was territory; the best hunting grounds and fresh water sources, but soon they competed for women, treasure and power. There were leaders in each tribe who pushed to assert their rights over everything within reach. The Ba'ath stepped in with guidance and wise counsel, and their intervention averted many conflicts, but there were too many factions. It was impossible to satisfy them all. After all, there were only thirteen Ba'ath to serve all the humans of the earth.

- From the Book of More

6

COBBS

THE NEXT MORNING, Thomas bundled the whole family into the carriage to take them on a tour of the little town. Although the town proper was within walking distance, it was a warm June day and being mindful of his wife's comfort, Thomas insisted they take the carriage. Neither Jack nor Abigail minded and they piled in as soon as the coach pulled around. Mr. Rutherford smiled and nodded his thanks to the coachman, Clive, who had unfolded the steps and now held the door open for Mrs. Rutherford.

Once they were all in and settled, Clive closed the door and pulled his lanky body up into his seat. With a quick snap of the reins he had the carriage moving and Jack and Abigail both leaned out opposite sides of the carriage to watch the scenery go by. Down the lane and out through the arched gate with the vine trellis, the carriage turned toward the main avenue. Trees lined both sides of the roadway, which kept the heat off as they trundled down the road, flashing through patches of light while the horses and the carriage wheels kicked up dust along the way.

Nearing the town Jack saw plenty of townsfolk walking about, greeting one another as they went about their business. As they approached the main avenue, Mr. French stood outside the mining office, wearing a bowler derby with a cigar pinched in his teeth and his hands in his pockets. Jack thought it funny his name was "French" while the man's brogue accent clearly proved him to be Irish. As Clive pulled the coach to a stop Mr. French waved at him to stay in his seat and stepped forward to open the carriage door.

"Good morning ma'am, children." He said, tipping his hat to them.

"Good morning, sir," said Elizabeth. She accepted his offered hand, stepping down from the coach and onto the wood-planked boardwalk facing the office. Thomas and the two children disembarked from the carriage and followed Elizabeth through the office door, also held open by Mr. French. Once inside, Jack looked around the office to see most of the walls had been covered with maps, charts, and other official looking documents. His father walked over to one particularly large and colorful map tacked on the wall. He explained to mother, "This is the map of our land purchase, all properly surveyed and registered." He used his finger to outline an impressive patch of territory.

"This is Cobbs," he said, pointing to an area bordering the property to the east. Jack had studied geography and had seen many maps, so he recognized most of the elements of cartography, like the navigator's compass in the upper right-hand corner of the map.

"We've started shafts here, here, and here," he said, thumping the map with his forefinger each time.

"In a little while we'll take the coach up to see the operation if you'd like," he said, looking at Elizabeth. As she smiled and nodded he turned back to the map and continued, "Thus far the mines have turned out some iron ore in good quantity, but both Mr. Dalby and Mr. French here assure me we've only scratched the surface. There are also signs that other types of precious metals may be in the area as well. If necessary, I am prepared to purchase another 200-acre parcel here," he said outlining another area adjacent to the first. Jack saw his mother's eyebrows arch in surprise. Apparently this was a development father had not discussed with her, but he pressed on, "Even so, with the demand for iron and steel increasing it's likely we will see a handsome profit on the ore we turn out," he finished, looking at Elizabeth with a smile. "Oh, and you may be interested in this," he said as he switched his attention over to another complicated looking chart posted on the wall. "These are the results of a test carried out using sulphur, iodine, and carbonate. They indicate..." and that's where Jack got lost.

His father continued on for several minutes, during which his mother paid polite attention, nodding her head and asking simple questions, but Jack couldn't even pretend to be interested. He noticed Abigail was in the same boat, yawning and shifting her weight from one foot to the other, bored to tears.

His father paused for a second, allowing his mother a moment to appreciate his explanation, and Jack jumped in, "Excuse me, Father," he said.

"Yes Jack?"

"Can I go look around? I'll take Abby with me. We'd like to see the town." He looked from one parent to the other.

Mr. Rutherford understood right away. "Of course," he said, "but stay on the main street so we can find you when we're ready to leave."

"Yes sir," Jack said, and taking her hand, he and Abigail scooted out the door. *At last,* Jack thought, looking up the main street and trying to decide which side to walk first. For no particular reason he moved to the right, and they began making their way past the shops and storefronts. People were riding up and down the street on horses or drawn carts, and it seemed there was a lively bustle about the place. The first shop they passed was a store that sold tobacco goods. An older man sat on a stool on the boardwalk, humming to himself while he braided some leather strips in his lap. He had silver hair, and a matching bushy mustache drooped down both sides of his mouth. His deeply tanned and lined skin, and the sturdy material of his clothing made him seem rough and hardy, if a bit worn. His eyes were a dark brown under thick eyebrows and stood out well against his complexion. The man eyed them as they approached and stared as he reached down to pick up a mason jar and take a great long drink. Jack could smell the wonderful aroma of tobacco leaves hanging in the shop, which were visible through the front window. It seemed the entire ceiling was covered as well as the walls. The man still watched them approach as Jack said, "Good day, sir." It was merely a polite greeting and Jack had intended to keep walking, but the man abruptly smiled and said, "Good day to you son, who's this pretty little lady?"

Jack stopped and said, "I'm Jack Rutherford, and this is my sister Abigail. My father is Thomas Rutherford, he owns the mines."

"Is that right?" the man said dryly.

Jack realized how pretentious that must have sounded and continued hurriedly, "We just came into town with my mother yesterday."

"Pleased to meet you Jack, I'm Tom Shaw," he said, extending a hand. Jack shook his hand, very impressed by this cowboy figure with the strong handshake. "And you, Miss Abigail, are the prettiest angel I've seen around here in a long, long time," he said as he took her hand and shook it also. Abigail smiled and curtsied, looking well pleased at the compliment.

"We're just having a walk around the town, trying to learn our way about."

"Well, there's no way to get lost in Cobbs, but don't let me hold you up," he said, still smiling.

"Yes sir, nice to meet you, Mr. Shaw," Jack said, as he bobbed his head and pulled Abigail along behind him.

As they continued down the walk Jack glanced back to see Mr. Shaw still watching them. A little strange perhaps, but he supposed they didn't get many new people here in Cobbs. He shrugged inwardly and turned his attention back to their inspection.

A beautiful saddle and leather hat were displayed in the window of the next shop, and they spent a few minutes strolling through the place, running their hands over the tooled leather pouches and chaps, and sniffing the fresh scent of newly oiled and polished boots.

The general store was next, which was larger inside than it seemed from the window, and contained an impressive variety of goods. There were tools of all sorts hanging from the rafters and stacked in barrels, along with numerous bins of hardware items, the uses for most of which Jack had no idea. Canned goods, bags of flour, spices, coffee, blankets, spurs, pickaxes, lanterns, nails, and so on.

Abigail tugged on his sleeve, and pointed to four or five glass jars with assorted candy canes and lollipops sticking out of them. They both had a sweet-tooth, so they stepped up to the counter. The storekeeper glanced over at Jack while he concluded a sale to another customer. She was a very worn-looking woman, who also looked briefly at them as she took her purchase and quickly left.

"What can I do for you young man?" asked the shopkeeper, placing his hands on the counter.

"We would like some of those please," Jack said, pointing to the jars. "Abby, which would you like?"

"May I have the butterscotch please," she said, standing on her toes so she could raise her mouth above the level of the counter as she pointed.

"Two please," said Jack.

"Those are my favorites," said the storekeeper. "Say, how old are you, miss?" he asked Abigail, reaching into the jar.

"I'm five," she answered, smiling and holding up the widespread fingers of her left hand.

"Oh, I see," he said, peering over the half lenses of his glasses at her. He laid the canes on the countertop, "That will be two cents."

Jack fished his half-dollar coin out of his pocket and handed it to the man. His father had taught him to carry a half-dollar in his pocket at all times, no more and no less. That way he could become accustomed to handling money and still learn to appreciate its value. Father administered an allowance for him, and Jack was a very responsible consumer. Still, from the shopkeep's raised eyebrows Jack could see few boys his age in Cobbs carried much money.

"Thank you," he said, as he pocketed his change, and handed one of the canes to Abigail. They turned and walked out of the store.

Cobbs wasn't a very big town, and with the exception of the saloon, which was directly across from the general store, there were only a few more shops to see. As they continued their walk, Jack noticed that virtually every man's face was begrimed, and his clothing and hands dirty as well. Black, sooty residue was ground into the pores of their faces, making every line and wrinkle seem that much deeper. Their clothing too, not just of the men but also that of the women, was plain, linens and cotton, canvas and denim. They wore drab colors and most of their clothes were well worn, if not downright shabby. He became more and more aware of how conspicuous he and Abigail looked with his new shoes, well-cut trousers and collared shirt, and she with clean stockings and laced petticoat. Suddenly, he felt uncomfortable at all the stares they were getting. There were socio-economic differences back in Philadelphia, but there were many more wealthy people there, so people generally stayed within their particular social circle. Here his father seemed to be the richest man in town, and Jack wasn't at all sure how they were being received.

They continued walking, and as they passed in front of the next shop over they heard the sounds of work coming from a smithy.

"What do you think, Abby? Let's go see what they are making," he asked, eager to exit the main street, away from all of the staring citizens. Abigail nodded, and he turned down the side road toward the open side of the smithy, where a red-hot furnace could be seen glowing.

As they stood there next to the smithy hand-in-hand, a group of boys about Jack's age were walking in toward the main street. They wore patched and faded trousers with suspenders over long-sleeved undershirts, or without shirts at all. Jack and Abigail stood out like sore thumbs, and the boys continued walking toward them, leering and making inaudible comments back and forth. Jack kept his eyes forward, occasionally looking down or at Abigail, anywhere but at them. He couldn't help but glance up as they passed by though, and saw a boy with shoulder-length blond hair smile and wave at them, only to be soundly punched in the arm by another stout looking lad.

"Bloody Hell!" Jack heard him say as he scowled, looking at the one who had hit him, rubbing his arm and continuing down the street with the pack.

He heaved a sigh of relief as they passed, and turned to watch the Smith work, but when nothing spectacular happened, Abigail quickly lost interest and started pulling on Jack's arm.

"Let's go Jack, we still haven't walked down the other side yet," she said, pulling harder to propel him into motion.

He let her guide him, turning from the smithy and heading back toward the main avenue. Back on the main street, they looked across the road and saw a small bakery shop. Jack led Abigail along as he stepped into the street after a passing cart. He could smell freshly baked bread and other sweet smells as they walked across, up the porch step and into the shop. The window inside displayed several bread loaves and pies, along with a number of preserved fruits and vegetables. On the counter, there were jars of pickled pig's feet and boiled eggs.

At the sound of the doorbell a woman stood from where she was seated behind the counter. She was fair-skinned, with a multitude of freckles covering her face and hands. Her red hair was kinky, and gathered at the base of her neck with a black ribbon, although stray strands had escaped and hung down on both sides of her face. The gray dress she wore was simple, but made of a bit better material than what Jack had seen around Cobbs thus far. The apron over her dress was clean and white. He supposed she was pretty in a way, and she gave him a little smile as he nodded and said, "Good day, ma'am."

"Good day, young man, can I help you?" she asked.

"Not right away, ma'am," he answered, "We're new in town and just wanted to make our way around."

"Well, that's just fine, take your time. We get some visitors, people interested in the mines you know, but not many new people come to stay," she said, walking around the end of the counter. "My, you two look quite handsome. What did you say your names were?"

Jack's face turned red, "I'm sorry ma'am, I'm Jack Rutherford and this is my sister, Abigail." He decided to leave out the part about his father this time.

"Oh, of course, I believe I saw you arrive on the carriage yesterday. I'm afraid you'll find Cobbs a very quiet little place." She turned and walked back around the counter, holding up a finger, "Just a moment, I have something you'll like." She knelt down behind the counter, and all Jack could see was her frizzy red hair sticking up. When she stood she held a jar of peach preserves. She put the jar on the counter, and retrieved a bowl with two forks. With a quick twist, she opened the lid of the jar and set it on the counter. She started sliding peaches into the bowl, and when she had transferred about a half-dozen slices, she replaced the lid and re-shelved the jar under the counter.

"Here, try these," she said, "These are some of my best this year." She held out a fork to each of them and they stepped forward to accept.

Jack speared a peach slice and held it over the bowl as the excess juice ran off. Abigail just popped hers into her mouth, unmindful of the drippings she left on the counter. The peaches were delicious, and they praised them as they ate. Abigail was up on her toes, having to stretch to get to the peaches, so the lady brought her stool around to the end of the counter and sat Abigail on her lap.

As they ate, the woman drew Abigail closer to her. First one, then both arms were around her waist, holding Abigail on her lap so she wouldn't slip off. Her head was cocked to one side as she studied Abby's face. They were exchanging words, the woman asking simple, meaningless questions; her age, her favorite color, did she have any dolls? Abigail chatted, oblivious to the woman's closeness.

As Jack finished off the last of the peaches, he set his fork in the bowl, "Thank you ma'am, those were delicious. I'll recommend them to our mother," he said.

"You're very welcome," she said, at the same time closing her eyes and giving Abigail a firm hug. "You'll come back and see me again, won't you?" she asked, turning Abigail to look into her face as she spoke.

"Yes ma'am," Abby said, nodding her head. The woman smiled, and gave her another strong hug. There was an awkward silence as the hug continued, Jack standing there waiting. Abigail looked at Jack, puzzled but not really alarmed. She squirmed a little, indicating she wanted to get down, and still the woman did not release her. Another second passed before Jack said, "Ma'am, I'm afraid we have to be going, our parents are waiting for us."

The woman did not look up, her face buried in Abigail's curls, and Jack tried again, "Do we owe you anything for the peaches?" he asked quietly. At that, the woman finally raised her face, kissing Abigail quickly on the cheek before lifting her off her lap and setting her on her feet. He was alarmed to see her eyes were glassy, on the verge of tears. She blinked them away, taking in a great breath, and with obvious effort smiled at Jack, "No, that was a free sample, be sure and tell your mother."

"Yes ma'am," Jack said as he took Abigail's hand and turned toward the door. He walked quickly, hurrying to leave, but she stopped him with his hand on the doorknob, "Jack?" she called out. He turned to see her walking toward him, their eyes locking as she approached, "Yes ma'am?"

The woman's eyes were wide, red-rimmed with spidery veins at the edges. "You have to be careful here in Cobbs. It can be a dangerous place." The hairs on the back of his neck suddenly stood up, and Jack stared back, held in her gaze even as he opened the door and pushed Abigail outside. "Yes ma'am," he mumbled as he quickly stepped out and pulled the door closed behind him. He grabbed Abigail's hand, and started down the walkway back toward the mining office. *What was that about?* Jack's heart thumped, and he hurried Abigail along.

They were now on the saloon-side of the street, and would pass right in front of it on their way back. As Jack walked, he noticed more people watching them. Wherever he turned someone was looking at him, the dirty, weary gaze direct and forceful. He walked a little faster, dragging Abigail along. Across the street past the general store, Mr. Shaw was still sitting outside the tobacco store, peering in their direction.

Without warning, Jack ran into someone, mashing his nose and knocking himself down, falling on his rear. Surprised, he sat on the boardwalk, goggling the four men exiting the saloon. They were obviously miners, with heavy clothing and the worn, dusty look of men employed for hard labor. The man he had run into didn't say anything, but looked at him for a second before shifting his quiet gaze to Abigail. Jack started to apologize, but his eyes caught the other three men all gawking down at Abigail as well.

Jack jumped to his feet and shouted, "I'm sorry, excuse me!" as he took off down the walkway, pulling Abigail along as fast as her little legs could run. It was only another hundred feet or so to the mining office, but when they made it to the front porch, Jack and Abigail were both breathless and panting.

Their parents and Mr. French were still poring over the maps and charts, mother now looking exasperated, and they all looked up as the children burst in.

"Excuse me," said Jack, still breathing hard as he gently closed the door behind them.

"Well," said their father, standing straight and clapping his hands, "you're just in time. I'm about to take your mother to see the mines. Would you like to join us?"

"Yes Father," they both answered at once, glancing at each other. Thomas beamed, "Wonderful, then into the carriage with you."

Clive stood holding the door open as the Rutherford family came out of the office and climbed into the carriage. After seeing them in, Mr. French mounted the horse he had tethered to the hitching post, and turned its head down the street, leading the way toward the mines. Clive clucked at the horses and rolled smoothly away, the carriage gently rocking as they passed through Cobbs.

Jack was practically crouching in his seat, only sitting high enough for his eyes to peek over the windowsill. Mr. Shaw still sat in his chair, and he nodded as the coach rolled by. Jack pretended not to see him, and faced straight ahead.

"So Jack," his father asked with a grin, "did you find Cobbs a bit different from Philadelphia?"

"Yes sir. I'm not sure I like it at all," he said.

"Well, I admit it's a little rustic and rougher than Philadelphia in most ways, but you'll get used to it. I find it quite invigorating, actually. Did you meet any boys your age? How about you Abigail, did you meet anyone?"

Abigail didn't answer; she was staring out of the coach window. Jack followed her gaze, and saw the red haired woman standing in front of her shop, her arms crossed. Strands of hair whipped around her head in the breeze, as she watched the passing coach. Elizabeth leaned forward to see what had captured the children's attention. When she saw the red-haired woman she asked, "Who is that?"

"She owns the bakery," Jack answered, "she keeps good peaches."

7

DANGEROUS WORK

THE SLOPING TRACK to the mines wasn't nearly as smooth as the road through town, and the carriage bounced along, squeaking and yawing on its springs. Both Jack and Abigail were thoroughly enjoying the ride, grinning and flopping around in their seats, exaggerating the action of the coach. Elizabeth wasn't half as amused, but she smiled at their antics.

It was a little over two miles to the mines, which were dug into the foothills as they rose towards the mountain peaks. Steep terrain lay on either side of the track; deep shadow-filled hollows that only saw sunlight when it was directly overhead. The rugged hillsides were completely blanketed in trees of every description, as if the forest couldn't make up its mind. Oak, ash, pine, cedar, maple, elm and poplar all grew in a profusion of small clumps, each variety trying to squeeze the others out. As they ascended, Elizabeth looked out the window, anxiously peering over the edge of the road as it fell away into the tops of the trees below them. She thought nervously of how dreadful a fall like that would be, and swallowed as she sat back in her seat. Behind them the panorama spread out like a painting. The patchwork colors of the trees textured the landscape, and in the distance, light glinted off a body of water. As the land rose, so did the winds, swirling around the shoulders of the foothills and breezing through the coach, bringing with it exhilarating scents. Hawks and other birds wheeled through the blue sky above the trees, their piercing calls lonely and strange. All in all, it was a beautiful, albeit dangerous, ride. Thomas sat across from her, seeming unconcerned; listening to the children play, he smiled to himself and breathed deeply of the fresh air as he too, stared out of the coach.

Along the way they passed men going to and from the mines. Those coming from the mines were covered in dust from head to toe, their eyes squinted, and breathing out of their mouths. Droplets of sweat ran down beneath their hats, cutting trails through the dust on their faces. They stumbled down the hill, raising a hand in greeting to Mr. French and glancing in weary curiosity at the occupants of the coach. There were one or two riding on mules, but for the most part they were on foot. Those on their way to the mines seemed a bit cleaner, and as the coach approached from the rear, they would usually turn and say a few words in greeting before continuing their trudge up the hill.

The track began to level out, and Elizabeth knew they were almost there, judging from the many sounds of industry that could now be heard. Rolling wagons, yelling men and chiming hammers were all intermingled in the air. Suddenly a tremendous, crashing *BOOM!* punctured the air, causing the ground to shake. The carriage team was not accustomed to the sound of dynamite and spooked, whinnying in fright and backing in their traces. Clive fought them for several moments before regaining control and sending them forward at a walk. Everyone in the coach had flinched at the explosion, even Thomas, although only for a second before he grinned, setting Elizabeth and the children at ease.

The coach pulled to a stop and the door swung open to reveal Mr. Dalby standing there smiling, the gap in his front teeth even wider than Jack recalled from last night.

"Good afternoon all," he said as he unfolded the steps and offered his hand to mother. As she stepped out of the coach he continued, "We've just blown another charge in the number two shaft so it'll be a while before it's cleared."

"Of course," said his father, as he turned back to lift Abigail under her arms, and lower her to the ground. A light cloud from the explosion still hung in the air, misting in to land fine dust on their shoulders and in their hair. Mother took father's proffered arm, fanning her other hand at the dust. Flanked by Mr. Dalby and Mr. French they all walked toward a cabin, leaving Jack and Abigail to follow behind. He took Abigail's hand and trailed them, at the same time looking around at the bustle of activity. Everywhere gangs of rough men were struggling with one task or another, swinging hammers against giant boulders, leading mules loaded with bags of rubble, or carrying boxes of dynamite toward the mine. The mine itself was a great arched cave; Jack thought it resembled a giant mouth and he imagined the mountain was yawning. Two large ore cars sat on a small track, which ran into the mouth and disappeared into darkness. He watched as four men flanked one of the cars and pushed it toward the opening.

They followed their parents into the cabin, but were disappointed to find the same maps and charts tacked to every surface along with a collection of rocks on a table. Piled in amongst all those rocks were several giant gold nuggets, some as large as a man's fist.

"Father!" he exclaimed in awe, "Is this gold?" he asked, moving over to the table, eager to touch one.

All the men laughed, and his father said, "No, Jack, we haven't been that lucky yet." Walking over to the table he picked up a gold piece and handed it to Jack, "This is iron pyrite, and pretty as it is, it's quite worthless. You can keep as much as you like."

His father picked up another large rock, which was unremarkable as far as Jack could see, and with a small hammer lying on the table tapped it until it broke in two.

"This is what we're after now," he said, showing the inner halves to everyone. There were shiny iridescent metallic streaks inside the rock. "This is raw iron ore, which is valuable if we can find enough of it, but we're still hoping to find more precious metals." He put the rocks down and dusted off his hands.

Jack and Abigail crowded each other at the table, each picking out their favorite chunks of pyrite as the four adults continued to talk about mine operations. He was only half-listening, just in case something interesting came up. Mr. Dalby and Mr. French were giving Mother a report on the mine's production. They were going to great lengths to impress upon her that the mine was producing something, and it was only a matter of time before they found iron ore in greater quantities.

"Elizabeth," said Thomas, "you'll recall I mentioned we've had problems with things going missing, slowing work down considerably - pickaxes and hammers and such." Mr. Dalby nodded, and took up the report, "Yes ma'am, and there was that pallet of dynamite that went missing as well."

"We questioned all the men, and threatened to dismiss and arrest anyone who was caught stealing, but it has continued until finally we've had to start locking up all the tools." Thomas finished.

Jack looked at the gold pyrite in his hand, but his ears were perked to hear more. Mother said, "Yes, well, now that you've taken measures, I presume the work is moving along well enough?"

There was a pause, while Mr. Dalby and Mr. French exchanged glances.

"Unfortunately, no, the problems have continued," said Mr. Dalby. "Oh, now it's not thievery so much, but still, problems..." he trailed off, looking at Mr. French.

"It's become a great nuisance," Mr. French said, in a loud, confident voice. "Logs have been laid across the road, the mules have been run off, the water troughs get knocked over and rocks have been thrown through these windows more than once," he said sweeping his hands around the room, "Small inconveniences to be sure, but enough to delay the work, sometimes by half a day."

Mr. Dalby cut in, "But the real problem is with the men. I've never seen such a superstitious lot. Grown men afraid of the dark, I mean really, they work in a mine for God's sake!"

"Despite the fact that something happens more often than not, the sentries have never seen anything, even when they are posted in pairs." He snorted, "If they would leave this cabin and walk their rounds like they should, I daresay we would find out soon enough who the vandals are."

"Unfortunately," Mr. French said, "they're too nervous and huddle inside, content to peer out the windows. We considered going to day and night shifts so the work could continue at a faster pace, but with limited manpower, that would only be dividing our workforce."

The conversation had Jack's full attention now and his father stood with his arms crossed, one hand coming up to cup his chin as he considered the problem.

"Alright, we've already talked about this. Mr. French, please post a reward of fifty dollars for the man who can identify the person or persons committing these acts," he said. "Raise a series of lantern poles around the worksite. The lanterns will be lit each evening before the crews leave for the day. This might help keep the vandals away if they know the sentries can easily see them."

Jack's father was a decisive man. A natural leader who instilled confidence in those around him and the two foremen were visibly relieved, simply from the way father had taken charge. He continued, "I also want a guard post constructed, one without doors or windows. This cabin is to be locked each night. Finally, we'll hang a bell large enough to be heard in Cobbs. If the sentries ring the bell, we will send help."

"What sort of help, sir?" asked Mr. Dalby.

"Well, I suppose five mounted and armed men would do it. Mr. French, I would like you to supervise, please. You may handpick the other four men as you like, but I suggest you choose some of the miners who came here for the work rather than natives, they'll be less likely to get spooked. Draw up a list and let me know how much compensation you think they deserve."

Mr. Dalby smiled and clapped Mr. French on the back, "Well, good luck with that crew."

"Yes, you should wish him luck Mr. Dalby," said father with a smile of his own. "Because if the problem persists, I will have no choice but to ask you to take up residence here," he said, indicating the cabin with a wave of his hand.

Mr. Dalby's smile withered, and now it was Mr. French who laughed, "Not to worry, I'll send you the best sentries we have," he guffawed, enjoying the look on Mr. Dalby's face immensely.

"Gentlemen, do we have anything else to discuss?" asked father.

"Yes sir, we will need more track for the railcars…" Mr. Dalby began. The excitement over, Jack turned away from the conversation. As his gaze moved to the front door he was startled to see an old black man standing there. Startled because the man's appearance was a shock; his clothing was more or less the same as everyone else's, but his right arm was deformed. It hung motionless from his shoulder, partly because he had secured it across his body with a length of cloth. The arm was long and thin; why, it would have reached below the man's knees had he left it to hang! The weird aspect of the man however, was his right eye, which was obviously blind, a milky blue-white orb in his socket, like a cotton ball in ice.

The adults noticed the man's presence. "Ah, Lucius, come in," said Mr. Dalby. "This is Mrs. Rutherford and their children."

"Good afternoon ma'am," he said, giving a slight bob of his head. Whether his business in the cabin was serious or not, Jack didn't get the impression Lucius was much inclined to smile. His mother politely greeted Lucius as Mr. Dalby went on, "Lucius here is a local, lived here even before the war. He's a good stout man, we're very glad to have him on."

"Thank you, sir," said Lucius.

"Yes, as you can see, Lucius has some physical limitations, but he helps out greatly in many other small ways. He takes care of the pack animals, issues out equipment, and travels to Charleston to receive goods and supplies for us. What is it Lucius?" Mr. Dalby asked.

"Sir, Mr. Peyton asked me to come tell you, the men have finished cutting in on the far side if you'd like to come see."

"Oh yes," Mr. Dalby answered, "Sir, he's talking about the north face, where we're planning on starting a fourth shaft. Would you like to inspect the site?"

"Yes, give me a moment. Elizabeth, you and the children can ride back down with the coach and I'll join you later, all right?" said father. Mother nodded, and the men all walked out of the cabin, moving through the worksite. As soon as they had left, Abigail wanted to show Mother her choice of golden rocks, and they spent several minutes going over their booty. The pyrite was actually beautiful, and Jack couldn't believe they were worthless. He stuffed as many nuggets as he could in his pockets, and Abigail carried several in her little fists as well.

"Well then," said Mother, "let's be off, there are still a few things I wanted to get done before the day is gone." They walked out of the cabin and toward the coach, which Clive had turned around, ready to return to Cobbs. As they climbed in and sat down, Jack saw the man named Lucius moving about the worksite. He walked with a slow and somber gait, like he was headed to the gallows. The coach started slowly rolling around the first bend in the road, and Jack watched Lucius until the mountain hid him from view. What an odd looking man, he thought.

* * * * *

Their wisdom and power could not be disputed however, and true to his nature Man pursued the Ba'ath. Once again competition to win was key as the kings of men flattered and courted the Ba'ath. Their roles as advisors were elevated and honored beyond all others. Kings presented them with gifts; golden statues in respect and admiration. Rituals of honor became elaborate ceremonies, celebrating the influence and kinship of the Ba'ath.

For the Ba'ath, there was as yet no reason for concern. In their own naivety they saw these acts as simple expressions of respect and they were pleased. They believed they were effective in their roles as advisors. In time however, the needs and desires of each tribe put them in increasing conflict with other tribes. The Ba'ath were consulted of course, but when contending with the passions of men, wisdom will often fail. Thus began the wars of Men.

-From the Book of More

8

SETTLING IN

THREE DAYS LATER was their first Sunday in town, and they were preparing to attend church in Cobbs for the first time. Jack and Abigail were raised Presbyterian, but the Holy Antioch Baptist Church was the only house of worship in Cobbs. Father said it didn't really matter as everyone was there for the same purpose.

Now, after having their breakfast and getting ready, with Mother making a dozen final adjustments, the family was finally loaded into the carriage and trundled off down the lane.

It was only a short ten-minute trip from the house, down the main street, then another quick turn down the first side road to the church. The bell had rung once already that morning telling everyone it was time to get ready for church, and now one hour later, it tolled again, calling everyone to worship. The bell still clanged as the carriage pulled up and Clive opened the door. Mother looked at Jack and Abigail and said, "Okay you two, on your best behavior, right?" They both nodded, and everyone climbed out of the coach.

Jack was surprised at how many people were in attendance. He hadn't thought there were this many people in all of Cobbs. Everyone had cleaned up; the ever-present dust had been washed off, and their hair was combed. Their clothing was still fairly drab and worn, but all in all, it seemed like a pleasant little assembly.

Standing at the top of the steps leading into the church was the man Jack would later learn was the Reverend Gideon Fetch. Jack couldn't help but stare as the reverend stood there wearing a long black woolen coat, with a bible in his left hand. He greeted people as they entered the church, but he was not smiling. His features were stern, with a long straight nose, furrowed eyes and a square jaw, outlined by a trimmed beard in the style of Abraham Lincoln. His face was shaded by a broad, straight-brimmed hat with a rounded crown.

By this time, father was shaking a few hands and introducing them, so Jack tore his eyes away from Reverend Fetch to be polite, and after a few moments they were moving towards the steps themselves. They moved through the stream of people and came face-to-face with Reverend Fetch at the doorway.

"Mr. Rutherford, God bless you," said the reverend in a deep, gravelly soft voice. "I had hoped your family would join us today," he said, extending his hand to father, who took it with a polite smile.

"Thank you Reverend, yes, of course," Thomas said. He introduced Elizabeth and the two children before moving them all into the church. It was a simple church, with rows of wooden pews which were quickly filling up. Even though it didn't have the massive vaulted ceilings and towering stained glass windows of their church in Philadelphia, a hushed, respectful atmosphere dominated the little building. A few minutes more, and everyone had filed in and taken their seats. Reverend Fetch had removed his hat and closed the doors behind him, as he walked down the center aisle to take his place behind the podium on the small pedestal stage. He motioned to a matronly woman standing off to one side, "Mrs. Fetch...,"

"Please turn to page 142 of your hymnals," the woman said, holding hers in front of her and waiting patiently for the congregation to find the song. As Jack reached for a hymnal in the back of the pew in front of them, his eye caught a glimpse of unkempt blond hair. The boy who had waved at them by the smithy sat next to a man with a good clean coat, a bushy mustache and a matching head of uncombed, shoulder-length hair. The boy noticed Jack, so Jack waved politely. The boy smiled back and waved, just as everyone stood for the hymn. Jack hurriedly found the page and held the book for Abigail, as the congregation began to sing.

There was no music, which was strange to Jack because their church services in Philadelphia always included organ music and sometimes other instruments. He had to admit though, the a' cappella song sounded somehow more heartfelt; a more sincere and genuine entreaty. After a few moments, the hymn had ended and everyone settled into their seats. Revered Fetch stood at the podium, and a respectful silence prevailed, as all the rustling and foot shuffling ceased, until not a sound could be heard. He turned a page in the bible lying open on the podium, and looked out into the congregation with a hard stare.

"There is NO WHISKEY IN HEAVEN!" he suddenly shouted, slamming his hand down onto the podium. Both Jack and Abigail jumped in their seats, and sat straight up. The sermon only got hotter from that point on. Jack guessed Reverend Fetch must have said "Hell" and "damnation" a dozen times before he was through. Other than the occasional "Amen," there was absolute silence as the reverend thundered on. This was certainly different from the services they were accustomed to, and by the time an hour had passed, Jack and Abigail were deathly afraid of alcohol.

After the service ended everyone began filing out of the church. There was little conversation that Jack could tell, and it seemed the congregation simply faded away in silence, like ghosts drifting out of sight. This also struck him as odd, as Sundays usually meant at least an hour of his parents' socializing while he and Abby stood listlessly by, bored to death. Father tried to make the most of the opportunity, making a point of shaking hands and smiling at people passing them, but Jack noticed many of them just walked past, staring like the Rutherfords were animals in a zoo, so he was thankful when Father finally nodded his farewells, hustled them back into the carriage and headed home.

The next few weeks were spent exploring the nooks and crannies of their new home, and getting to know the household staff. Being from the city, they delighted in things common to life in the country, but that they had never seen; a root cellar, the barn, and the smokehouse. They particularly enjoyed the barn, spending hours watching and petting the animals they found there. They hadn't had any pets in Philadelphia, and now they had dozens! Jack loved the horses best, while Abigail loved the pot-bellied pigs. There were also cats in the barn, chasing rats through the straw, and curling up beside the other animals at night. Jack helped Abby climb to the loft, and they would sit in the loft window, letting their legs dangle over the side. Once, Jack thought it would be fun to grab onto the lifting strap and swing out over the yard, but his mother had seen him and forbade him from doing it again.

Besides Lucille, Mr. Rutherford had also employed several other servants to help around the house. There was Ambrose and Charles, who tended the animals and maintained the house and grounds. They took their orders from Mr. Severn, who also kept up the smokehouse, ordered necessary provisions from the general store, and would be giving Jack and Abigail riding lessons. Esther was a young black girl who helped Lucille with the wash and housecleaning chores, and of course Clive. Mr. Dalby, Mr. French, Mr. Severn and Clive all lived in the small white guesthouse in the back three acres of the fenced property, while the rest lived in the two-room servants' quarters just off the main house. The Rutherford property stretched beyond the fence another thirty acres or so, but this place was still so wild there were no fences to mark the boundaries.

The whole month of June had passed, and now it was the 1st day of July. The days were hot, the sun blazing down with prideful strength. Neither of the children was accustomed to spending so much time outside. In Philadelphia much more of their time was devoted to study and social events, not to mention they simply did not have the sort of space available to them now. By the end of the first week, both were beet-red from the sun, smarting from the burns on their faces. After a few weeks however, the first burn had peeled and now their fair skin began to take on some color.

The Independence Day celebration in Cobbs was a bit of a disappointment, nothing like the grand displays in Philadelphia. Father had arranged for a decent fireworks show, which was well attended, with plenty of snappers and sparklers for the crowd. They "Oohed" and "Aahhed," but otherwise the holiday came and went without much fanfare.

Jack had accompanied his father to the mines several times, which he was now beginning to enjoy. Watching the men work, listening to them plan and coordinate the operations. He found it exciting, and he went with his father whenever he could. It was during one of these trips to the mine he had met Elijah, the blonde-haired boy from church. Elijah's father had immigrated to America from Australia, and was employed as a demolitions expert at the mine. When he introduced Jack to his father, Jack took the offered handshake and was shocked to discover the man only had three fingers on his right hand, the result of an accident early in his career. The man laughed at the look on Jack's face, making him smile as well. After that, the two boys spent a lot of their spare time together. Elijah actually worked at the mine with his father, so Jack often had to wander about alone until he was available. Elijah, "Eli" as everyone called him, had grown up in frontier towns and was a real rough-and-tumble sort, but for some reason, he and Jack had hit it off. On the occasional day they were able to sneak off for some fun, they usually went running off into the woods, adventuring like pioneers. Often, Eli brought his father's rifle, and they had taken turns shooting at squirrels and pinecones. Jack had never shot a gun before, but he found he enjoyed it very much. Eli was a crack shot and Jack envied his skill, but Eli complimented him on his shooting, declaring him a natural. True, he hit his target more often than not, and when he brought the gun up into his shoulder he was as steady as a rock. Jack contemplated how to ask his father for his own gun.

These weeks also gave them a chance to become more familiar with the town and its' residents. Jack's mother had met Emma James, the woman who owned the bakery. She made wonderful pies, and Mother purchased several, as well as some baked goods. On the occasions Abby accompanied Mother, Emma would go on about how precious she was, but otherwise showed no signs of the odd behavior from their first meeting.

Emma was one of the few exceptions however; most of the locals Jack encountered had a cool reserve about them. Not quite to the point of being rude, but certainly not very inviting towards outsiders. The problem for them, was that nowadays, with the influx of workers for the mines, there were a lot more outsiders.

Workers had streamed in from small towns and big cities alike, eager for work. The miners had established a camp at the base of the foothills leading to the mines. Their tents and shanties were spread out on either side of a clear, shallow river that ran along the base of the foothills before wandering through their camp. A series of large stepping stones had been arranged to allow them to cross back and forth without having to walk all the way down to the bridge a hundred yards downstream on the main road. The camp consisted of just over one hundred people including the women and children. This addition brought the overall population of Cobbs to approximately two hundred and eighty souls.

Jack had visited the miner's camp several times with Eli. It was always a lively scene, with folks laughing, playing cards or doing chores, and the smell of something cooking wafting through the air. A more permanent housing site was being planned, but for now this was their home.

One of the townspeople Jack met was a man named Tim Button. He walked into Cobbs every morning from his little shanty house, which was back across the bridge and sat off the main road in the tree line. He wore a wide-brimmed hat pulled down low, and leather gloves on his hands at all times. He was only in his early-forties, but there was a palsy in his hands, which jangled at the ends of his arms as he walked. His lips constantly mouthed words, gibbering quietly as strands of greasy hair hung down over his face.

One morning, Jack made the mistake of greeting him. "Good morning," Jack said, as he walked toward the mining road. It was just a routine greeting, but the man's wide eyes looked at him in annoyance and anger. He started screaming at Jack, telling him to mind his own business, cursing and excitedly throwing his arms around. Of course, he scared the hell out of Jack, who quickly moved away. Jack later learned that many years ago, while still a young man, Tim had been a farrier. By all accounts he was a happy-go-lucky person who was quick to laugh. While shoeing horses one day, Tim was kicked in the head by a heavy plow horse. His brains were nearly dashed out and he lay in bed for over three months, with his fingers and toes tightly curled, barely responsive. Slowly, over time, his mother had nursed him back to health, but he never truly recovered and he became a moody creature of habit. Frequent outbursts of anger and cursing were tolerated by the community, and were mitigated by his mother who tried to keep him at home as much as possible. When she died several years before, it sent his already fragile mind into a deep depression. His outbursts were disturbing, and some of the younger boys started calling him names, which of course made things worse. He was not able to work, but the community and his mother had provided for him and now he only came outside twice a day. He walked to the saloon every morning to eat the same breakfast; three boiled eggs, pan-fried potatoes, and a beer. When he finished he would walk back home, not to be seen again until evening, when he came outside to feed his chickens and the few pigs he kept in a pen. Sometimes he was seen standing out by the pen, bucket in hand as if he had forgotten what he was doing. After their encounter Jack decided it was best to just avoid him altogether.

9

TAKING SIDES

In THE DANK UNDERBRUSH of a fading twilight, he entered the ring of elm trees in a puff of black smoke. These trees were dead, and he looked around at their empty hearts, the outer bark no impediment to his sight. His confederates were hidden there, immaterial but present and awaiting his arrival. A thick layer of fog swirled in to surround the trees and cover the ground between them.

There were six present, but he could feel the approach of the seventh. This was a very good sign. The seventh was new to this council, and was a very important ally. As one, they stepped out into the center of the ring, black smoke wisping off their shoulders as they phased into material form.

"Well met," he greeted them. They all nodded in return. This was not the ideal meeting place, but the other side was no longer safe for these discussions. Even as they grew stronger, their position grew more dangerous. Everything depended on utter secrecy. He turned as the seventh appeared in a puff of black smoke. "We are honored by your presence, welcome." This Ba'ath was dressed in mail and armor like the others, but it was hacked and chewed worse than any, worn in ten thousand battles. The metal was burnished, dark and tarnished, almost rusted through in places.

"Yes Bael, I am here, though I don't really know why I agreed to come. I hope you have something new to say." There was acid in the words, and Bael choked down his first response. He needed this one.

"I have nothing new to tell you," he said, keeping his gaze level and direct. "However, I believe you've finally come to realize Micah is wrong. His way isn't working; has never worked." The others were standing silently, watching their exchange. "This argument between the brethren cannot go on forever. We want peace as much as you Samael, but this time it will be on our terms. Do not pretend to be ignorant of our intentions. You are here of your own free will, are you not?"

"I am, but if you are wrong, it will undo everything. All that has been accomplished these many thousands of years past. Even if you are prepared to bear that burden, it is all of us who will pay the price."

"The price? What price have we already paid these past millenia? Our methods are what they must be, in part due to the stubborn resistance of your fellows. What is to come is as much their doing as mine." His forceful gaze stabbed the Samael, "Besides, it seems you have given up on your duties long ago. Thick as flies they are..."

Samael looked down, his jaw clenching. "That is not my fault, there is nowhere for them to go."

"Of course, we all know that, but that is also why we must finish this. Come, all will be explained to you, and we shall help you." Samael had a miserable, haunted look on his face. "Before we continue, we will require an assurance from you. Something...binding."

"Binding? I think not. You asked me to listen, more than that, I cannot promise you."

Bael closed his eyes and shook his head, "Nevertheless, it is required. Make your choice." The circle drew closer and Samael looked at those around him.

"Grim," he said, speaking to one of the other Ba'ath, "you are resigned to this course?"

Grim lifted his left hand. Only a small lump remained where the last finger had been. "I am."

"And you Azel?" he asked, turning to another. Azel bowed her head in a nod, fanning her hand out as well. Despair filled him, *How have we come to this?* he thought. Another moment passed before he slowly nodded, and stepped over to one of the trees forming the circle.

Samael placed his left hand on the rough bark, splaying his little finger out wide. With his right hand he slid a dagger out of its sheath, putting the first inch of the blade on top of the finger. With a quick forward and downward push, the finger was off.

It tumbled, dropping through the fog to land in the leaves. A thick drop of dark blood welled out, and Samael watched it wriggle for a moment before taking his hand off the tree. He noticed a wet smear of his blood remained on the bark, but that was of little consequence. There was little pain of course; he had known much worse than this, so it was really only a small discomfort. He turned to look at Bael.

"Now I'm committed, are you satisfied?" he asked, pointing the dagger at Bael.

"Yes, of course," Bael said, but all he could think about was the finger squirming in the leaves. His triumph threatened to burst his heart, and it was all he could do to keep from scrabbling to snatch the thing from the ground. "Why don't you go on over brother, heal that and come back. We will be here."

Samael nodded, "I'll be back," and he shimmered, dissipating into a black mist.

Bael stepped over and bent to pick up the finger. He smiled to himself, before pulling open a bag that hung at his waist and dropping the finger in. Seven fingers now lay in the bag, including his own, crawling over each other like grubs. He pulled the bag tight and secured it on his belt again.

"Surely his fate was a cruel joke," he said, turning to face the others. "Perhaps he has finally realized that. Now, let us discuss our next step."

* * * * *

Mankind brought the progress of millennia to bear on their fellow humans and the slaughter was terrible. The Ba'ath were dismayed and tried to settle the conflicts by entreating with the leaders, appealing to their people. The box had been opened however, and man's greed would not allow it to be closed again. Their craftiness would outmatch the Ba'ath's wisdom as they mouthed words of understanding and appreciation. They built temples to the Ba'ath, honoring their power and magic. They gave them new names in the myriad of human tongues and from the human perspective, created deities.

-From the Book of More

10

STRANGE BEDFELLOWS

JACK'S BUTT WAS STARTING to hurt. He sat on one end of the wooden wagon seat, bouncing along next to the driver as the four-horse team wound their way along a dirt track. The mid-July heat was fierce, humid and sweaty, but the steady breeze of their passage and a wide-brimmed straw hat kept Jack from feeling the worst of it. The road led to Charleston, which was the only city within one-hundred miles of Cobbs where supplies could be bought and received in bulk, due to the confluence of the railroad and the Monongahalee River.

As their school lessons had not yet resumed, Jack and Abigail were having something of a vacation. With few duties around the house, or the social obligations of life in Philadelphia, they found they had a lot more time to themselves. Much of that time they spent together at home, playing with the animals in the barn, horseback riding, and whatever else they could find to amuse themselves. Jack had also been spending more time with Eli. The two were becoming fast friends, for which he was thankful. His reception among most of the other boys in town had been less friendly.

Jack also spent considerable time up at the mines. Eli was usually there working with his father anyway, so Father would always find a few tasks to keep him busy, which is how he ended up on this wagon.

After wandering around the mine site all morning, he had retreated to the operations office and sat slumped in a chair bored to death. Father was speaking with Mr. Dalby and mentioned the wagon would be leaving shortly to go pick up supplies. Jack sat up thinking, *"It might be fun to see what a bigger town looks like."*

"Father," he said when Mr. Dalby had left, "could I go with the wagon to get supplies?"

"What? It's a long trip Jack, they won't be back for several days," Thomas said, flipping through the pages of a ledger.

"That's okay, besides, this way I could learn where the supplies come from, and maybe I could help with the loading," Jack said, trying his best to sell the idea.

Thomas looked up from the ledger, considering Jack a moment. "Well, I suppose it wouldn't hurt for you to lend a hand." Thomas stood and walked to the door of the office, opening it and calling out to Mr. Dalby. After explaining that Jack would be accompanying the wagon he turned back to Jack, "I'm expecting you to do your part, and mind what you're told, deal?" Thomas stuck out his hand, which a smiling Jack grabbed and shook, "Deal!"

Now, eight hours later he began to regret volunteering for this particular assignment. The creaking of the wagon had long since lost its bucolic charm and the dusty clip-clopping of the horses' hooves became almost hypnotic, lulling Jack to sleep. The driver was a local – a weathered, thoroughly wrinkled man who introduced himself as "Hank," wiping tobacco juice off his chin as he extended a hand in greeting. Hank turned out to be much like the various cattle they passed from time to time; uninteresting and smelly. Jack soon found himself almost as bored as being back at the mines.

In the bed of the open wagon sat the old black man Jack had seen his first day at the mine. *Lucius,* Jack thought, recalling the man's name. He sat with his back against the wagon's sideboards, looking back the way they had come, his left arm resting along the top of the sideboard while his right arm remained in a sling. Fingertips stuck out of the sling, but they were covered by a coarse leather work glove. Hank had only exchanged a few words with Jack during the ride, while Lucius had said nothing at all.

Several hours later, the wagon pulled into the outskirts of Charleston. Jack perked up a bit, and a short time later they were all three climbing down from the wagon and stretching their legs. The two men got the horses out of their traces and stabled, then headed down the main street to look for rooms for the night. Jack strode along with them, his head on a swivel, taking in the fresh variety of new sights.

Now this is a town, he thought. Charleston was a much more robust frontier town, more like what he had imagined when Father had first told them about moving out to Cobbs. Yes, it was still very rustic compared to

Philadelphia, but at least it had a rail station, mercantile stores, two hotels and lots of people.

They found the hotel shortly, and arranged for dinner and a room. The hotel dining room was crowded, but they managed to find a table in a corner. After ordering a meal of roasted chicken, they sat back with drinks and waited for the food to arrive. Once dinner was delivered they made short work of it, leaving nothing but a pile of bones. Hank was picking his teeth and leaning back in his chair while Lucius sipped a beer. Neither Hank nor Lucius offered any conversation, and he thought it was strange they hardly spoke to each other. The three of them sat in silence watching the people around them. Jack caught himself staring at Lucius' blind eye occasionally, the cataract both repulsing and fascinating him at the same time. With nothing else to do, Jack listened in on the louder talk around them. Several men were discussing upcoming local elections, while others talked about purchasing livestock, their plans to play cards later or the charms of various ladies.

Hank belched and said, "Jack, we're gonna have to take care of a few errands and it's getting late. Why don't you head on up to the room and get some sleep? We'll have some work to do tomorrow, so you're gonna need it."

He didn't feel all that tired, but remembering his father's words he replied, "Yes sir," and rose from his seat.

"Good lad," Hank smiled, as Jack started up the stairs. The buzzing conversation began to fade as he topped the stairs, walked the few doors down to their room, and went inside closing the door behind him. It was almost nine o'clock, and after leaving most of the raucous noise behind fatigue started to settle on him. Jack was a little surprised to see the room had only one bed. He was accustomed to having his own room and his own bed, so needless to say he felt uncomfortable sharing a bed with a stranger, but he supposed he really didn't have much of a choice. He quickly splashed some water over his face and hands from the basin on a small stand, then dried off and sat on the bed. Taking the suspenders off his shoulders and kicking off his boots, Jack turned down the lamp and crawled under the thin coverlet. Within a few minutes Jack could hear his own heavy breathing as he hovered on the edge of sleep, before consciousness faded and he began to dream.

For a moment he thought he was still dreaming as he heard scuffling, but came fully awake as he realized someone was at the door. His eyes slowly opened, but otherwise Jack lay still and listened. Light streamed in as the door swung open, creaking slightly as the silhouetted figure of Hank entered the room. He lurched into the room, boot heels clopping on the wooden floor and the odor of smoke and whiskey wafted in with him. Hank fumbled around for several minutes before tumbling into the bed, and within seconds was snoring loudly. With a sigh, Jack closed his eyes and went back to sleep.

The next morning, Jack awoke as early dawn sunlight crept in the window. Hank still snored away, so he got dressed as quietly as he could and eased out of the room. He closed the door behind him, and made his way downstairs to the dining room. He was surprised to see Lucius already seated, finishing breakfast.

"Good morning," Jack said, as he pulled out a chair and sat down.

Lucius glanced up at him. "Morning," he responded, spearing the last piece of sliced ham on his plate. "Hank awake yet?"

"He's still sleeping," Jack said. "I think he may have had a few drinks last night."

Lucius' eyebrows arched, and a wry frown appeared on his face, "Well, that ain't nothing new. Looks like you and me gonna have a full day of work ahead of us. Get something to eat and meet me down at the stables."

"What about Hank? Should I wake him?" Jack asked.

"Don't you worry about him, he'll be along presently. Until then, we can probably get a lot more done without him. I'll be expectin' you shortly." With that, Lucius stood and walked out of the hotel.

A few quick bites to eat, and Jack hurried down the boardwalk to the stables. Lucius already had the horses harnessed to the wagon, and motioned for him to jump onboard. With Jack settled, Lucius chucked the horses into motion, moving the wagon smoothly out onto the street. The mercantile warehouse was only a short drive away, and soon Jack stood amongst a bustle of activity as men and animals worked all around him. Lucius went to speak with the man who seemed to be in charge, and handed him the list of ordered supplies.

Within a short time several men were bringing sacks,

bales and crates of goods which they passed off to either Jack or Lucius. It wasn't long before the two were sweating in the mid-morning heat. Since his arm was in a sling, Jack had assumed Lucius wasn't going to be very capable, but the man labored away as well as anyone with two arms. By picking up a sack with his left hand, then using his knee to lift it to waist level, he could trap the sack under his right arm in the sling and carry it to the wagon. Jack also saw Lucius using the fingertips of his deformed arm to pinch and hold, or steady an item against his chest. In this way the two of them made steady progress, and by mid-morning, had the wagon nearly full. Hank had shown up shortly after they began loading, looking like a train had run over him. He groaned with every step, and eventually just sat down on a pallet of flour sacks, holding his head in his hands.

"Alright," Lucius said, wiping a sheen of sweat from his forehead, "You getting' hungry yet?" Jack's cheeks were red with effort and his sweaty hair stuck to his face as he nodded. They stopped long enough to get a quick lunch, but went right back to work, finishing the last bit of loading. Hank had climbed up into the wagon and wedged himself into a comfortable spot between some flour bags and crates and lay back, head lolling as he laid his hat over his face. Lucius finished with the merchant and motioned for Jack to get aboard.

With a quick flick of the reins, the horses stepped forward, straining to pull the fully loaded wagon. The animals fell into step together and the wagon began rolling down the street, headed out of town. As tired as he was, Jack took a last look around Charleston, and regretted he hadn't had more of a chance to get to know her.

Several hours later they came to a small stream, and Lucius decided this would be a good place to stop for the night. The last golden rays of the sun were winking out as they blocked the wagon wheels, and released the horses from the traces. Lucius sent Jack to gather firewood, while he took the horses down to the stream to drink. The wagon ride hadn't done anything to improve Hank's condition, but he gathered a few stones together and constructed a hasty fire ring. As Jack brought back an armload of twigs and branches he found lying on the ground, Hank snapped them into different lengths and fed them into a small blaze within the ring of stones. Lucius returned and hobbled the horses where they could graze, then started cooking the night's supper. A short while later they were eating beans, biscuits and bacon, and washing it down with coffee. It was simple food prepared in a way Jack was unaccustomed to, but he thought it was delicious, and he had never felt more like a frontiersman than he did right now. As he ate, he rubbed at the new blisters he had earned. There was some pain, but it was fleeting and he felt proud he had pulled his own weight today.

The night deepened, and the crickets were giving it their best, while the occasional owl or nightbird broke their rhythm. As soon as he had finished dinner, Hank threw his tin plate in the empty pot and reached for his bedroll. With a "G'night y'all," he rolled into his blankets and turned his back toward the fire. That left Jack and Lucius sitting around the campfire staring at the glowing coals. It was Jack who broke the silence first.

"Lucius, can I ask you a question?" Lucius looked at him expectantly with a raised eyebrow. "What happened to your arm? Did you hurt it in an accident?"

Lucius snorted and stared back at the fire before answering, "Well, I wouldn't exactly say it was an accident, but I was in the wrong place at the wrong time. It happened when I was just a boy, even younger than you. I get along with it though," he said, flapping it like a bird wing. Lucius started poking at the fire with a stick, "I got caught in a mill, lucky I got to keep it at all."

"Oh," Jack replied wincing. They sat in silence a few moments, and he noticed how quiet and deep the darkness had settled in around them. The fire had died a bit and now only lit a small circle. Jack had never camped outdoors before. It was thrilling, but also a little spooky.

Hank was softly snoring as he lay on his side. Jack smiled to himself and asked, "Does Hank usually leave you to do all the work?"

Lucius looked over his shoulder at Hank, then back to Jack. "Ah, leave him alone boy," he grinned. "No, Hank's usually a pretty good fella. Most times he's a good hand, but sometimes he's even worse off than this."

"So you two are friends?" Jack asked.

"No, I didn't say that, but we work good together. He's a trial sometimes, but I let it pass. He's been through some hard times." Lucius poked at the fire again. "No, don't reckon I have any real friends 'round here."

"Eli and I are friends," said Jack.

"Are you now? Come to think of it, I've seen the two of you traipsing around together. He's your friend, is he?" Lucius' eyebrows were raised, a challenge in his tone.

"Yes, he's my best friend."

"What do you know about him?" Lucius asked, furrowing his brow and poking the fire again, sending sparks into the night air. Jack told Lucius where Eli was from, about his work with his father, and that his mother had passed away years ago. Lucius shrugged, "Is that all? I know that much about him, does that mean we're friends?"

"No, but we also do things together, like fishing," he explained.

"Well, that's a start. Friends are important, that's for sure. Believe me son, it get harder to find them the older you get." He paused, "Think you could trust Eli with your life?" Lucius looked at him in an unsettling way.

He thought about it a moment, "I don't know..., yeah, I guess so," he began, but Lucius cut him off.

"So the answer is 'No'," he said. He turned back to poking the fire, "All I'm saying is it's easy to get along with someone, like me and Hank over there, or you and Eli. It's a lot harder to find someone who'll stick with you no matter what." Jack nodded, but kept quiet. Lucius stared into the coals, but it was obvious he was seeing something else, perhaps something pulled from his memory. "I'll tell you, you can't trust nobody in Cobbs," he said in a low husky voice. He stared back at Jack, and the good eye and the dead one were both glaring now. "You hear me boy? Don't you trust nobody in that town, nobody. Understand? That goes for your family too." His voice had changed to a vicious whisper, and he threw a glance over his shoulder at Hank before once again nailing Jack with a feral stare. Three quick heartbeats passed and Jack still didn't know what to say, so he just sat there with his jaw hanging open.

Lucius abruptly stood and walked over to the wagon. "We'd best turn in, we'll be leaving early in the morning so we make it back in good time." He spread his bedroll out on the opposite side of the fire from Hank and lay down, intertwining his fingers over his chest and closing his eyes.

Jack went to retrieve his own bedroll, but decided to make a spot in the wagon amongst the goods. As he made his nest, the fire died to nothing more than a sullen glow, the smell of wood-smoke barely noticeable now. Standing in the wagon with darkness all around him, he could just make out the silent forms of the two men lying on the ground. The fair breeze blew through the camp, bringing smells of moist earth and animal spoor. Jack wedged himself into a space and threw his blankets on top. It wasn't the most comfortable position, but it wasn't as exposed as sleeping out on the ground. Still, it was at least another hour or so before he finally drifted off to a fitful sleep.

* * * * *

Samael was the first of the new gods. When a human died, it was his duty to guide their soul to the portal of Heaven. The short-lived humans were ever afraid of death, and soon prayers were being sung to Samael. Images representing the god of the afterlife were carved and worshipped. This became the practice in virtually every civilization around the world. Images of the other Ba'ath were carved as well, but even as they praised them, the humans were set upon their own agendas.

-From the Book of More

11

TROUBLE

JAMES DALBY SLAPPED at a mosquito as he sat in the cabin, penning a letter to his cousin Cecil in Tennessee. Cecil would share the news with the rest of the family, so he tried to catch him up on all the latest happenings here in Cobbs.

Despite Mr. French's efforts, there continued to be trouble at the mine. Ore carts had been found lying on their sides, pushed off the tracks spilling a ton or more of rubble that had to be shoveled up once again. The cart-rails had been torn up in two of the shafts and most serious, someone had dislodged several support timbers, which could have led to a tunnel collapse. This vandalism was dangerous, and someone was going to get hurt. It had to be the work of some of the miners themselves. Was there some discontent over pay or conditions? He thought not; in his experience this was a routine operation with accepted standards for wages and good equipment. No, it was more likely an attempt by some of the more unscrupulous sorts to cause delays, thereby lengthening their employment.

He ordered his thoughts as he wrote, making light of the situation to Cecil. He was not prone to exaggeration and anticipated a reasonable explanation when they got to the bottom of the matter. Although, he mused, it had been several weeks since the subject had first been addressed with Mr. Rutherford. The precautions put in place seemed to have reduced the incidents, but they still occurred often enough to cause costly delays and were becoming more dangerous. True to his word, Mr. Rutherford instructed him to take up residence here.

It was really no great hardship, as he regularly took his evening meals in town before returning to the cabin. He also still had sentries posted, so he had the freedom to manage his schedule as he pleased. Which reminded him, *I suppose it's time to look in on the boys,* he thought, checking his pocket-watch.

James stood up and reached for his hat. His reflection in the windows stared back at him, and the glow of the oil lamps filling the room made it difficult to see outside. He pulled open the front door and surveyed the cleared space leading to the mouth of the mine. The lanterns created a wide, diffusely lit space around the mine's entrance, clearly illuminating the nearby sentry shack. Besides his horse and the two mules hitched on the side of the shack stamping and softly snorting, all seemed peaceful and quiet.

As he walked across the open space James felt exposed and vulnerable. *Good,* he thought, *that's the effect I'm going for.* He could see the glow of a lantern spilling out of the shack and two men sitting inside.

"Evenin' George," he called out, raising a hand.

"Evenin', care to join us?" George replied, indicating a deck of cards. Nathan Guilford was the other sentry, and he waved a greeting to James as well.

"Well, let's see now, what's the game?" he asked, pulling a small crate over as a seat. The cards were dealt, and time passed as the three men played. At one point, the mules began braying and the men looked back over their shoulders. That side of the cabin was outside the circle of pole lanterns however, and shrouded in shadows, but the braying quickly subsided and they turned back to their game.

Another hour had passed and James thought it was time to make his way back to the cabin and finish his letter. He was about to excuse himself when the braying began again. This time though, there was an unmistakable urgency in the mule's alarm, and all three of the men quickly stood.

"What in the hell?" George started, reaching for his rifle. Nathan grabbed the lantern and they started toward the cabin as they heard the sound of breaking glass.

"It's the vandals!" James hissed, "After them!" They broke into a run toward the cabin, George levering a shell as he moved. James had enough time to slap his side and curse himself for leaving his gun belt in the cabin.

His horse was loose somehow and it thundered away at an angle from the men as they approached. The mules' screaming suddenly ceased and James slowed to a quick walk, coming around the side of the cabin. The lantern light shined over the area, revealing the mules were gone. Not without a trace though; James saw an arc of blood on the cabin wall and a shower of droplets on the ground.

James grabbed the lantern from Nathan, "Quickly! Cut them off on the other side!" The cabin was backed up to the edge of a forty-foot cliff face with tall trees growing just out of reach, rising tentatively behind the cabin like saplings. Except for a small apron on the backside of the cabin there was nowhere for the vandals to go.

Nathan raced away as James and George quickly moved to the back corner of the cabin, looking out over the chasm and along the back of the building. Within seconds, Nathan appeared at the other end silhouetted by the pole lanterns. He shrugged his shoulders and shook his head.

James looked out over the cliff's edge, searching for some kind of path or stairway down, but he already knew there was none, and certainly not one you could get a mule down. They scanned the cliff face, expecting to see the culprits desperately clinging to a ledge. There was no one there, but in the dim light that just reached the base of the cliff they saw dead mules on the rocks below, broken limbs splayed out grotesquely.

"Bastards!" James shouted, "You've gone too far this time!"

Crash! They whirled at the sound of glass breaking. George and Nathan raced back around to the front. James had started also but a sudden instinct made him think,

Maybe they're under the cabin! He still had the lantern and he knelt down to peer under the cabin floor. The lantern's dim rays shone around the support beams and pilings, revealing nothing more sinister than a few large stones that had been pushed into place as support for the wood-planked floor. James shifted the lantern for a better view, when something hard smashed into the back of his head, knocking the lantern out of his hand. A gunshot broke, as the ground rushed up to slam into his face. He rolled onto his back just in time to see something leap over him against the backdrop of a starry sky, before everything went black.

* * * * *

Attempting to stem the rising tide of disobedience to their wisdom, the Ba'ath resorted to demonstrations of power. With their strong magic they commanded the winds and rains. They possessed powers of illusion and persuasion, glamors and charms. By all appearances they were immortal; kings were born, grew old, died and still the Ba'ath were there. Over the centuries the power and mystery of the Ba'ath became ingrained cultural traditions for humans. They could not be everywhere however, nor were they all-knowing. Once humans understood this, they took advantage of the increasing absence of the Ba'ath to decide things for themselves. Wars continued, with slaughter and tragedy, until the Ba'ath decided there was no choice but to force humans to obey.

-From the Book of More

12

AFTERMATH

THOMAS WAS STANDING at the foot of the bed when Mr. Dalby woke. He had been awakened himself in the middle of the night by an urgent knocking on the door. It was Nathan Guilford, sweating and out of breath. He told Thomas there had been an attack at the mine and urged him to come see to Mr. Dalby, who had been carried insensible to the guest house. Doctor Keene had also been summoned, and eventually there was a crowd of a dozen men standing around talking about the incident.

Thomas watched as Dalby's eyes flitted a few times, then opened and looked around the room. He groaned and tried to put his hand to his head, but found it was wrapped in bandages.

Doctor Keene leaned over him, pulling his eyelids up and looking into each of his eyes. He nodded and said, "You're going to have a fierce headache for a few days, I suspect." He turned to begin putting his instruments back in his bag, "You took a pretty good knock on the head, but you'll be fine. I'll check back in on you in the morning."

He picked up his bag, nodded his goodbyes and left.

"You get some rest, we'll talk tomorrow. If you need anything, just call for Clive," Thomas said quietly, and followed Dr. Keene outside. Nathan was still outside, talking excitedly with the other men, but stopped as Thomas came out.

"What happened up there tonight, Nathan?" he asked.

"Well, like I was tellin' the boys here, them vandals was breaking into the cabin, so we run over to catch em' but there warn't no one there."

"Was it just you and Mr. Dalby?"

"No sir, George was on guard duty too. Yeah, me and George seen something, or someone... well, we thought it was a man, standing on the roof of the cabin, but I really can't say what it was. It attacked Mr. Dalby, and he went down real hard. George fired a warning shot, and it run and *jumped off the cliff!* Clear out to the trees, I swear it on my soul! The branches was crashing and waving for a few seconds, then it was gone. George shot at it but we didn't see or hear anything else."

"So, are you saying it was an animal?" asked Thomas.

"I...I can't rightly say," stammered Nathan, "that's what I been thinking about this whole time. It all happened real fast and I just saw it for a second. I just can't really say, but,..." he paused, "there's some more bad news Mr. Rutherford."

"Yes, go on."

"Well, Mr. Dalby had the lantern with him and when he fell it broke and caught the grass on fire. By the time we run that thing off and dragged him away, it had spread and caught the cabin. Me and George tried to put it out, but it was no use, and he sent me to get help. By the time I got back, it was beyond saving."

"The cabin has burned down?" he asked incredulously.

"Yes sir. Oh, and the mules were killed."

Thomas was furious, and he struggled to maintain his composure. "Well, that is enough!" he gritted. He and the men mounted horses, and rode to the mine just in time to see Mr. French and a gang of miners putting out the last of the flames, though the charred structure still smoldered, and copious amounts of smoke rolled into the pre-dawn sky.

The men were tearing charred planks off the building and stamping out embers. The sky grew lighter as Thomas walked around the site with Mr. French. There wasn't much to be recovered from the building itself, which had contained many of the maps and mineshaft plans. If there was anything left, it was being covered by the dirt that was being shoveled on the smoking timbers.

Men were sent to the base of the cliff to tie ropes onto the mules' broken corpses, so they could be hauled up and carted away. While down there, they looked around for signs of the bandit, but found no clues. Thomas and Mr. French stood at the cliff's edge looking down at the men as they went about their task. Thomas looked out at the trees that rose up past him. The nearest thin branch was at least ten feet from his ledge, and he couldn't see how anyone could have made a leap to safety from there. He scanned the ground below the tree, thinking he should see the body of the attacker lying in the leaves, but nothing was there.

"How could they have made that leap?" he mused out loud.

"I don't know," said Mr. French, "but when Nathan came to get me, he was spooked out of his socks."

"Came to get you? Why didn't they ring the bell?" Thomas asked. They both looked at each other, then toward the post where the alarm bell hung. The only thing on the pole now was a scrap of the rope that had secured it there. From behind them, they heard Nathan's voice, "Oh Mr. Rutherford, they also stole the bell."

* * * * *

Thus began the wars of divinity, wherein the Ba'ath directly participated. They were terrible in battle, amplified by illusion into towering giants in black armor who breathed fire. A single Ba'ath could slaughter thousands on the battlefield, and the fear they inspired prevented many battles. They began to regain control, progress of a sort until they found themselves on opposing sides. With so many competing kings to advise and appease, it was only a matter of time before the Ba'ath ended up facing each other. The great capital city of Agra was the battleground, now lost to the ages. Two of the most powerful Ba'ath, infected by long years of interaction with the human's passion, hurled insults and spells at each other. They were Bael and Micah, and men were slain in heaps around them as they tore at each other's armies. In the midst of this slaughter the

Creator withdrew His presence, causing them both to flee the field in shock and dismay.

-From the Book of More

13

ODD FISH

JACK WAS EXCITED as he hurried down the lane towards the front gate. It was very early; so early the sun had still not risen, although the sky was lightening with dawn's approach. It was late August and the morning would already be hot and humid, but for the breeze blowing down off the mountains. Jack hiked up his gear and stepped faster as he looked ahead to see Eli waiting for him. He had promised to show Jack his favorite fishing spot today, and since it was a long hike, they were getting an early start. In their previous fishing trips to nearby streams, Eli had shown Jack how to set his tackle up. Fishing was something else Jack had limited experience with, and outside of shooting, the most fun he'd ever had.

The two set out, talking excitedly about the day ahead. In addition to fishing tackle, Eli had brought his rifle, so it promised to be a red-letter day.

They walked down the main street and out of town. They continued on another mile, until they passed the miners' shanty town at the foot of the mountain road. Eli turned west at the wide stream that ran past the shanties and headed toward the trees. The woods were quiet, but that was a deception. There were probably a dozen pairs of tiny eyes and ears on them at any time, as they walked through the forest. With the stream on their left, Eli picked a game trail to follow, which made for easier walking and they moved quietly up the stream.

The sun was still below the horizon, but the air around them warmed quickly, and Jack eyed the stream of rushing water. It was clear and inviting, with trees overhanging the bank on either side. He was tempted to start his fishing right then and there. Occasional exposed boulders wallowed in the rushing water like bathing golems.

"Eli," he whispered, "how about here? This looks good."

Elijah looked back and smiled, "Patience mate, it's even better up ahead, you'll see!"

They hiked on for another fifteen or twenty minutes before Jack heard the sound of rushing, thundering water. The stream had grown wider by this point, but also shallower so most sections were only knee-deep.

"There it is," Eli said, pointing ahead. Jack moved around him to see a great waterfall, plummeting from a rocky overhang perhaps a hundred feet high. As they moved closer, Jack could also see another much wider branch leading from the stream off to the south. *Eli was right*, he thought, *this is perfect!*

After dropping their gear and setting their tackle, the boys moved into spots on the stream just as the sun burst into view. Eli moved up near the waterfall, while Jack moved down to some rocks in a shallow section.

The fishing was everything Eli had promised it to be, and Jack was having the time of his life! Eli pulled in white bass from under the waterfall, while Jack had landed several trout and a few sunfish. Throughout the morning, they managed to string up a dozen good keepers. By midday though, the fish had stopped biting so they took a swim to cool off, stripping down and jumping from the rocks into the waterfall's pool.

After a while, Eli started a fire with his flint. He showed Jack how to clean the fish, removing the internal organs with a quick slit up the belly and washing out the cavity. They cooked a couple of trout, roasting them over the flames on green switches, and picking off the clean white flesh with their teeth. There was no salt, lemon or butter, but to Jack it tasted amazing.

As the afternoon waned, the sun moved west over the mountains, and the stream was once again covered in shade. More than once Jack had heard it said the sun sets fast in these mountains, and now he knew what they meant. Without the brilliant sunlight penetrating its depths, the clear water of the stream looked black and deep, with the pebble and boulder-strewn bottom now hard to discern. It didn't seem to bother Eli however, and both boys picked their poles up to carry on with their fishing.

Jack had moved back to the spot he favored, a shallow area with water flowing around several boulders that he could cast around, while Elijah went back to the waterfall. Jack was soon mesmerized by the flowing water, trying to make the perfect cast and land the giant monster he knew lurked just on the other side of that rock; or maybe *that* one.

Suddenly, he heard a yell and saw Eli squatting on the boulder struggling with something. Jack's first thought was of a prize fish, but Eli's line snapped and he fell backwards to land on his rump.

Eli leapt to his feet and began sprinting towards Jack shouting. Jack scrambled back from the water, "What happened?!"

"It got all our fish!" Elijah shouted, as he grabbed the rifle and turned to run back to the waterfall. Jack was hot on his heels and the two of them ran through the rocks to jump back up on the boulder.

"I had just caught a bass and was bringing up the stringer when something grabbed it from me! It was something big too; I had the stringer in both hands and if I hadn't let go it would have pulled me in!"

Eli worked the action on his carbine, levering a cartridge into the chamber as Jack stared into the water. He knew the depth here was ten feet at most, but in this light it might as well have been forty.

"There!" Eli shouted as he threw the rifle into his shoulder and fired off a round, making Jack jump. Jack saw the water erupt as the slug punched the surface, but he didn't see anything else. Eli chambered another round, and for a moment they both stood, searching the depths.

Suddenly, Jack saw a silver glint moving toward the waterfall, and he realized it was their stringer of fish!

"Eli," he whispered, putting his hand on Eli's shoulder and pointing.

"I see it," Eli answered, again raising the rifle. They both watched as the stringer moved steadily toward the boiling hammer of the waterfall. Eli held his shot as the fish disappeared in the foam. Then they both saw it; through the curtain of water, a dark shape pulled itself onto the rocks. Eli was right; whatever it was, it was big. There was a lot of water though, and there seemed to be shadow behind the waterfall, so now Jack couldn't see the thing at all.

"Bloody Hell," said Eli, "take my catch will you?" He aimed the rifle and fired through the waterfall.

A blood-curdling, yowling scream rent the air, bouncing off the rock wall and echoing out over the water.

The scream startled them both and they nearly jumped out of their skins before turning to run back to their gear. Eli's fright scared Jack even more and he scrambled to grab his tackle, keeping one eye on the waterfall. Eli did the same, and they both stood as yet another scream erupted, sounding like the victim of some horrible murder. They turned to flee back down the trail. Eli and Jack ran neck-and-neck, tearing through the woods, leaping fallen logs and slapping branches out of their way.

They ran on for another few minutes before slowing to a quick walk, breathing hard and looking over their shoulders.

"What was that!?" Jack asked.

"I dunno," Eli answered, "but whatever it was, I don't want to run into it again."

Another few minutes of fast walking brought them back into the sunlight. Even filtered through the trees as it was, it lifted the gloom that had enveloped the forest around them and they both felt their confidence and courage returning.

"Did you get a look at it?" Jack asked.

"Not really, I mean, it grabbed the stringer as I pulled it up and all I saw was this dark shadow under the ledge of the boulder." Eli's brows furrowed, "Come to think of it, I'll bet it was a beaver, or perhaps an otter."

"Really, do they get that big?" Jack had never seen either animal, so he had no idea.

"They must, right?" Eli said with a smile, "I mean, what else could it have been? Whatever it was, it's probably dead. That sounded like a death cry to me."

Jack nodded with bravado and said, "That's what it gets for stealing our fish."

The boys went home, feeling stronger and tougher in the aftermath of their adventure. At dinner Jack told the story to the family, embellishing it here and there for the sake of entertainment. His parents were obligingly interested and his hero status in Abbey's eyes grew larger.

Meanwhile, back at the waterfall, a creature sparsely-covered with coarse black hair slobbered over the remaining fish, biting the head off of one and crunching it up. It savored the morsel as it chewed, spittle running down its' chin. The pain of the bullet tearing though its' thigh and splattering on the rocks was gone. As was the hole of torn flesh; the injury had already knit itself, stitched and grown back together as if it had never happened.

14

CONFRONTATION

MICAH STOOD IN THE ARCHWAY staring at the table in the center of the room. The room itself was a circle with five arched openings and no ceiling. It was open to the sky, but there were no signs of neglect; no leaves or debris piling up in the corners. The table was large and round, made of granite and placed on a dais. It had been here before him, since the beginning. It was perfectly formed with crisp edges and a smooth surface that showed no signs of decay or wear. The table was surrounded by thirteen stone seats. They were simple in design, but graceful and majestic; high-backed, with a single name inscribed on each. His eyes traveled around the inscriptions he could see from his position.

He didn't need to read them, he knew the name on every chair intimately; *Erus, Micah, Fale, Urba, Azel, Vesh, Kraka, Grim, Durz, Bael, Samael, Pahn and Golga.* He also knew it had been a very, very long time since this table had served its purpose. He stepped onto the platform and slowly walked around the seats to the one reserved for him. His fingers traced the inscription, written in the old tongue by the Creator himself. These very stones were divine, yet it had been so long since he had been here to touch them.

"Go on brother, take your place," came a quiet voice from behind him. He resisted the urge to turn and look, and calmly stepped around to sit in his chair. It felt good; it had been too long indeed.

"Brother, is it? I'm so glad to hear we're on good terms again," he said. He stared straight ahead, waiting for the speaker to show himself.

The other appeared to his right, walking around the table counterclockwise and stopping behind a seat. "Well, that may be going too far, but come now, why start that old saw?" he said with a grin, draping his arm over the back of the chair.

"Wonderful, does that mean you're here to mend your ways? This is the best place for it after all," he said, smiling back at Bael in his most disarming way. There was a flash of irritation in Bael's black eyes, and Micah smiled even wider.

"Oh yes, the Sacred Chamber, meeting place of the Immortals. The seat of our arcane power, the lens of our communication with the Creator – that's the claim isn't it?" Bael's lip curled in a sneer, "So what does He have to say today brother?"

Now it was his turn to be irritated, but he kept the pleasant smile. "Perhaps if we all sat down…" he began. Another Ba'ath entered from his left, and he turned to look at Grim, who sauntered over to his place and sat down. "Michael," he said in greeting, nodding his head.

"Careful Grim, I believe he's sensitive about that name," Bael said. "What is it you're calling yourself these days? Blick? Some elfin name I hear." Azel walked in behind Bael and stood there regarding Micah.

He smiled, "Oh, you know, whatever comes to mind."

He started to stand, but Bael made a sit-sit motion with his hands, "No, no, please, let us talk," he said as he slid into the chair.

Micah was shocked; there were very specific rules in this chamber. He carefully smoothed his face, "Ah brother, I'm afraid you've got the wrong seat."

Bael cocked his eyebrows in surprise, and looked over his shoulder at the name inscribed on the chair, *Samael*. He looked back at Micah. "No, I think this one will do nicely," he said with a subtle but unmistakably triumphant smile.

The confidence and satisfaction on Bael's face stunned Micah, and he struggled to keep his composure as the implications of what had just happened raced through his mind. "Where is Samael?"

"Why, attending to his duties I suppose, as he has always done. We can talk about him later though. I've come to speak to you about our arrangement," Bael said, staring intently at Micah.

"No," Micah said, shaking his head, "not here. Your philosophy is inappropriate in this place. I'll not speak with you unless you're willing to discuss reconciliation."

He stared back at Bael, the undercurrent of tension beginning to simmer.

"Of course we can talk about reconciliation, brother. Why not? I believe I can speak for all of us when I say, we would welcome you with open arms." Bael threw his arms wide for effect, "What do you say?"

Micah gave a small smile and slowly stood up. Bael's sarcasm was meant to wound and harass him, and if it were true that Samael had defected, the consequences would be profound. He turned to leave, but Grim moved to intercept him, just as Fale stepped out of the nearest arch to block his path.

He eyed Fale cooly - he could not possibly think to offer Micah combat in this room. Fale raised his empty hands, but did not move out of the way. He turned back to face Bael.

"You are wrong," Micah said. "You have always been wrong and you are compounding your errors by recruiting others to share in your sins. There will be a reckoning."

"Listen to you, laying down judgments. You almost sound like your old self again! Remember those days Micah? Why don't you use your old Nomme de Guerre? I liked that name, it suited you; but spare me the lecture, we both know you're in no position to judge."

Micah gritted his teeth, "Perhaps not, but you will be judged. Your duty never included provisions for your vanity."

"Say what you like, we are committed to seeing it through. We've tried it your way for far too long. I will restore things to the way they were. Wasn't that our charge?" Bael asked, thumping his fist on the table. "We are moving forward, with or without you."

Micah clenched his fists, his anger rising. "You're a fool Bael. Samael will come to his senses, and your plans will come to naught. Besides, the Compact remains." He turned and pushed his way past Fale, striding through the archway even as Bael shouted after him.

* * * * *

The Creator had been with them from the beginning, His divine presence their virtual life-force, but once the Ba'ath fell into discord He vanished like a candle's flame in the wind. Their anguish at His absence was breathtaking and the effect immediate. They lost all but a fraction of their powers and as one, they fled the world. All thirteen retreated to the other side, a world beyond a magical curtain that only the Ba'ath could enter. It was but a poor copy of earth; there were no seasons, no life of any kind. The Ba'ath called this place "Lumis."

The only residents of Lumis were the Ba'ath and the ghosts of humans. Upon their deaths, their souls fled there, walking around endlessly, confused, forlorn and tormented. They remained in this state of limbo until Samael came to guide them into the presence of the Creator. Unfortunately, he could do nothing for them now. The portal of heaven was closed.

-From the Book of More

15

ENCOUNTER

JACK CAREFULLY SLID THE RIFLE forward on the fallen trunk. The squirrel he eyed was noisily thrashing in the leaves, running from this tree to that, stopping every so often to chatter at something.

His father had finally bought him a rifle, and the lever action seven-shot .25 caliber was perfect. He had already burned up most of the ammunition his father had given him, so he was rationing his last box until he could get some more. Today he was determined to bring something home to show off his developing hunting skills. He knew squirrel wasn't going to make the menu in his house, but miners in the camp would happily put it into a stew pot.

He sighted down the barrel, lining up the beaded front sight with the notch in the rear. The squirrel was twitchy, flashing this way and that, but the next time he stood still for a second, Jack told himself, he would fire – but he never got the chance.

The noise of crashing brush came from the tree line across the field from the finger on which he stood. He froze as a stag erupted from the trees, only fifty yards away. The stag was under attack by a gang of animals, the like of which Jack had never seen. Two of them hung onto the deer's back, wrapping long arms around its body. A third was trying to force its head down, having attached itself to the front of the buck's throat, grabbing its antlers, and biting the stag's muzzle. The deer stumbled across the field, bleating piteously as the creatures ravaged it. Others bounded across the field, using their long arms to propel themselves faster. Are they monkeys? Jack wondered to himself. The struggling stag had almost made it to the bottom of the slope, and Jack quickly lay down. The hairs on the back of his neck were standing up, and he knew he did not want to be seen. The stag fell on its side, it's bleating now a gurgle, as the creature had almost bitten its nose and lips off, blood spurting freely over the grass. The creatures hooted and barked, and began tearing open the deer's body. The sparse dark hair on their skinny arms dripped with blood as they tore at the internal organs. The stag finally lay still, and the creatures dove in, tearing at the flesh and eating. Several of them clapped and gamboled around in a queer kind of celebration. Jack slowly pushed himself up on his hands to try and get a better look, but as he did, his toe pressed down and broke a twig with a loud snap.

At the sound, one of the creatures snapped its head to look in Jack's direction. Jack froze, as he saw the creature's gaze. Its eyes were cataracts, without iris or pupil, like that of a dead fish. The creature stared with feral intensity at Jack's hiding spot.

Oh no, oh no! Jack's mind screamed as he slowly lowered his eyes, hoping he had not been seen. He counted to five, before slowly cutting his eyes back to the feeding frenzy, only to see the creature making its way up the slope. Panicking, Jack grabbed his rifle and leapt to his feet, running down the opposite side of the slope as fast as he could! He heard a hoot behind him and knew they were on his trail. Jack flew down the hillside, leaping and jumping with every step. Branches slashed across his face and tried to trip him, but he kept moving, knowing if he stopped he would be caught. As he tumbled down into the bottom of the slope, he found himself in a narrow draw, dark and humid from moisture. Pine trees and cedars filled the space, dropping a thick, silent carpet of needles on the forest floor. Frantically, Jack threw the rifle down and leapt at one of the pine trees, hugging the trunk and trying to scratch his way up to the nearest branch. He still clung to the trunk when the whole pack of gibbering creatures crashed into the pines. They quickly surrounded him, rolling in the needles and clapping their long fingered hands together.

Terrified, Jack looked down to see the creatures leering up at him, smiling. Small pointed and broken teeth lined their wide mouths, and their froglike faces crinkled as they smiled. At such a close distance, he could see them more clearly. Against his will, his eyes were drawn to stare at their grotesque forms, which were only about four feet tall, yet they emanated an unmistakable feral strength. Their squat heads sat on squat bodies, with flat, pinched features. Long greasy, stringy hair hung down from their heads, matted and tangled with long pointed ears sticking out. Dark hair ran down the lengths of their arms, back and legs. Their arms were abnormally long and spindly, like the spider monkeys Jack had studied, with long, dexterous fingers and dirty nails. They were all naked, filthy and vulgar.

"Come down, little boy," one of them spoke! It was a strange croaking voice, but there was no doubt the creature spoke to him. Jack felt his bladder release as he stared into the empty blue eyes, feeling terror such as he had never known. They laughed all the more when they saw he had wet himself, and began throwing pinecones at him. Jack felt his grip slipping, and he looked helplessly at the branch still two feet above his head. He stretched his arm upward, desperately trying to grab the branch, but with a loud scraping sound, he slid down the trunk to the ground.

He sprawled at the base of the tree, and was instantly spun around to find himself looking into the face of one of the creatures. Its breath stank worse than any odor he could describe, and he choked, almost vomiting in the creature's face. If he was terrified before, he was in a state of shock now. The creature casually picked up a long switch, and hit Jack with it, whipping it across his arms and face, cackling with glee. The pain startled him out of his stunned condition, and he put his arms up to protect his face from the creature's slashes. The others grabbed sticks as well, and were poking him painfully, in the ribs, the neck, and his legs. Curling into a fetal position, Jack was afraid for his life.

Suddenly, there was a flash of light, like the magnesium flash from a photo-pan, but without any sound, and the abuse stopped. After a second or two, Jack looked out between his arms to see the creatures shuffling around, staring at a place to his right. Jack turned, and for the second time today, saw an odd creature.

The creature was small, perhaps a foot tall, and had large green eyes like that of a frog, but there the similarity ended. Covered in papery, leaf-like layers, it bounced and jiggled, emitting a burst of hums and clicks, sounding like a whole menagerie of insects.

One of the creatures giggled, and thwacked Jack on the head with a stick. "Yes, yes, we know, we know, but does he? What a curious boy!" It cocked its head to one side and whispered, "Perhaps he would like to stay?" Its' eyes bored into Jack's, and he found himself looking deeply into them, trying to find something in the cloudy blue swirls. *Stay? Why not? Why not stay? Stay.* Suddenly the eye contact was broken as the smaller creature ran up Jack's arm, interceding between him and the monster, it's tiny hands gripping Jack's hair. He shook his head and tried to remember what he had been thinking. The frog-eyed creature buzzed and clicked furiously, pressing toward the gargoyles.

"Calm yourself, Master Worm, we'll go, but we know you now Jack. We will find you, find you!" The creature pointed the stick at him, laughing. Just like bullies on a school playground, the rest of the troop followed suit, spitting raspberries and making other rude gestures before backing out of the pines. Jack noticed they didn't turn their backs on the smaller creature. Then they were gone.

Breathless, Jack sat looking at the petite creature now standing on his knee. His mind spun, and he didn't know what to say. "Th-thank you," he finally sputtered.

He flinched backward as the creature began to hum softly, and its' eyes seemed to grow even larger. As he stared, he felt his vision flooding with light, until it blinded him. Bathed in sunlight, he smiled as the smells of a spring flowering washed over him.

Jack stood on the porch of his father's house, swaying as the light faded from behind his eyes. He shook his head, confused; how had he come to be here? He took a step toward the front door and gasped at the burning sting he felt all over his arms and legs. His rifle was in his hands, but his palms were scraped and bleeding. His forearms also had scratches and were beginning to bruise. He had no idea how he had received his wounds, but he knew he would be in serious trouble if his mother saw him in this condition.

Creeping around to the horse stable, Jack leaned his rifle in a corner, removed his clothing, and quickly doused himself in the horse trough. The cold water burned his cuts, and he scrubbed everywhere it burned. It was still early September, so the water wasn't too cold, but Jack jumped out of the water and stood shivering in the straw of the barn. It was almost full dark now, and Jack knew he had to make his way inside the house soon. He quickly donned his clothing, doing his best to make himself presentable. Coming out of the barn, he made his way across the yard. He had the sensation he was being watched, and he looked back toward the trees, but there was nothing there. The hairs on his arms stood up, and he stepped faster, practically running up the steps to the porch and through the side door into the kitchen.

Lucille stood in the kitchen, cleaning up from dinner. She took one look at Jack, and gasped, holding her hand to her mouth and furrowing her brow in concern.

"Oh my lord, what happened to you?" she asked loudly, setting down the dishes in her hands.

"Ssshhh! Lucille please," Jack pleaded, clasping his hands and making his most desperate face at her.

"Jack? Is that you?" his mother asked, her voice floating in from the front parlor.

"Yes, Mother, just on my way upstairs, good night."

"Just a moment, Jack." Her footsteps clicked on the wood floors, coming toward the kitchen.

Lucille stepped over and threw her arm around his shoulders and pulled him tight against her, almost smothering him against her breast. He returned her hug, encircling her girth with his arms.

Elizabeth entered the kitchen to find Lucille giving Jack a hug, ruffling his hair and grinning at him. "Ma'am, this rascal knows he missed dinner and was down here trying to chivvy some leftovers." She looked at Elizabeth, "I'll just make him a plate he can take up to his room." She turned him and marched him to the stairs leading up from the kitchen.

"Go on, I'll be up there in a few minutes with your supper." She gave Jack a little shove and he ran up the stairs, trying not to look like he was in too much of a hurry.

His mother called up the stairs after him, "Jack, from now on I expect to see you at the dinner table promptly, is that understood?"

"Yes Mother, I'm sorry, it won't happen again," he answered, quickly taking a candle from the hall, entering the room and closing the door behind him. He ran over to the washbasin by his bedside and lifted the small hand mirror. He saw what had so alarmed Lucille; he had a series of bloody scratches across the right side of his face, and swelling under his eye. His face screwed up in confusion, Jack probed at the scratches with his fingers, trying to figure out how he got them. He heard Lucille coming up the stairs, and turned to meet her as she knocked and came in the room. She carried a large plate covered with a cloth and a jar of tea. An oil lamp swung from her pinkie finger as she set the dishes on his bureau.

Lucille walked over to Jack, lifting the candle to better see his face. "Boy," she said, "don't you ever ask me to do that again. I don't like tricking your mama like that."

"I know Lucille, thank you, but you know how mother would carry on if she saw me like this," he said, gesturing at both his scratches and his clothes. Jack had come up with a story, and tried it out on Lucille, "I was taking a shortcut back from the mine through the woods and I took a wrong step and fell into some thorn bushes."

"Uh-huh," she said, clearly unconvinced. "Well, that must be the reason your trousers smell like they need a good wash; you must have rolled in something."

"What?" Until that moment, Jack hadn't even noticed he stank of urine. "Ugh! Y-Yes, I must have gotten into something in the leaves. I'll change right away. Thank you Lucille." Red-faced, Jack hurried to change out of his clothing as Lucille exited the room. Now in his nightshirt, he bundled his soiled things and stacked them in his hamper.

He walked over to his bureau and lifted the cloth from the plate Lucille had brought for him. It looked delicious; sliced ham with mashed potatoes and green peas, and a huge biscuit. Jack suddenly realized he was famished. He fell to eating with gusto, spooning up the mashed potatoes and peas, and washing it down with big swigs of sweet tea. After a minute or two, he had taken the edge off his hunger, and he picked up his plate to take it with him to the bed, where he could sit down and eat in comfort. He returned to his meal, making quick work of the ham and biscuit. Jack placed his plate on the dresser and noticed a small tin. He set the plate and his tea down and opened the tin. It was a salve, and Jack could smell camphor and eucalyptus. He silently thanked Lucille again, and padded over to the mirror to apply it to his face. After his face, he had enough to do his hands and some of his forearms. It stung a little, but the smell of the salve was invigorating, and Jack felt better already. He crawled into bed, blowing out both the candle and the oil lamp.

As he lay on his side, listening to the noises of the house creaking, and the muffled sound of his parents talking downstairs, Jack tried to piece together what had happened that night. The last thing he remembered was leaving the sluice and heading for Lucius' cabin, but it was no use. Try as he might, he couldn't remember a thing after leaving the mines.

16

GRUESOME DISCOVERY

JACK WAS STILL SLEEPING the next morning, as Thomas stood over the mess in the center of the stable floor.

Thomas had been shaving when Ambrose came to tell him Mr. Severn needed to see him in the barn. He wiped his face and followed Ambrose outside. As they came around the corner of the house, he could hear one of the horses neighing loudly and apparently kicking the wall of its stall. The loud insistent booming threatened to break the slats and Thomas hurried his steps. He entered the barn as Charles managed to grab the halter and throw a blanket over the horse's head. As he patted and soothed the animal, Thomas, Ambrose and Mr. Severn studied at the remains lying on the floor. It was a stag, bearing eight points on its antlers. With that exception, it was difficult to tell what kind of animal it had been, since its head had been gnawed terribly. The carcass had clearly been fed upon, the white bones of the rib cage gleaming through the gore, but the organs of the deer had been flung all over the barn. The limbs were also torn apart and scattered in no particular order. Thick looping strands of blood splattered the walls and the straw. It was a gruesome sight, and Mr. Severn motioned for Ambrose to help him clean up the remains. As they gathered the pieces, it was obvious the deer had been dismembered by some predator, but there was still plenty of flesh left uneaten. He supposed the panicked horse must have scared off whatever was feeding. Perhaps the animal had rabies. They put all the pieces they could find in a wheelbarrow, and Ambrose took it away to dispose of it. Charles would rake out the stalls, replace the hay, and wipe the blood off the rails and walls. From now on, they would have to ensure the barn door was closed, Thomas told himself, but for now he needed to get ready for work.

As the morning sky brightened into full daylight, Jack sat up in bed, unable to sleep any longer. He was not feeling particularly rested, but his body was accustomed to rising early, and now he was fully awake and alert. Moving to the bureau, Jack rummaged through his drawers for a change of clothes, and began dressing. As he pulled a clean pair of trousers on, he noticed the salve tin, and he put his hand to his face. He could feel the scratches beginning to scab, and he retrieved the mirror to see what his face looked like in the light of day. Hmm, he thought, that's not too bad; perhaps his lie about the sticker bushes would fool his mother. *Well,* he reasoned, *maybe I whacked my head when I fell, and since I can't recall what happened, that's as likely the truth as anything.*

He had just pulled on his shoes when he heard the quick little patter of Abigail's feet as she ran down the wooden hallway. She burst into Jack's room and he smiled at her, "Good morning Abby."

"Good morning Jack. Will you please come down and... Oh, Jack! What happened to your face?" she asked, walking over to him as he sat tying his shoes. She raised a hand and gently laid it on his scratches. Her hand was soft and cool, and it felt good on his face. He hoped the scratches weren't becoming infected. Jack was touched by her concern, and he put his hand over hers, pulling it away and kissing her palm. "It's nothing Abby, now what were you saying?"

"Will you play some croquet with me, please? I have no one else to play with, except mother, and she is having Miss Celia over again for lessons."

"Is Miss Celia already here? Downstairs?" Jack asked. Since she had been coming over for piano lessons with their mother, Jack had taken every opportunity he could to be around when she was at the house. Today was a different story however, with him looking the way he did. He wasn't sure what she would think about him being all scratched up; maybe she would think him a hooligan. The truth was, she was sixteen and far too old for him, but she was a beauty.

"No, but I heard mother asking Lucille to make some refreshments and plan lunch, because Miss Celia would be visiting shortly."

"Oh, I see. Well, all right, let's go then." Abigail's smile widened and she grabbed Jack by the hand, pulling him out of the room and down the stairs.

* * * * *

There was one other being present on Lumis and the Ba'ath sought her out; she was Mother Nature. She was more ancient than they and her power was strong. Even at the height of their glory Mother might have destroyed any one of them, but in their weakened state her advantage was colossal. Mother did have one weakness however, because she was almost completely restricted to her duties. She controlled all the powers of the earth; volcanoes, earthquakes, floods and the seasons, but for all that, she had little ability to act on her own. It was predictable therefore, when they asked her counsel she advised them to return to strict service to the Creator. Their problem of course, was after so many years of confusion and conflict they were no longer sure how to interpret His will.

-From the Book of More

17

OVERHEARD

ELI STOOD WITH everyone else as the service ended. He turned to leave, but stopped abruptly when he saw Elsa Cutter standing in the doorway. Eli had come to church with his father as they did every Sunday, but Elsa had seemingly taken a shine to him. Over the past several weeks she had become more and more attentive, and now she always found some reason to speak with him. *Just my luck*, he thought; Elsa wasn't particularly attractive, and it filled him with dread to see her blocking his escape. He lingered, wading through the adults as they all shuffled in a quietly chattering gaggle out of the church. Elsa had moved out of the church, but now stood on the steps, scanning the crowd. Desperate to avoid her, Eli hung back until he was the last person in the building. He stood back from the doorframe so he could just barely see Elsa, yet remain hidden.

Why isn't she leaving? He leaned out slightly to see Elsa speaking with another girl, who shook her head. Elsa huffed and turned to walk back up the steps.

Eli jerked back and looked around for somewhere to hide. The pews and the pulpit were no good, but maybe he could fit into the small closet just off to one side at the back of the room. He flung the door open and jumped inside, pulling the door closed behind him as quietly as he could. He winced as his foot bumped something that sounded like a pail, and he held his breath and listened. Elsa clopped around the hall, and then, "Elijah?" It would be awkward to explain being in the closet, so he certainly wasn't going to speak up now.

He put his eye to the crack between the door and frame, and saw Elsa walking up the side aisle toward him. He quietly took hold of the doorknob and gripped it hard, fearful she would try to open the door, but she did not. He watched as she stood for a moment with her arms crossed, looking annoyed and flushed, before walking out of his line of sight. It sounded as though she had left the building, but having escaped thus far, he wanted to remain hidden a few moments more just to be sure. He resolved to wait another five minutes or so before leaving. Sitting in the darkness, he listened for any signs of Elsa's return and had just decided it was safe to leave when he heard a heavy clumping coming up the church steps.

Oh No! His heart started pounding and he looked out to see who walked through the hall. It was more than one person; Eli could tell several men had walked into the church, perhaps as many as six or eight. He peeked through a crack to see them take their seats in the pews, while Reverend Fetch resumed his position behind the pulpit. Now he really had a problem; hiding from a girl was one thing, but this could mean serious trouble. He considered bursting out and making a run for it, but he would probably get caught, and besides, so far none of the men showed the least interest in the closet. *No*, he decided, *I'm going to stay right here and keep my mouth shut!*

Other than Reverend Fetch, Eli could only see the faces of three of the men, but he recognized each of them; Mr. Pearson who owned the dry goods store, the stable owner Mr. Egan, and Judge Cole. So, it was a gathering of the town leaders, but he wondered what they were meeting about, and he placed his ear by the slit to better hear the conversation.

The men seemed solemn, not talking among themselves and only the occasional squeak of a wooden pew breaking the silence until Reverend Fetch began, "The event will take place on the twenty-third. Are we all still in agreement about the Rutherfords?" Eli saw heads nod, and presumed the rest were doing the same. "Very well. Remember, if the worst happens, they will need our prayers. It will be a time of trial, as it has been for many people in Cobbs these past years."

"Let me remind you all you are doing nothing wrong in the eyes of the law," said Judge Cole. "This matter will be decided by divine providence, and none can be blamed for unhappy chance."

"Other folks might not see it that way," said a man Eli couldn't see.

"This matter is not to be discussed outside these walls,"

said Reverend Fetch. "What we do here, we do in the sight of God for the good of our own kin. Do not speak of this even to your womenfolk. They will not understand." He paused for a moment before asking, "Does anyone wish to speak before we adjourn?"

Another moment of silence passed, "Then go home and ensure your families are prepared for the season. There are no guarantees."

With that, the men stood and shuffled out of the church. Eli listened for several minutes before he thought it was safe enough to open the closet door. He peeked out, and seeing no one in the hall, stepped out of the closet. He saw the doors of the church closed, and he walked over to a window to look outside. Several buggies pulled off down the road, and a few other men were walking on foot.

He slowly pulled the door open, watching for anyone who might see him. When the coast was clear, Eli slid out of the building and shut the door behind him. One last look around, and he jumped off the steps to one side and scampered away.

He quickly walked down the street, heading back to his father's shanty in the miners' camp, nervously looking around as he walked, imagining someone watching him leave the church. His mind whirled as he tried to make sense of what he had heard. Of course, he would tell Jack tomorrow when he saw him at the mine. *Tell him what?* he thought. He didn't really know what they were talking about, just that it didn't sound good. Eli made it back to the shanty and spent the evening troubled and restless.

After a good night's sleep, Eli felt a bit less anxious about what he had overheard. He walked up to the mine to work with his father, but after a few hours took a break to find Jack. This particular morning he was nowhere to be found, so Eli's father allowed him to leave to search for him. He walked the mile back to Cobbs and made his way through the town, stopping at the mining office before continuing over to the Rutherford's house.

Lucille answered the door, and told Eli to look for Jack out in the barn. Eli reached the barn to see Jack filling the horse's feeding trough with oats.

"Oy mate!" he called, waving as he sauntered into the barn. "I looked for you at the mine this morning."

"Yes, sorry, Father loaded me up with some work here for the day," Jack said with a smile.

"Well, I came by to tell you something."

"Ok, what is it?" said Jack. He could tell Eli had something on his mind. He put the bucket down and followed Eli over to a pile of straw, where they both sat down.

"Listen," Eli began, "I heard something yesterday you should know about." Eli told Jack everything he could remember about the affair at the church. When he had finished, Jack sat there with his hands clasped over his knees. "What do you think they were talking about? Are they angry at my father for something?" Jack asked.

"I don't know, but it sounded like they were serious, so I just wanted to let you know you should keep on the lookout for them."

"But Judge Cole? He and his daughter come to our house on a regular basis. They seem to like us well enough." Even as he said it, Jack recalled Lucius' words the night they returned from Charleston. *Don't trust nobody*, he had said.

"Well, Reverend Fetch told them not to tell the women, so Miss Celia probably doesn't know anything about it. Are you alright then? We can talk some more later, I have to get back to help Da."

"Okay. Hey, Eli?" Jack said.

"Yeah?"

"Elsa Cutter?"

"Shut-up!" Eli grinned, throwing a handful of straw into Jack's hair.

Eli left Jack sitting there in the barn. He turned Eli's news over and over, wondering what he should do about it. In the end, he decided it must be a matter involving the mine. What else could it be? If that was the case, Jack was sure this was a matter his father would be capable of handling with no help from him. Besides, he didn't want Eli to get in trouble for spying on the meeting, so Jack decided to keep the information to himself, at least for now.

* * * * *

For more than a thousand years the Ba'ath remained on the other side, trying to decide where they had failed and how to proceed. In the end they could not agree and separated into two factions. One felt they had gone too far in trying to influence the affairs of men. This faction was led by Micah and he proposed going back to reassume their roles as advisors, hoping to regain the human's cooperation through diplomacy and wisdom. Bael led the other faction, whose members felt they needed to take the offensive against humans to regain their obedience and restore order by any means necessary.

-*From the Book of More*

18

THE TOWN DRUNK

DUSK APPROACHED as Jack and Eli walked back toward Cobbs from the mine. They were still making their way down the shoulder of the mountain when Eli turned off to head to the miner's camp while Jack continued alone. On this eastern side of the mountain, the light faded quickly and the sky had already turned a dark blue-purple.

As he walked along he occasionally passed a miner coming or going, but unless he was familiar with them he kept his head and eyes forward and marched on.

It had been almost a week since Eli had told him about the meeting at the church, and Jack still hadn't seen cause to tell his father. It was true that when he walked through the town lately people stared or turned their backs, and continued to talk in a huddle. The reception in Cobbs had never been warm, but lately it was downright frigid. Perhaps it was this way every year near harvest time. The mood certainly wasn't affecting the business at the saloon though; Jack could hear the faint tinkle of music and laughter at all hours of the night now. Drawing near the outbuildings of Cobbs, he saw a good number of people walking up and down the street. Maybe it was the pleasant weather that brought people out in droves, with the streetlamps lit and many stores staying open later than usual.

Jack entered the town, but for all the attention he was paid, he might as well have been a ghost. He saw the saloon entrance ahead, which had ten or fifteen men standing outside talking and laughing. He moved off the boardwalk and across the street to avoid having to walk through them. As he walked past the saloon several of the men turned to look at him, and he saw their smiles freeze and quickly disappear as they ducked their heads, or turned their backs. He quickly passed, and continued walking on the far side of the street. Despite their cool distance, Jack didn't feel particularly threatened by their behavior, which made it easy to ignore.

He absently looked over as he drew near the church and saw lanterns stuck on poles in the cemetery. They were illuminating the dark fertile soil of a fresh grave; the final resting place of Tim Button.

Yesterday the church bell had begun tolling. Being it was a Thursday Jack didn't know what it portended, but he heard the rest of the story later from Eli. That morning, Button had not shown up at the saloon for his breakfast as usual. When the lunch hour passed, and he still hadn't come by, one of the girls at the saloon asked a few of the men to go by his house to check on him. When they arrived, Button's feet were sticking out of the open door. The talk of the town however, was that his face was stuck in a rictus, eyes wide and mouth stretched in a silent scream. The superstitious among them were very nervous, but Doctor Keene had declared it perfectly normal, explaining that in the throes of death the muscles in the body may draw up. When this happened to the face all manner of grotesque and frightening expressions were possible. It seemed reasonable, particularly because there were no signs of violence on the body. Although he was relatively young, Button had the health problems of a much older person and his untimely death had been attributed to a weak heart.

The normal tradition was to conduct funerals and bury the dead after three days of mourning, but Tim's body was quickly prepared, and planted in the ground that very evening. Lanterns had been put up in the cemetery and the townspeople took turns watching over the grave. This was the first funeral that had taken place since the Rutherford's arrival and there was no explanation for this strange custom.

Something on the ground near the headstone moved, and in the weak light of the lanterns he could see it was a person. He stopped for a moment, watching as the person rolled behind an adjacent gravestone and pushed themselves into a sitting position. The hairs on the back of his neck started to rise, but he shook it off. *Maybe they're hurt*, he thought, and headed toward the lanterns.

The headstones seemed to shift ranks to block his view

as he traversed the open ground and approached the cemetery. All he could see were the legs of the person laid out straight and unmoving. Coming alongside the row of headstones, Jack saw it was a man, leaning back against the stone, chin on his chest. His hair fell over his face and his arms were lying limply at his sides. Now within a few yards, Jack could see a whiskey bottle in the man's right hand.

He was making an odd sound and it took Jack a moment to realize the man was sobbing; quiet, mewling sounds, like that of a child.

Jack cleared his throat and asked, "Sir, are you okay?"

The man gave a small jerk and looked in his direction, searching for the voice. The red bleary eyes turned toward him and Jack recognized Hank, the wrinkled face a ruin of sadness, wet with tears. He looked at Jack as if pleading and shook his head.

"No, can you give me a hand up?" he asked in a hoarse whisper. He thrust his hand at Jack and tried to sit upright. Jack grasped his wrist and tried to pull Hank to his feet, but he was heavy and his balance was poor. The odor of whiskey was so strong Jack almost choked as Hank grabbed the front of his shirt with the other hand, pulling himself the rest of the way to his feet. He still hung onto the whiskey bottle, the last third left in the bottom sloshing out onto both of them.

Hank stood with one arm over Jack's shoulders and the other hand wrapped in Jack's shirt. Jack started to turn to walk Hank back to the street, but Hank's feet were rooted in place as he stared out over the graves. Jack had no choice but to stand there supporting him.

He released Jack's shirt and pointed out at the stones, waving expansively as he said, "I got a bunch of my kinfolk buried right here. I've lived 'round these parts all my life."

Jack didn't know what to say, so he remained silent. Hank glanced at him with bloodshot eyes before continuing, "You want to know what's wrong with this town," he slurred, "all you got to do is look out there."

Puzzled, Jack looked out over the gravestones. This cemetery had been here for at least a hundred years, and there were a variety of headstones, from simple stone blocks or wooden crosses, and even a marble obelisk or two. It seemed like any other graveyard.

Hank looked down at him and smiled ruefully, "You don't see it do you?" he asked. "That's alright, nobody does. At least nobody that ain't from here."

Jack winced at the alcohol in Hank's breath. He still didn't know what Hank was talking about so he said, "Here, I'll help you home," pulling on Hank to get him moving. Instead, Hank took his arm from Jack's shoulders and hooked it around the back of his neck, pulling Jack into him. He lurched forward, "Wait, I'll show you," he said, still pointing with the bottle.

They staggered together up the row of graves, stopping at each one where Hank would ask, "How old was he? I knew her... What about that one?"

Jack would quickly do the math, "Seventy-two, Fifty-three, Nineteen, Forty-six..." Jack's neck and back were starting to ache from supporting Hank, but they only stopped once they were beyond the lantern's glow and it was too dark to read any more. Hank removed his arm from around Jack's neck, but gripped his sleeve and held him at arm's length. He looked at Jack with an expectant squint, daring him to guess the answer, but Jack had no clue.

"You don't see it boy, because there's nothing there." He grinned at his wit, but the grin melted and his face collapsed again in an expression of agony.

"I'm sorry, Hank, I don't understand what you're trying to tell me," he said. Standing in the cemetery with a distraught drunkard was starting to feel very strange.

"Life is hard in a town like this boy, a frontier town, a mining town. For a long time there warn't no doctor. Accidents, disease, they all take a toll, you see?" He swept his arm over the graves, "How many children are buried here?"

Jack's eyebrows rose, and he obligingly looked around. Come to think of it, he only remembered seeing one young child in the rows they had reviewed. What was Hank saying? He felt a chill run up his spine.

"My boy isn't here," he said sniffling. "Lost to me fifteen years ago - I never found him, God forgive me. I couldn't even bring him home for a decent burial and now his bones are scattered and lost!" Hank shrieked, breaking down to sob again. It was terrible to hear his pain and a frightened Jack tried to take a step back, but Hank wouldn't let him go. He threw the bottle down and grasped Jack's shirt with both hands. "This town is cursed!" he shouted, shaking Jack. A snarl twisted his face and saliva drooled from one corner of his mouth. Jack tried to twist away but he couldn't break Hank's grip.

"Hank, let me go!" He wrestled with Hank's fingers, trying to pry himself free, but the man was too strong for Jack to escape. He fell to his knees and hung there in Hank's grasp, afraid for the first time.

"Let him go, Hank," said a calm voice out of the darkness.

Hank froze, and he and Jack both looked toward the voice. Lucius had stopped a few feet away, watching Hank, his good eye alert and dark, his blind eye pale and dead. Time stood still for a few seconds before Jack felt Hank's grip begin to loosen, and he pulled away from his grasp, scuttling backward. Hank looked down at his hands and glanced at Jack. He mumbled something before turning away to sit down on the nearest headstone, rubbing his face with his hands.

"See, I told you he's worse sometimes. He's just drunk, don't hold it against him boy," Lucius said, "you go on home now."

Jack nodded and stumbled back toward the church and Main Street. Looking back, Lucius was talking with Hank, both men ignoring him altogether. He hurried down the road now, feeling better in the lights of town and by the time he turned down the lane to the house, he was recovered, if still a little shaken by Hank's behavior.

19

THREAT

Dᴵᴹ ʟɪɢʜᴛ ꜰɪʟᴛᴇʀᴇᴅ ᴅᴏᴡɴ from the overhead opening in the high rock walls surrounding the little grotto. A dribbling waterfall fell from on high to splatter on the rocks thirty feet below. This fed a shallow pool, which in turn, surrounded a small island. The island, covered in short grass and tiny white flowers, also had a single old weathered tree stump in the center.

It was critical that everything was in place, nothing left to chance. Bael had carefully prepared this chamber, weaving spells of strength and power into the stones. Even so, the humans came closer with every passing day, chewing their way through the mountain like termites through dead wood. They were close enough now that the muffled thumps of dynamite blasts reverberated through the chamber, but there was still time.

Bael looked around the walls at the goblins he had placed throughout the chamber. There were perhaps twenty of them, and they stood by obediently, their dull blue-white eyes eerie in the semi-darkness. Before each goblin was a stone, set in the earth and marked with a rune of ancient power. All was in place. *And so it begins*, he thought.

He stepped into the pool and waded out to the island, scooping water in a small golden bowl as he walked. He stepped onto the island and approached the stump. Holding the bowl in his left hand, he made several passes over it with his right while intoning a charm.

"*Il nath tor da braukin fer*," he chanted in a soft sing-song voice. The glow from the golden bowl became brighter and he held it out over the stump, slowly pouring the water out. Like tiny glittering diamonds the droplets splattered on the wood to run along the surface into the cracks and crevices. The water disappeared into the stump, except for a few glowing beads that remained standing in tiny hollows. Bael tossed the bowl to one side and walked back across the pool to take his place. His was the most dangerous task, but it could not be entrusted to anyone else.

The charm was a simple summoning spell, but if he had prepared correctly it would be the key to his success. He signaled the goblins with a clap and as one, they began to hum. It was a froggy, raspy sound, which at first was very annoying, but then the tone smoothed out and settled into a deep buzz. The goblin's arms were out wide, with their long hands lying on the ground palm-up. Their heads lolled back but their eyes were wide open. Bael slowly lifted his hand and wafted it in a lazy pattern. The goblins began to speak the incantation in rhythm with his movements and Bael watched the tree stump. Now that it had begun, he would not stop, but the danger was appalling. This was something he had never attempted before, and he felt excited, nervous; *Is this what fear feels like? I'd almost forgotten.*

He saw movement at the stump and he watched as a tiny green shoot sprouted from the center of the wood. Tendrils slowly slithered out and down the sides of the stump. The green shoot grew thicker and taller until it was almost as tall as Bael.

Bael watched intently as a pod formed at the tip of the shoot and began to swell. He sped up the pattern of his hands, the goblins matching pace. Even as the shoot swelled in girth and height, it bent over with the weight of the translucent white bulb, pulsing like a heart. Again Bael quickened the pace and the goblins grew louder, their heads thrown back as they chanted.

More tendrils flowed out and over the stump, making their way across the grass and into the pool. The shoot was now as thick as a man's arm and swelling every second. The bulb began to sway and thrash about. Bael quickened the pace again, his hands flashing through the air while the goblins howled in perfect unison at the top of their lungs. Their hands were rigid claws, while saliva frothed and flew from their mouths as they sang.

Bael saw two dark spots form beneath the surface of the bulb. He almost lost his courage then, but pressed on. The new tree continued to swell and grow. It changed colors from bright green to mottled gray. Branches shot out to the sides and were whipping around in a fury. The bulb now sat atop the trunk which remained flexible, wobbling around as if it might fall over. Two of the larger branches reached for the bulb, grasping. The tree was definitely moving on its' own accord now, thrashing to and fro while clasping the bulb. The noise in the grotto was deafening and Bael started to feel the strain of keeping up the spell, when the bulb began to split.

The branches pulled at the tear, ripping the fleshy petals away from a pale head with two dark eyes; eyes which were glaring at Bael with the most terrible anger. The head emerged with a horrific roar, so loud even he was shocked at its' savage power. His loss of concentration caused the goblins to falter as well, but the deed was done. He dropped his hands and the goblins fell silent, panting and gasping. Several fell to the floor.

Mother had arrived. She assumed her typical form, the branches smoothing and tightening into corded muscle, forming clawed hands.

"BAEL!!" she roared, "WHAT IS THE MEANING OF THIS!?!" The trunk rose, elongating until she towered over Bael. "You dare to summon me? By FORCE!?"

Bael quickly knelt on the ground and bowed his head in submission; this was the most dangerous moment.

"Mother! Please calm yourself, hear me!" he yelled at her, true fear helping his tone sound sincere.

She looked around the grotto, taking in the rune stones and the goblins. Hissing in fury, she flung one arm out, smashing into the rock wall and a ton of debris crashed down on a pair of goblins. Another motion of her arms and a wave of water stood up out of the pool and slammed into several more, smashing them into the walls. Some of the goblins did not move or get up again. She began an incantation of her own and Bael could feel the eldritch power crackling through the air before she released a bolt of lightning that blasted every rune stone into dust and shards. *Such power!* he thought.

She leaned toward Bael, spreading her arms wide and he took a step back putting his hands up in supplication, "Mother! Wait!" he shouted. She growled, but hesitated.

"The Thirteen are divided Mother, as you well know. I need your guidance, and I took this precaution so we could speak in private. Will you hear me?" he said, watching her. She could destroy him if she wanted.

She bared her teeth in a feral snarl. The branches of her tree were still whipping and flailing around, and goblins were whimpering in pain in the background. "You have overstepped yourself! What are you playing at with these magics?" she asked as she pointed at the goblins and the rubble of the rune stones.

"My apologies Mother, I meant no offense. It was imperative we speak in private and this was the only way I could assure that."

"Speak then!" she snapped.

"Samael has joined me Mother, we are Seven. I want to reopen negotiation of The Compact."

"What?!" she said, drawing back, clearly surprised. "Where is Samael?"

"He is carrying out his duties, but I can assure you, he is committed."

She regarded him for a moment with a gaze that was always unsettling; like a wise and ancient serpent, dangerous and implacable. "So be it. Call the Thirteen. Nothing can be changed unless all are present," she said. *Clever*, he thought, *She knows Durz refuses to come down from his mountain, and Erus and Golga haven't been seen for two centuries. No matter, I have solved that problem.*

"Yes Mother, we will call when all are assembled."

"Bael," she hissed, leaning down to within an arm's length. Anger and malice radiated from her like fire, "If you ever summon me against my will again, it will be your end, do you hear? I will not destroy one of the Creator's tools, but I will bury you in iron beneath mountains at the bottom of the sea." Bael felt the ground beneath his feet turn to slush and he looked down in time to see liquid earth up to his mid-shins re-harden, locking him into place. A shiver ran down his spine at the thought of such a fate.

"I understand, Mother," he said, bowing his head in humility.

She stood back up to her full height, her head almost reaching the top of the grotto wall. Her limbs stiffened, while her skin became rough and tree bark enveloped her face. In a matter of seconds, a true tree stood silent and still before him. Mother was gone.

Bael sighed, wriggling and pulling until he stood free of the dirt. Escape would not be that easy if Mother carried out her threat, but he wasn't going to give her the chance. Bael smiled to himself. He had her right where he wanted her.

20

REVELATION

IT HAD BEEN THREE DAYS since Jack's run-in with Hank in the cemetery. Hank's behavior, and his declaration about the town being cursed nagged at Jack. In the middle of some mundane task, he found himself staring off into space, replaying the scene in his mind. He wanted to go back to the cemetery to look at the gravestones again.

Today though, he was at the mine watching the men rebuild the cabin. The charred timber had been removed and the new framework had been erected within a few days. Now they were in the process of putting in the windows and nailing up the wall slats. Mr. Dalby bustled around the site, apparently none the worse for wear after the incident that injured him. Jack had heard the details from Eli, who was privy to all the talk in the miners' camp.

It was late in the day, and he decided to go down to the sluice run-off to see if anything turned up that day. Mr. French had educated Jack on what to look for in the screens and sludge that washed down out of the mine's rubble. The tailings were being screened to watch for signs of precious metals like gold and silver, even copper, but the mine's main output was iron ore. This was brought out by the cartload, packed onto wagons, and transported to foundries for processing.

Still, the occasional nugget would come rolling down the chutes, passing through a series of screens until it could go no further. It would then be picked out and taken to the mining cabin to be weighed. Jack wanted to find one himself, so he occasionally wandered down to slosh around in the water.

But he had no luck today either, and gave up after an hour or so. Jack walked down to the stream at the bottom of the ravine to wash. Wiping his wet hands on his trousers, he looked up from where he knelt to see the last rays of the sun wink out over the mountains. Darkness fell quickly, especially down in the ravine, and Jack found himself foundering over dirt clods and stepping through water as he tried to find his way around the hillside to the roadway. He had never been so far down on this side of the mine site though, and somehow got turned around in the darkness. A small degree of error in his course took him stomping through ever denser foliage. He had walked far enough that he should have made the road by now, but somehow it still eluded him. He looked for the lights of the miners' camp, but saw none.

Being out in woods alone at night was more adventure than he wanted, and his heart fluttered as he tried to stay calm. His hearing sharpened and he squinted hard to see into the shadows. His senses were on high alert when he picked up the delicious smell of someone cooking. With an enormous sense of relief, Jack stumbled through the brush, following his nose until he came within sight of a building. A lone cabin with light streaming from the shuttered windows and door sat in a small clearing in the trees, an early moon casting blue light over the roof shingles. His mouth watered at the smell of cooking meat. *Smells like ham*, he thought, as he stepped quicker.

He approached the cabin from the front, not really thinking about whether he would be welcome or not, otherwise he might have considered shouting a greeting from a distance so he wouldn't startle whoever was inside. He mounted the two steps onto the boardwalk porch and knocked lightly on the door. A second or two later and the door swung open. Silhouetted against the yellow lantern light, Lucius stood with his eyebrows lifted, looking quizzically at Jack. His dead eye was still unsettling.

"Oh, hello Lucius," he began, "I didn't realize this was your house." When Lucius continued to stare at him, he continued, "I'm sorry to bother you, but I was at the mine when it got dark and I was trying to get back to town, and somehow..."

Lucius sucked his teeth and looked around behind Jack as if he might have brought friends. He stepped back, swinging the door wide open, "Well, come on in then," he said.

"Thank you," Jack mumbled as he stepped past Lucius

and into the cabin. It was a sparse little place; a small table was in the center of the single room, with a chair and a two-foot section of tree trunk that served as a stool. A pot-bellied stove stood in the corner with a coffeepot and a skillet of thinly-sliced ham on top, popping and sizzling. The windows didn't have any glass in them, but they had shutters, which were slightly open. Lucius' bed was pushed against the wall across from the stove, so as to take advantage of heat radiating from the stove in cold weather. All in all it seemed rather cozy.

Jack turned and was startled to see Lucius' arm out of his sling. The long, skinny arm formed an exaggerated triangle when Lucius tucked his hand into his pocket. It was strange but he quickly averted his eyes and said, "Can you point me to the road so I can get back home?"

"Sure I can," Lucius answered looking sideways at Jack as he returned to the stove, "but my dinner is almost done. As long as you're here, might as well have a bite. If you're hungry, that is."

"It smells good, thank you," Jack said with a smile. He was beginning to like Lucius. Maybe he appeared a bit odd, but he had always been nice to Jack. Lucius motioned for him to sit down at the table, and took two plates and cups off a shelf next to the stove. He opened the lid on a small larder sitting on the floor, removed a linen bag and took out two big biscuits. Throwing those on the plates he sliced the meat in the skillet and divided it, pouring the grease on top of the biscuits. Lastly, he grabbed the coffeepot and sat down at the table.

"What are you doing out here so late?" he asked as he poured coffee for them both.

"I was doing some screening, and I lost track of the time."

"Uh-huh," Lucius replied, taking a bite of his biscuit. "Did you find anything?"

"No." They ate as they talked and Jack winced at the strong bitter coffee. Looking around the shack, he noticed several chains hanging on nails on the wall. There were chains draped across each window sill, one coiled like a snake on the floor by the bed and a good length lying across the overhead rafters. When they had finished eating Lucius picked up the plates and stacked them in the skillet. Curiosity got the best of him and Jack finally asked, "Why do you have all these chains in here?"

Lucius looked at him. "You wouldn't believe me if I told you," he said with a slight grin.

"Of course I would."

"Let's just say they keep the animals out. You know, living out here by myself, I got to be careful." Lucius reached to pull the chain down from the rafters. It took Jack a second to realize, *Lucius used his bad arm!* He had reached up with that long arm and plucked the chain off the rafter. Now he wrapped the end of the chain once around his left hand. He saw Jack looking at him with wide eyes and said, "What, you've never seen a chain before?"

Jack mouth hung open and he clamped it shut, trying to keep his eyes from staring at Lucius' arm.

"That's alright boy, take a good look." He held his right arm up and opened his hand. Jack couldn't help it; he stared at the long slender fingers, which he suspected were almost twice as long as his. The arm was much thinner than Lucius' good arm, with long, striated muscle. "Yep, it works, but you got to promise not to tell nobody, okay?" Jack nodded dumbly while Lucius continued, "It looks strange, and that bothers folks, especially around here, so I keep it tied up."

"Can you use it like normal?" Jack asked stupidly.

"Oh yeah, almost better," Lucius answered. He extended the arm to its' full length, which was probably a good ten to twelve inches longer than the other.

"So it grew like that after being crushed in the mill?" he asked incredulously.

"No, that warn't exactly true either, but that's another story and it's getting late so we better get you home." Lucius stood and put his suspenders over his shoulders then reached for the linen wrap that served as his sling. After putting the work glove over his hand, he placed his arm in the sling and grabbed his hat from a nail by the door.

Jack got up and walked out as Lucius held the door open. He stepped off the porch and down the step to stand in the moonlight, as Lucius pulled the door shut behind him. Lucius stuffed a three-foot length of chain in his sling and Jack fell in beside him as they started walking down a well-cleared path leading north. Jack had obviously arrived at the cabin from another direction because he hadn't come across this path before. It was wide enough for a cart to drive down, although both sides were flanked by a thick border of foliage and trees.

A few minutes of walking and the lights of the miner's camp came into view. The sounds of voices and laughter drifted through the air and Jack was relieved to recover his sense of direction.

"I think I can manage from here. I appreciate the meal and your help."

Lucius looked around before nonchalantly saying, "That's okay, I'll walk on in with you. I might even stop at the saloon for a glass."

Jack shrugged and said, "Okay."

They walked on for another minute before Lucius plucked his sleeve, bringing him to a halt. "Remember now, don't tell nobody about my arm, not even Eli. I got your word now?"

Jack nodded, "Of course."

"Fine, fine. One more thing; it's real dangerous in these parts at night. Real dangerous, you understand? Try not to make this a habit."

Jack nodded again and they turned back to the trail.

* * * * *

To avoid open confrontation in the future, Mother was asked to mediate an arrangement. This arrangement was called The Compact, and it allowed both Bael and Micah an opportunity to pursue their agendas without interference from the other. Every equinox, one faction stepped forward to assume the leadership, while the other retreated into the shadows. Each of the Ba'ath agreed to all articles of The Compact, and spellbound by Mother, an eldritch magic they could not hope to overcome.

-From the Book of More

21

SECOND WIND

JOHN WAS PRACTICALLY hypnotized by the story, but Grandpa Jack was wracked by a wet, hacking cough, jarring him out of his listener's trance. The cough continued, and Grandpa Jack gripped the coverlet, while holding his other hand over his mouth. He bent forward as it grew more violent, causing the carved box to snap shut and slide off his lap.

John reached out to make sure the box didn't fall, and he felt the bones shift inside, like something trying to get out. Revulsion shivered through him as he steadied the box. Grandpa Jack had trouble getting his breath back, and another fit of coughing took him.

"Grandpa, are you okay?" he asked, moving closer.

A rattle in his throat, Grandpa Jack sucked in a breath and asked, "Maybe a glass of water..."

Nodding his head, John grabbed the pitcher and glass from the bedside table and ran downstairs. It was getting later, the sun falling behind the distant mountains, and Mother would be calling him soon for dinner, but all he could think about right now was the incredible story he was hearing.

Imagine, he thought, *if this were all true...faeries and goblins?* But it would be impossible for him to consider a lie from Grandpa Jack; as strange as the sun rising in the west. No, this was genuine, and it was real, and it was important...and it was amazing.

He ran back up the stairs, taking them two at a time, but careful not to slosh the water out of the pitcher. By the time he reentered the room the fit had subsided, but Grandpa Jack took the glass just the same, swallowing a mouthful before placing it on the nightstand.

"Ah, that's better, thank you," he said, reaching a little further for the pipe and pouch of tobacco which also sat on the table. John shook his head a little, but Grandpa Jack filled the pipe bowl and stuck a lit match to the material, puffing it into a glowing ember. The delicious aroma of pipe smoke wafted through the room, and Grandpa Jack seemed content, but John was not. He wanted the story to continue – he had so many questions.

"So...if you didn't remember anything after the goblins trapped you in the woods, how could you tell me what happened?"

Grandpa Jack was wreathed in smoke and had once again pulled the box onto his lap. He nodded, "A very good question. There a great many things I didn't know at the time, which I learned later. Is that really what you want to hear about now, or would you like me to finish the story?"

22

SMALL GAME

THE RUTHERFORD'S CARRIAGE trundled down
Main Street and out of Cobbs. They were heading to the
Plunkett farm, which was a little over two miles away, just
southeast of the miner's camp. Jack remembered passing
by the farm on their first day in Cobbs. That was over
three months ago and he was amazed to see fields with
rows and rows of cornstalks at least a foot taller than him.
Apparently, the Plunkett's hosted the town's festival at
their farm every year to celebrate a successful harvest. All
families in the community were invited, including the
miners.

There were a number of other buggies, carriages,
wagons and carts on the road as well as people walking or
on horseback. It looked as though it would be quite a
gathering.

Father and Mother were looking out the windows,
occasionally waving or nodding their heads in greeting,
but Jack leaned back in his seat and rested his head in the
corner of the coach. He felt tired; the strange events of the

past few weeks were weighing on him. Something in the atmosphere of Cobbs had changed. The townsfolk were as drab and mute toward him as ever, but lately they were staying up late into the night. They socialized amongst themselves at the church, at the saloon, or at their homes. Maybe it was Lucius' warning, the trouble at the mines, or Hank's ramblings, but he felt a growing sense of unease. Something nagged at him, as if he were on the verge of remembering something he had forgotten. Whatever it was, he had no idea what to do about it.

Jack was so tired he almost fell asleep with the swaying and creaking of the carriage, but his rest was interrupted by Mother saying, "We've arrived, Jack, sit up." He sat up and groggily peered out the window. They were just pulling into the lane leading to the Plunkett's farmhouse. Clive had to slow the horses to a walk for all the people coming and going. He pulled the carriage around and to a halt before jumping down to open the door. They exited the coach and were immediately met by Judge Cole and Miss Celia. Jack watched warily as the Judge and his parents exchanged pleasantries.

"Hello, hello! Good evening madam and sir," said Judge Cole, grasping both of Father's hands in his and pumping away. Miss Celia greeted Mother and the children warmly, with Jack's face flushing hot as she shook his hand. The whole group was escorted around to the space between the farmhouse and the barn. The grass here was trimmed low, but behind the barn was a great cornfield stretching away into the darkness. Tables were set up and there were perhaps a hundred pots, pans, and plates stacked with food. All cooked and brought by the ladies of the community, everyone contributing to the feast. A whole pig and a half side of beef were being roasted on spits along with a dozen chickens; the smell made Jack's mouth water. Mother had brought two pans of cornbread and a pecan pie Lucille had helped her bake and she and Celia took them over to the tables. There were other tables set up that held a dozen jars and decanters of tea, lemonade, cider, wine and three beer kegs. Jack stood there holding Abigail's hand surveying the scene. People were standing in small groups or walking around, talking and laughing. They walked toward the barn where there were a number of children playing just inside the doors. These were smaller children, some even younger than Abigail. Jack didn't really know any of the adults standing around the children, mostly women, and he quickly became bored. Abigail smiled as she watched the kids chasing chickens and Jack knew she wanted to join them.

"Abby, you stay here and play, okay? I'm going to see if I can find Eli, he's supposed to be here tonight." Abby nodded, and Jack kissed her hand and left her to her fun.

After a few moments he spotted Eli standing with a group of boys near the spits and he headed toward them. His approach was noted by one of the boys, who promptly nudged a large brown-headed boy nearby. The boy turned and smirked when he saw Jack. They all watched as he walked up to their circle. The big lad took a step toward him with his hands in the pockets of his trousers, which were too short. His brown hair was longer than most, and parted down the middle above a large nose.

"Hullo, Pinkie. Lost your way? The children are playing over there," he said, smiling as he pointed toward the barn.

"Leave off, Tad," said Eli, stepping between Jack and the boy. "What's the matter with you? I told you he was alright." Eli glared at Tad and steered Jack away from the group. They walked away, Jack looking back over his shoulder once to see Tad and the other boys still watching and laughing at him. "I'm sorry about him," said Eli, "sometimes he's a real idiot."

"What has he got against me anyway?" asked Jack.

"Ah, don't worry about him. He's just a big fish in a small pond and he wants to keep it that way. You move into town, your folks are rich – you know, he's jealous."

Jack nodded his head, "Hey, let's get some cider."

Eli winked, "No mate, let's get some beer!" He laughed and they headed off to get drinks. They stood around nonchalantly for a few minutes until the coast was clear, then filled their cups and quickly walked off, grinning ear to ear. They walked over and sat at the base of a haystack, talking as they sipped at the dark, frothy beer. Jack had tasted wine before, and but never beer and he was not impressed with the bitter taste. Eli seemed to have no problem with it though, and he quaffed his down.

They finished their drinks and went to grab themselves some food. Reverend Fetch had opened the festival earlier with a prayer, so it was a serve-yourself free-for-all. Jack piled a plate with chicken, sweet potatoes, corn and squash. Eli went to fill his cup again, but Jack opted for the tea. They ate their fill, watching the people around them. The men had hung lanterns all around the area, so there was plenty of light. There was music too, with men playing fiddles, banjos and harmonicas - one man had even brought a flute. Jack and Eli walked around, watching the girls who were watching them back. Elsa Cutter waved at Eli and he threw her a little wave before turning to walk in the other direction.

Perhaps it was the beer, but Jack felt pretty good. He was relaxed and not thinking about everything that had been bothering him. Now he was just enjoying himself.

Loud claps got his attention as one of the men began slapping two thin boards together.

"Everyone gather 'round, gather 'round!" he shouted. He repeated this call a few more times and everyone made their way over to the head table where Judge Cole stood. Once the crowd had gathered, Judge Cole stepped up onto a bench next to the table so he could be seen by all.

"Now it's time for the event you've all been waiting for. Children, get ready for the Fox Hunt!" There were squeals of delight from some of the young children and polite clapping from adults. He reached into an open-topped nail keg on the table and drew out a small wooden tile.

Holding it in the air, he explained, "All of the children's names are in here, so I will now draw the name of our Fox!" He dropped the tile back in the keg and reached in to stir them. He rattled them around a few times before stopping and picking one out. He made a show of not looking and handed it to Reverend Fetch, who looked at it, turned it right-side up and looked at it again.

"Abigail Rutherford!" he shouted, waving the tile in the air. Jack smiled in surprise and looked around to find Abby. A woman standing next to Jack let out a whimper and he saw her clutching a young girl perhaps a year older than Abby. Jack returned his attention to the front. Someone had pushed Abigail up to where Reverend Fetch stood. As she stood there he said, "Congratulations, Abigail, you get to be our Fox!" Abby beamed and clasped her hands behind her back. Jack saw his parents standing a short way behind Judge Cole, Mother's arm through Father's, both of them smiling.

"But first, we need to turn you into a fox," he said, motioning to a lady standing to one side. She smiled as she brought out a small russet hood with a set of pointed black ears sitting on top. She slipped it over Abby's golden curls and tied the string under her chin. The women all clucked and cooed at the sight of her.

Jack saw the woman rapidly whispering into the little girl's ear. She looked panic-stricken and she held her hand cupped over her mouth so no one could see or hear what she was saying. *What is she going on about?*

Judge Cole took Abigail by the hand and shouted, "To the field!" and began walking toward the cornfield. Everyone streamed in that direction. Jack walked with everyone else, but noticed another woman, white-faced and stiff as she pulled her son along, mouthing things to him in a very low voice. Of the people around him, some were in a fine spirits, laughing, talking and having fun. Others though, were markedly different. If he had to put a name to it, he would have to say they looked *frightened*. Jack and Eli had gotten separated and he now found himself alone at the back edge of the crowd.

They arrived at the edge of the cornfield and Judge Cole turned to face them. "Now, for those children new to Cobbs, here are the rules: The Fox will get a head-start into the cornfield, then all of you 'Hounds'," he said, making a circle motion to encompass the other children, "race to see who can find her first. Both the Fox and the Hound who finds her first get a prize!" He peered down at Abigail and said, "See Dear, you've already won."

There was some commotion at the edge of the crowd nearby and Jack saw a woman jerk her arm away from someone and stomp off toward the farmhouse. It was the red-headed woman who owned the bakery. *Something is wrong*, he thought.

Judge Cole turned Abby toward the cornfield and said, "Now Abigail, don't let these hounds catch you! Ready, go!" He gave her a little push and she ran into the corn rows, disappearing almost immediately. Jack's heart jumped a beat and he glanced over at his parents. They seemed a little discomfited, but not overly concerned. Judge Cole counted out loud, but all Jack could hear was something buzzing and clicking in his head. *This is not right, this is not right*, he thought, starting to push his way through the crowd.

Jack saw several women hooking the hands of two or more 'hounds' together, making them hold on to each other. He moved faster.

Judge Cole finished his count, "Nineteen... Twenty... GO!" The Hounds began rushing into the cornfield, many to the sounds of their mothers yelling last minute instructions, "Hold onto Suzanne!"

Jack plowed into the corn rows, pushing through the stalks as fast as he could. His heart hammered as he cut through to find the clear lane between rows and he sprinted down it, looking and listening for any sign of Abby.

"Abby!" he hissed, "Abby!" He ran a good hundred yards, before stopping to listen, his chest heaving with anxiety. The only sounds he heard were the crashing of the Hounds. He took off again, slapping through rows, quickly looking each way before smashing through to the next. He ran on until he reached the far side of the cornfield. He was far ahead of the other Hounds, who were being diligent about searching each row for the Fox. As he came to the edge of the crop, there was a little cleared space, twenty feet or so, to the tree line. Out here away from the lights of the lanterns, the three-quarter moon was bright and crisp. He stopped, trying to listen over his panting. "Abby!" he yelled. Jack ran along the edge of the cornfield, calling her name. Somewhere off in the distance he heard a wolf howl, and he froze. The hairs on the back of his neck rose and a chill ran from his scalp all the way down his back. A shadow moved up ahead, just under the boughs of the trees. The hair on his neck stood even taller and some primitive instinct knew there was danger here. He wanted to run, to flee to safety, but he screamed, "Abby!" and ran toward the shadow, praying it was her. The buzzing and clicking in his head was insistent now, but still he ignored it.

The shadow slipped into the forest and Jack stood at the treeline, squinting to penetrate the blackness. He had the overwhelming sense he was being watched in return. Scanning the foliage, his eyes caught something, a faint blue luminescence. He found it again; a pair of pale eyes, barely visible, stared back at him. Jack stood rooted, watching, but the eyes made a lazy blink, and disappeared.

The sounds of the other Hounds finally making their way across the field broke the spell, and he backed away from the trees and started calling his sister's name again.

High above the field in an old hawk's nest, the Watcher gazed down, green eyes watching as Jack stumbled away, his young voice plaintively warbling out into the night. *Master must be told*, it thought, and the small puff of smoke went unseen as it vanished.

Another hour passed and Abigail had still not been found. The adults had joined in the search and torches and lanterns filled the field as nearly two hundred people called and searched for her. One of the children found her fox-eared cap in the middle of the cornfield, the tie still in a bow. Men had brought out bloodhounds and they were now trying to catch the scent, but with so many people tramping around it was doubtful if they would be able to track.

Jack's mother was almost hysterical and had to be corralled by some of the other women. His father was still in control, organizing the men and barking orders. Jack was oblivious to this as he was still out looking for Abby. He had almost screamed himself hoarse and frantically rushed from one patch of bushes to another. The search continued through the night and when the sky began to lighten the next morning, Abigail had still not been found.

Jack trotted back to the farmhouse, filthy, with his shirt and trousers torn in a dozen places. The tracks of tears showed on his dirty face and a hundred things were going through his mind at once. The buzzing and clicking noises he had experienced had stopped hours ago and along with it, the sense that Abby was nearby.

He stomped through the field broken-hearted, heading back toward the farmhouse. He stopped in his tracks as it suddenly occurred to him, *yesterday was September twenty-third*.

23

A RUCKUS

PEOPLE WERE HURRYING AROUND in a bustle of activity to and from the barn. Men on horseback cut through the cornfields and trees calling Abigail's name. They had been at it for hours and the sun had risen. It was strange to see the promise of a clear, bright sunrise on such an anxious day.

One of the men told Jack his father had just returned and he hurried to the barn. There were all sorts of people coming and going, with perhaps twenty inside huddled around his father.

"Mr. Webber's hounds have tracked Abigail to this point," he said, stabbing a finger at a map on the wall. "There has been no trace of blood or clothing found, so I have every reason to believe she is still out there, safe but lost. I want every available man on foot and horse. Mr. French, all operations at the mine will cease until she is found. Every man will be paid his full wages to help search for my daughter." There was a murmur and men looked around at one another. "And," he continued loudly to make sure they were all listening, "I am offering a reward of five thousand dollars to the man who finds her alive!" That was more money than these men could expect to make in ten years and there was a mad rush as they flew from the barn en masse into the fields and trees. As the press of men cleared out, Jack made his way to his father.

"Jack!" he shouted, and grabbed him in a hug. "Son, I need you to get back to the house and look in on your mother. She is very upset, and seeing you will help calm her down."

Jack nodded, "Yes sir, but I need to tell you something. I think it's important."

Thomas looked at his son and said quietly, "Okay Jack, what is it?"

Jack blurted out the story Eli had told him about the meeting at the church.

"Then I remembered last night was September twenty-third," he finished. "I'm sorry Father, I should have told you sooner. I just didn't know what to make of it and I didn't want Eli to get into trouble."

Father patted him on the back, "Not to worry, it probably has nothing to do with Abigail. Don't give it another thought, but I really need you to go check on your mother. Will you do that for me?"

"Yes sir," Jack nodded, clearly relieved. He turned and ran toward town. It was almost three miles to the house, but Clive had taken Mother home in the carriage, and father would be using his horse to search for Abby. He raced down the road, settling into a quick jog.

As his son disappeared around the corner of the farmhouse, Thomas clenched his jaw and turned to Mr. French. "Can you catch up to him and give him a ride home?"

"Of course, sir, I'll return shortly," he answered and trotted out of the barn toward his horse.

As Thomas watched him leave, he considered Jack's story, but shook his head and thought, *We'll see to that another time. Right now I've got to focus on finding Abigail.*

24

DISCORD AT HOME

JACK HAD MADE IT a good three hundred yards down the road when Mr. French trotted up and pulled his horse to a halt in front of him.

"Here Jack," he said, reaching down with his arm, "get up here and I'll take you home." Jack took the proffered hand and was pulled up onto the horse behind Mr. French.

"Hang on back there," he said, kicking the horse into an easy gallop. They made good time down the road and around the wide curve leading across the bridge and into town. Mr. French slowed the horse to a canter through town, but kicked into a gallop again when they were through. It was only a few moments before he reined up in front of the house.

As he helped Jack slide off the horse, Mr. French said, "I have to get back and help your father, you take care of your mother." Jack nodded and ran up the steps into the house.

The house was filled with visitors, mostly women, although there were a few men coming and going. He could tell several had been crying and fear tickled his chest. He noticed Emma James standing in a corner with her arms crossed and three or four women talking to her. Assuming his mother would be in her bedroom, he ran upstairs, past a line of women all gabbling like birds.

Mother lay in bed still dressed in her gown, although her shoes had been removed and a coverlet lay over her feet. Her face was blotchy, while her eyes were red and swollen. Jack had never seen her so undone before and it upset him. Mrs. Fetch sat on the bed, placing a damp cloth on her forehead and trying to comfort her.

"Mother?" he queried quietly.

Her eyes went wide as she recognized him. Her face broke into an expression of anguish and she started crying as she reached out to him. Jack fell into her arms and felt like a small boy again as she clasped him to her. She was trembling and frail and he tried to soothe her.

"Mother, it's going to be fine," he said, "Everyone is looking for her and Father has put up a huge reward. We'll find her before the day is out." Several of the women murmured and cooed in sympathy and agreement, but Jack just wanted them all to leave. She just nodded and continued to squeeze him.

As Jack lay in her arms she seemed to calm down, breathing more easily and allowing Mrs. Fetch to pat her face dry. He sat up, still holding her hand.

"Father is very worried about you. Can I go tell him you're alright?" She sniffed and nodded, squeezing his hand.

Her voice cracked as she said, "Yes, but tell him I need word sent to me as frequently as possible so I know what is happening." He nodded and kissed her hand before walking out of the room.

Making his way down the staircase he noticed Emma was still in the corner, but her hands were now in fists by her sides and she was clearly angry. The tension was obvious even without the fact that one of the other women had the shoulder of Emma's dress balled up in her hand.

"Sister Emma, keep your voice down," another of the women hissed, "this is not the time!"

"Oh, I agree, this should have been discussed long ago! Why weren't we consulted?"

"It is not your place…"

"Don't you dare tell me it's not my place! I've already paid for the right to have my voice heard, there's nothing you can do to frighten me now. Let me go!" she yelled, wrenching her arm away. A half-dozen women crowded around her, not offering violence, but clearly not willing to suffer her outbursts any longer. Jack eased down the staircase as the women nudged Emma out the front door, then shooed her down the steps and into the yard. Jack followed them out and stood in the back, but moved to one side so he could see what was happening. Once again several strands of her red hair had come undone in her tussle with the women and they hung down over Emma's face as she glared at them. The women exchanged a few more barbs until Mrs. Fetch came bustling out the door.

"What is all the commotion about?" she asked in a hiss.

"I thought we had agreed to do away with the lottery?" Emma asked loudly.

Mrs. Fetch rushed down the steps and slapped Emma across the face, knocking her to the ground, "You shut your mouth this instant!" she hissed, leaning over, pointing her finger. Emma laid on the ground with her hand over her face, staring in shock at Mrs. Fetch who slowly stood up straight. The other women watched, completely silent and Mrs. Fetch continued, "Before you make yourself too much a martyr you should recall you are not the only woman here to suffer loss! We didn't pick the poison, but many of us have drunk from the same glass." Her eyes narrowed coldly, "And this was not a lottery! You do not know of what you speak!" She practically spat the last words before turning to walk back up the steps. With the wall of women behind her, she ordered Emma, "Go home."

"What's going on?" Jack asked. Caught up in the exchange with Emma, none of them had noticed him standing there. A dozen women turned in his direction, but they said not a word. Like a barn full of owls they stared at him, simply watching. Out of the corner of his eye he saw Emma get to her feet and run out through the trellis gate and down the lane. Their mute answer intimidated him and Jack backed away down the porch before turning to run around the corner and out to the barn.

He was by no means a master horseman, but he had learned enough in his lessons with Mr. Severn to handle his horse, a fifteen hand pony he had named "Buck." Jack normally didn't get to ride him outside the fence, but he didn't care today. He quickly threw on the blanket and saddle, mounted the horse and kicked him out of the barn. He rode past the front porch, but the women had gone back inside and he spurred Buck out of the gate and down the lane towards town. It had only taken him a few minutes to saddle his horse, so he expected to see Emma on the road, but she was gone.

There was little traffic on Main Street, so Jack let Buck out a little as he galloped through and out of town. All the way to the Plunkett farm he let Buck have his head and by the time they arrived, sweat covered the horse's neck and he was blowing hard. He reined in next to the barn, but his father's horse was gone and of the few men standing around, none knew exactly where he was.

Jack spent the next several hours riding around the surrounding countryside frequently running into men, horses and dogs as they crisscrossed each other's paths. As the day waned he was at a loss as to what he should be doing. What he felt certain of however, was something sinister was going on in Cobbs and his family was now involved. He turned Buck back toward the main road.

Jack rode across the bridge, before turning west down the track leading past the miner's camp and to the south of the mines. The few people he passed either stared at him or shook their heads in sympathy. Jack ignored everyone and kept riding, pushing Buck along at a quick trot. *Something is wrong with this place*, he thought, *and I think I know who can tell me the truth.*

He pushed his exhausted horse into a clumsy gallop again and tore down the trail, Buck breathing hard as the cabin came into sight.

"Lucius!" he yelled as he approached. "Lucius!" Jack jumped to the ground, ran up the steps and almost right into the old man as he swung the door open. "My sister Abby's missing! I don't know what to do. I need your help." Lucius stepped back into the cabin and motioned him inside. They both sat down at the table and Jack told him about the meeting in the church, Abby's disappearance and the incident with Emma. He blurted it out as fast as he could and when he came to the end, he noticed the man's face was as sad and forlorn as he had ever seen him. Panic was welling up inside of him when Lucius spoke.

He looked down at the table and let out a long trembling breath. "Oh Lord, what have they done?" he said shaking his head.

The ominous statement confirmed Jack's suspicions and he nearly shouted, "What are you talking about? Tell me!" Fear and frustration caused his voice to shake.

Lucius met his eyes, nodding his head, "She's been taken."

25

AN UGLY SET

THERE WAS SILENCE in the cabin as the words sank in. Abigail had been missing for almost eighteen hours. If Lucius knew something about who she was with there was hope they could find her.

"I know who took her," Lucius said, "and I can show them to you if you want."

Jack nodded his head as Lucius spoke, "Yes, yes! We should get my father and some of the men..."

"No, listen to me, it ain't going to matter how many men you bring, they can't help with this. You're going to have to trust me."

"What are you talking about Lucius? Let's go!"

"Jack, you remember when you first saw my arm? I said you wouldn't believe the real story if I told you? What's happening right now is like that and before I can help you, I have to make you understand." Lucius reached out for his hat, "If we leave now we can be there before nightfall."

Jack gulped as he stared at Lucius. He was so tired of

not knowing what was going on, of things happening around him. Could he put his trust in Lucius? He wasn't completely sure, but this was not the time to be timid; Abby needed him.

"Alright, then, let's go."

Lucius led the way as they pushed through the undergrowth and trees, not following any track Jack could discern. He had left Buck at the cabin after Lucius told him they would make better time on foot. He knew nothing of their destination, but Jack would have followed him anywhere if it would help him find Abby. The sky was overcast, but it was still warm enough that twenty minutes of hard hiking had sweat rolling down his chest and beading his forehead. He hadn't slept much over the past two days and he could feel fatigue knocking at the door, but he held it at bay; there would be time to rest later. Lucius looked back occasionally to make sure he was keeping up, but otherwise kept marching at a fast pace.

They made their way up hills and down into gullies, slipping on moss covered stones as they splashed through shallow rivulets of water only to toil back up the opposite bank. Lucius came to the top of a rise and stopped, looking back and waiting for Jack to catch up. When he drew abreast, Lucius stopped him with a hand on his chest.

"Now listen, you ain't never seen anything like what I'm about to show you, but don't be scared; as long as I'm with you, you got nothing to be worried about." He looked Jack in the eye, "Are you sure you want to see this?"

"Yes, I'm sure," he answered. The truth was he needed to see what Lucius was talking about. Everything about this experience was so unreal and the only way he could deal with it was to find some answers.

Jack followed Lucius over the crest and down a slope covered in waist-high grasses. At the bottom of the slope was a pond, like dozens of others that occurred naturally in terrain like this. These natural depressions filled with water from rains and runoff and were home to all sorts of life, both plant and animal. It was almost completely covered with duckweed, which to an unwary hiker might seem like dry land but for the few clear spots on the surface where the water reflected the gray sky. This pond was odd though; no plops of tiny frogs leaping into the water, no dragonflies buzzing over the surface, no water-bugs. It harbored no apparent life, and the dead calm water seemed eerie. Lucius didn't even break stride as he stepped into the water up to his shins before turning to Jack.

"Wait here," he said, sloshing deeper into the pond. It was only eighty feet or so across and he waded out to the center, the water up to his waist. He held his chain above his head as if to strike and stuck his long arm down into the water. He felt around for a moment before taking hold of something, and turned to walk back toward Jack, pulling a mass along in his wake. Jack's eyes widened as he saw what Lucius had dragged from the bottom.

Although it was right in front of his eyes, his mind fought to rationalize what he was seeing. It was something straight out of a fairy tale.

Lucius dragged it out onto the bank, holding it by the chain fastened around the neck. He dropped it on the ground with its feet still floating in the water. Jack stood several feet away from the creature.

"What... what is that?" he breathed. Even as he asked, he took a step closer.

"That is a goblin."

The creature's dank stringy hair framed a brutish, pale face with a greenish cast and pointed ears touched the ground on either side of its head. A wide mouth sagged open and was lined with sharp, irregular teeth. The thick keg of a body was out of proportion to the long skinny arms, which were strikingly similar to Lucius' deformed arm, except their skin was rougher and the hands had long filthy nails, broken and cracked. Jack took another step forward and leaned over to look into the face, but quickly jumped back.

"Is it dead? The eyes don't look right," he said, pointing to the pale blue-white eyes peeking out from under barely open lids.

"No, it's asleep. See, look here," Lucius leaned over the creature and lifted its' eyelid with his thumb. Clouded over a milky blue, the eye sat there unmoving, like a dead fish.

"They can't abide metal, especially iron. If you bind them with a chain, they fall into a deep sleep. As long as that chain is on, they won't wake up; but that's easier said than done. They are strong and damn mean."

Jack saw the chain was fastened with a piece of wire. "What if the chain falls off?" he asked.

"Well, then you got a problem."

Jack shivered, "What are you doing with it?

"This ain't the only one, there are about a dozen in here. I have to hide them to keep the others from setting them loose again."

"Asleep? Why isn't it drowned?"

"I don't know, that's just how the magic works."

Lucius let Jack look at the Goblin for a few minutes. He even reached down and picked up the creature's hand before quickly dropping it in disgust.

"Now do you understand? I had to show you this, or you would never have believed me." Lucius asked. Jack nodded his head dumbly. His face suddenly flushed red and hot tears welled in his eyes as it finally became real to him. The tears slid down his face as he stood staring at the disgusting creature. He was angry, sad and hopeless, all emotions with which he had only minor experience. He was filled with pathetic despair, "Is Abby dead?" He cried in earnest now, and Lucius put his arm around Jack to comfort him. Jack composed himself and stood back, looking at Lucius with pleading eyes.

Lucius' face was creased in a grim smile, "Hell boy, why do you think I brought you out here? No, she's not dead." He patted Jack on the arm and turned back to the goblin. He grabbed it by the chain again and dragged it back out to the center of the pond. He pushed it back down to the bottom and held it there with his foot, until he was sure it wouldn't rise to the surface, before wading back.

"Let's get home now, we got work to do, and it's getting late." He led the way again, this time pointing out landmarks to Jack so he could find his way back to the pond if necessary. Jack tried to keep track, repeating the clues in his mind and hoping he could remember.

The hike back seemed a lot quicker than the trek out to the pond but dusk set in just as the cabin came into view. They made it inside, Lucius tossing his chain onto the table and hanging his hat.

Jack was anxious for answers, but he was almost afraid to ask the question on his mind, "How do you know Abby's still alive?"

Lucius sat down and nodded his head, "Trust me boy, she's alive." He sat down, motioning for Jack to do the same. "Now comes the hard part," he said.

26

TALE OF WOE

"I TOOK YOU OUT THERE so you would believe what I'm about to tell you next - you need to hear the rest of the story - at least my part in it anyway."

"When I was a child, I was a slave on a tobacco plantation in South Carolina. At the time, I was lucky, because all of my family was together. My Momma and Daddy, and I even had an Aunt and two cousins in that same place. I also had my twin brother, Isreal with me there.

"One night, we were fishing down at the river, about twilight, just trying to catch something extra for the frying pan. That's when they came for us." Lucius stared down at the table, but his eyes were focused on another time altogether. "They grabbed both of us, and carried us off into the woods. I ain't never been so scared in all my life, and me and Isreal was hollering for help. They threw us down, grabbed hold of our arms and legs, and started some kind of spell." Lucius wrung his hands as he spoke, and Jack saw his eyes glisten with unshed tears. "The pain was unbearable, so strong I thought I might die right then, but I could still see Isreal fighting with them. He was giving them hell and they broke up the spell on me to go take care of him first. I watched as they laid onto him, and pulled him until his bones came out of their sockets. His pain was so bad, and we were both screaming so loud I thought my head would bust. But I couldn't do anything. I was just laid out on the ground like a sack of potatoes, but I couldn't move. I watched them change him. They changed Isreal into a damned animal. Covered with hair and snarling like a rabid dog. They changed him into one of them." Lucius gritted his teeth and hissed out the words. "They were coming for me next, and they were just about to lay hold of me, when a gunshot broke. It was one of the overseers, making his rounds. He thought we were being attacked by some animal, so he shot to scare them off, and it worked. But Isreal took off with them, and I was in bad shape." Lucius lifted his goblin hand to Jack. "This is what they done to me, but they didn't get to finish. When the overseer saw what had happened to me, he took me back to the Master. I tried to explain what happened, but I was only eight years old, and they didn't listen. The white preacher came to look at me, and said it was the work of black voodoo magic. There was a woman who helped us when we got sick, her name was 'Effie', and she was a kind soul, but the preacher said she was a witcher-woman. The Master had her whipped nearly to death, and everyone started looking at me like I was the Devil's child. At first, I used my arm like normal, because it was strong, but it made people scared of me, so I started pretending like it hurt real bad, and carrying it in a sling. My eye was different too. Everybody thought I was wounded and blind in this eye, but I could see real good with it, especially at night."

"I couldn't stop thinking about Isreal. I wanted to find him and bring him home. I looked for him all through the woods, day and night. Folks started calling me crazy, 'Crazy Lucius.' I was living in the woods more than I was living with people, but I never found Israel."

Lucius reached his hand up to rub his eyes and take a deep breath. "I had been looking awhile, didn't find nothing, but that's when they found me." He looked into Jack's face, his good eye a deep pool of misery.

"The one thing you got to know about them, is they are dangerous, whether they say they're your friend or not. They'll help you sometimes, and sometimes they'll help you whether you want them to or not. And sometimes they'll just kill you, if you don't know the rules."

"The goblins?" Jack asked.

"Yes, them too, but the goblins are slaves, just like I was. I'm talking about their masters. They're the faerie-folk."

He squinted at Jack, "How old do you think I am boy?"

Jack blinked in confusion, "What?"

"How old?" Lucius insisted.

"I don't know,..." Jack studied Lucius' lined face, the hard-worked hands, and the slightly sagging jowl. Lucius' hair was graying throughout, but his stance was erect and strong. "You're probably fifty or so," he said, confident he was close.

Lucius gave him a strange grin, and his eyes seemed to water. "I was about eight when they took Israel, and that was in 1739. Near as I can tell, I'm about one-hundred-and-fifty-one years old."

Jack stared at him open-mouthed. It almost seemed funny, and he started to smile, but Lucius wasn't smiling anymore. In fact, he seemed quite serious about the whole thing.

"How could that be?" Jack gasped. Another thought began to creep into his head, that Lucius had become unbalanced. It was quite impossible for a human to reach such an age.

Lucius swung around on the chair and stood. Picking up his length of chain, he went over to one of the shutters, and with his goblin hand, unlatched and threw it open. It was full dark outside, and a cool breeze blew in.

"I'm getting to that." He lowered himself back into the chair. "Anyway, it was one of the faerie that found me wandering in the woods. His name was Blixt. Everybody else had pretty much given me up for crazy. Hell, the overseers didn't even seem to care where I was or what I was doing. I was about ten by then. One night I was camped out there, listening to mosquitos, when he just walked right up to me. With my new eye, I could see him plain as day, but with my regular eye, he looked like a little lightning bug, floating along. He told me to get up and follow him, and for some reason I was glad to do it. I know now he laid a spell on me, but I followed, and he took me to the other side. He explained some things to me, and told me they were going to keep me there, to keep me safe. I was in danger, he said, because the bad ones wanted to finish me off." Jack saw him tug the chain between his hands taut like a garrote. "But I didn't like it there. Sometimes Blixt or one of the other ones would talk to me, but most of the time they just left me alone. Their whole world is barren, not even an ant. I didn't feel any thirst or hunger, but the sun never went down, and the seasons never changed. It almost drove me mad. That was where I started practicing with my arm and my eye. When I got so I could see the curtain, I decided I would come back. I worked it out, and finally got past the curtain. The first time I was there, they kept me for three years," he held up three fingers to Jack, "but thirty-six years had passed here."

"Thirty-six years!?" Jack exclaimed. He struggled to wrap his mind around what Lucius was saying.

"Well, I still don't understand it completely, but my body got left behind when I crossed over, and was preserved somehow. I suppose it was magic, but I woke up buried in thirty-six years of bushes, thorns and leaves. My clothes had been damned near chewed to pieces by the insects, and the animals had burrowed under and against me through the years. I tore out of there, filthy as a man could ever be, and I walked to the river. It was getting' late in the day, but I waded in anyway, and once I spit all the filth out of my mouth, eyes, ears and nose, there wasn't a scratch on me, except the fresh ones. I left the river and walked to the plantation. I didn't know how long I had been gone see? I was surprised to see how much more land had been cleared in the three years I was gone, but I was looking forward to seeing my family again. I didn't have hardly a stitch on when I walked into the slave camp, and my sling was long gone. There were several new outbuildings, and it seemed Master was doing well for himself. The first person who saw me was a girl, a slave-girl who took one look at me, screamed and ran like the devil. I didn't know what to do, so I just followed her. As I entered the camp, there was some men and women who gathered around me. 'What's your name child? Where you from?' They kept their distance though, and I could tell they were scared of me. I didn't recognize any of them, and I asked for my Momma. I told them my name was Lucius."

Lucius sighed, and shrugged his shoulders, "You never saw so many people fly into a fit. They were screeching and pointing, calling for the Lord. Well, presently there comes this old lady. She's walking real slow, and her hair is all gray. That was my Momma. She stood there looking at me for the longest time, because I looked eleven years old. She didn't know what to think, but I said, 'Momma, it's me, Lucius.' and she finally came over and put her arms around me. We went off by ourselves and talked for a long while. She told me Daddy had died a few years ago; just dropped dead while he was working out in the fields. She thought the heat got to him. Then she told me

Master had died almost twenty years ago, and his son was the Master now. He was harder than his daddy, and the overseers used the whip much more regular now."

Jack flinched at that. Slavery was an abomination, and it shamed him to hear of people being treated so cruelly.

"I was trying to stay calm, but I just couldn't believe what I was hearing. 'Momma,' I cried, 'what is this year?' 'Seventeen hundred-seventy-seven Lucius,' she told me. I damned near fainted. Anyway, she found some clothes for me, and told me I should put my arm back in a sling, so I did. It was hard at first, because nobody trusted me, and they was scared of my arm. I kept it bound up real tight though, and didn't say nothing to nobody. I helped Momma with chores, and whatever I could do with one arm. After awhile, people just left me and Momma alone.

"The new Master had bought himself a bunch of new slaves, and nobody noticed one more slipped in, especially because I kept myself quiet as much as I could. But Momma was right, these overseers were mean sons-of-bitches, and they'd as soon whip you as look at you. Maybe because my arm was slung and I looked like a cripple, they never lashed me, but it was a regular thing, let me tell you."

"Did you ever tell your mother about Blixt?" Jack asked.

"Yeah, Momma died about two years later, but we spent all the time we could together. I told her everything about the other side, because she was the only one I could tell it to. She listened to me, and tried to help me figure things out. We talked once about what happened to Israel, but it made her too sad, and we never spoke of it again."

So many questions ran through his mind he didn't know where to start. "Whatever happened to Isreal? Did you ever find him?"

"I only saw him once more. That was probably close to a hundred years ago." In the momentary silence that followed, Jack noticed the sound of rain drops pattering on the roof.

"It's gettin' dark boy, we need to get you home."

"Home?" Jack asked, "Why am I going home? Aren't we going to go find Abby?"

"Patience, we're going after her, but we need to make some preparations first. Besides, you need to go home and see your folks. It wouldn't hurt for you to get a good night's sleep too, tomorrow is going to be a very important day."

Jack had been so sick with worry for Abby he hadn't even had time to think about his parents. He remembered he had promised his mother he would tell father to keep her updated, but he hadn't seen his father after that.

"Yes, you're right, I need to check on Mother," he said.

Lucius picked up his hat, slung his arm and laid his length of chain in the sling. "Let's get you home before it gets too late."

Lucius swung the door open to reveal a sullen rain pouring off the porch cover. Jack was about to ask if they should wait it out, but Lucius stepped off into the spatter, and Jack had no choice but to follow.

27

SHOWDOWN

THE SUN WENT DOWN on that day, and still there was no sign of Abigail. Thomas was doing all he knew to do, and thus far had achieved nothing. After learning her daughter was still missing, Elizabeth had been so beside herself Dr. Keene gave her a sleeping draught to keep her at peace. Jack was also missing now, although Thomas wasn't worried about him in the same way. He felt certain Jack was in the company of one group of searchers or another, looking for his sister. The incentive of a huge reward had kept many of the men out looking, but the weather wasn't cooperating, and now began to thunder and rain. The occasional crack of lightning strobed the landscape, but otherwise it was dark as pitch. Frustrated, he pulled his horse's head around and rode towards home to check on Elizabeth.

The rain had pushed all but the most determined searchers indoors, but as he rode through Cobbs Thomas noticed there were lights in the church, and he changed course to head that way. The steady patter of rain on his hat brim blocked out all other noises, so those inside might have been singing hymns for all he knew. Dismounting, he threw the reins around a post and walked up the steps. He pulled the door open and stepped inside to see a crowd of townsfolk, mostly men, staring at him. The interior was only dimly lit by a dozen or so short candles. Reverend Fetch was the first to address him, saying, "Brother Thomas, please come in out of the rain."

Thomas nodded and walked down the center aisle, but he wasn't looking at Reverend Fetch. He looked at the people sitting in the pews.

"We are gathered here to offer our prayers for the safe return of Abigail." Thomas heard Reverend Fetch speaking, but the atmosphere in the room distracted him. Something was wrong.

He reached the pulpit and let Reverend Fetch turn him toward the crowd and put his arm around his shoulders. There were perhaps thirty people in the church and he scanned the faces. He recognized several of them; had talked to them, laughed with some, and shared meals with still others. Yet the expressions on their staring faces made them complete strangers.

Reverend Fetch began a prayer, something about mercy for the innocent, but Thomas wasn't listening. He realized the townsfolk looked... frightened.

Then he noticed Judge Cole, sitting in the aisle seat of the second pew staring straight ahead, clearly not willing to look at Thomas. Underneath the judge's seat he saw the nail keg from which he had drawn Abigail's name. The story Jack told him sprang to mind, and his suspicion raced ahead of reason. Leaving the reverend in half-sentence, Thomas strode toward the judge, who still refused to meet his eyes. Without a word he quickly reached down to snatch the small keg from under the judge's seat. Judge Cole reacted with surprising speed, trying to trap the keg against the pew with his heels, but failing that, grabbed Thomas' wrist in a hard grip.

"Here now, what are you doing?" he asked, but his panicked reaction had told Thomas all he needed to know. He shoved the judge hard, causing him to fall prone onto the pew seat, but the judge's grip on his wrist also caused the keg to spill, the wooden tiles clattering all over the place. Everyone gasped and several men leapt to break the two up, but even as they pushed Thomas back toward the pulpit he grabbed a handful of tiles and thrust his fist in the air.

"Let me go!" he shouted, shrugging the men off. In the dim light of the candles and a solitary lantern, he looked at the tiles in his hand. They were all blank. He turned an incredulous face to Reverend Fetch, holding the tiles in front of him. The reverend's face was closed. He deliberately refused to look at the tiles and stared into Thomas' eyes, but said nothing.

"Why?" he asked, turning to the crowd, but there was no answer and the sea of faces stared mutely back at him. Thomas flung the tiles down in disgust and felt Reverend Fetch's hand on his shoulder. Without conscious thought, he quickly swung around and struck the reverend full in the face. It was a powerful blow that sent the man to the ground, felled like a tree. Thomas stood over him ready to follow it with more, but a half-dozen men pushed him against the wall and wrestled to restrain him. The scuffle only lasted seconds before Reverend Fetch's voice boomed out, "Enough!" He stood now, but Thomas' blow had likely broken his nose, and a spray of blood covered the front of his shirt.

"How dare you do violence here? This is a house of God!"

"What was so important about September 23rd Reverend!?" Thomas roared back, straining against the men.

Reverend Fetch's face blanched, "Get him out!" The men half-carried Thomas to the door and flung him out into the rain, to land at the bottom of the steps in the mud. He thrust himself to his feet and faced them. Reverend Fetch pushed through and Thomas pointed at him, "Where is my daughter, you bastard?"

"Control yourself man, your grief and exhaustion have caused you to jump to conclusions. Go home. The rest of your family needs you."

At that, Thomas pulled the pistol from his holster and pointed it at Fetch. There was silence as Thomas stood swaying, his finger on the trigger.

"My family is none of your concern." He grabbed the reins of his horse and swung himself into the saddle. Thomas pointed the pistol at Judge Cole, "You pulled the tile," then again at Reverend Fetch, "and you called her name. You will both answer to me if she's not returned safe." With that, he turned his horse and rode home.

28

MATERNAL DISTRESS

THOMAS RODE DOWN the main street, now churned by the rain into a wide muddy swath. He left the town proper and headed towards home, seething over the incident at the church. The rain still fell in big fat drops, but it seemed to lessen by the moment. Another fifty yards would bring him to the front gate of the house.

It was pitch-black and he was lost in his thoughts, which is why he didn't see the figures on the roadway until one of them called out, "Father!"

Startled, Thomas saw Jack waving at him from the gate. He had Buck by the reins and someone else was with him, and as Thomas drew nearer he recognized Lucius by the sling on his arm.

"Jack! What are you doing out in this rain? Any news?"

"No sir, but Lucius and I have been out looking for Abby."

Thomas looked down at Lucius. The milky, blue-white eye seemed to fluoresce slightly in the darkness. "Thank you for looking out for him. Let's get indoors."

They followed Thomas down the lane to the barn, then helped him unsaddle and stable his horse before all three trekked across the yard to the house.

Jack felt some trepidation as they walked inside; after all, the last time he had been home Mrs. Fetch had slapped Miss Emma. There were several women scattered around the living room, sitting and talking, while others poured tea or coffee and set out food. They rose as one and began fussing over the men, bringing them towels, and pushing hot cups of coffee into their hands. Jack and Lucius accepted the coffee and stood in front of the small fire in the fireplace to dry off a bit, but Thomas turned to go upstairs to see Elizabeth.

Mrs. Fetch stood in his way. "Ah, Mr. Rutherford, so good to see you've made it home. Any news?" she asked, concern wrinkling her brow.

"No, Mrs. Fetch, I'm afraid not. I need to speak with Elizabeth if you don't mind." He started to pass Mrs. Fetch, but she stepped to block his path.

"I understand sir, but she has been in a terrible way all day long, and has only just gotten to sleep a short bit ago. Can't your bad piece of news wait until she wakes?"

Thomas regarded her, seeing sympathy and pity in the lines of her face, but all he heard was Reverend Fetch's false words. "Mrs. Fetch, I will tend to my wife now. Thank you for your concern, but I believe you may be needed at your own home; I understand the Reverend has taken some injury," he said cooly.

Shock registered on her face, but she quickly composed herself. "Surely nothing serious..."

"I couldn't say, but you should probably check in on him just to be sure..." He turned to call down, "Jack, please have Clive bring the carriage around for these ladies." He gave Mrs. Fetch a nod and pushed past her and up the stairs.

As he entered the bedroom, he saw there were fresh flowers in vases and their clean, soothing scent filled the room. The only light was from the dim glow of a few yellow candles. Altogether, it was a pleasant and relaxing atmosphere, and he was grateful Elizabeth had apparently been well-cared for.

Moving to the bedside, Thomas watched Elizabeth's sleeping form, her chest rising in long, deep breaths. She was sleeping deeply, and Thomas decided Mrs. Fetch had been right after all. Moving quietly, he sat down in a chair which had been pulled close to the bedside, and settled back to wait for her to awaken. How was he going to tell her Abigail was still missing?

Downstairs, most of the women had left, but Clive would have to make a second trip to get them all. While the rest were waiting for him to return, Jack and Lucius had helped themselves to the meal standing prepared on the table. It had been a very long day and only when he smelled food did Jack realize how starved he was. There were roasted chickens and peas, baked potatoes, cornbread, and a buttermilk pie. Jack had never had buttermilk pie before, but it was delicious, and he ate a second piece before letting Lucille take his plate away.

Lucius had pushed away from the table as well and he stood and motioned Jack outside. They stepped out onto the porch, and Jack followed Lucius as he walked around the porch to the side of the house. The rain had let up and was now only a drizzle. Lucius looked at him for a moment, and it seemed to Jack he was trying to make a decision.

"There's something going on out there," he said, waving vaguely toward the darkness. "I've never them so stirred up and bold. The trouble at the mines is their work for sure."

Jack nodded, but Lucius could see he was confused, "Well, that's neither here nor there right now. Look, I'm going to try to help get your sister back, but I also told you about Isreal, and how I never found him."

Jack leaned against the porch rail, his head bowed.

"I know a lot more now than I did back then though, and I've got an idea," Lucius said, putting his good hand on Jack's shoulder. Hope sprang instantly to Jack's heart. "Now I'm not promising you anything, but if you're willing to trust me, we can try to go see someone who might help us."

"Who is this person?" Jack asked, wondering that there was yet another person even more informed than Lucius.

Lucius sighed, "You ain't going to believe this." He paused a second, "'She' is Mother Nature." He watched Jack's stunned face, and went on, "They call her 'Nai'ah,' the Earth Mother. I've only seen her a time or two, but she is powerful, the most powerful of them all."

"Yes!" Jack exclaimed, "That's an excellent idea Lucius, why can't we go now? Where is she?"

"It's not that easy. I can't find her here on earth, at least not in a physical body. To see her, we have to go to the other side, to Lumis."

"Alright...," Jack began slowly, "How do we get there?"

"Like I said, I have a plan but it's dangerous for you, both the means and the journey. I think I've got it worked out but if I'm wrong, it could mean your life. That's what I want you to sleep on tonight, okay?" Jack nodded.

"You think about it real good tonight, and if you're still willing to chance it meet me at my cabin tomorrow, before noon. Come alone and leave your horse here. Now go get some sleep, you're going to need your rest." Lucius turned, stepped off the porch, and walked off into the darkness.

29

THE CROSSING

As JACK MOVED THROUGH the trees toward Lucius' cabin, he nervously watched the woods around him. Now aware of the real dangers the forest held, his head jerked around at each sound, eyes searching every moving thing. His rifle helped his confidence greatly, and he held it at the ready, a shell already levered into the chamber, ready to fire.

He had not slept well last night, tossing and turning while dreaming fitfully of goblins who were trying to eat him. As he lay there during one of his lucid moments however, staring at the ceiling in the darkness, he recalled his conversation with Lucius on the return trip from Charleston. He said real friends were those you could entrust with your life. It appeared Jack had decided Lucius was a real friend, because he came this morning ready to put his life in the man's hands.

Speaking of friends, he had wanted to find Eli, to see if he could bring him along as well, but Lucius had told him to come alone, so when he came within sight of the miner's camp, he skirted wide around it, not wanting to be seen.

His nose found the smell of wood smoke coming from Lucius' cabin and he felt a welcome sense of relief he was almost there. He hurried his steps and as the cabin came into view, the old black man was there on the front porch, leaning on the rail and looking in Jack's direction. Lucius' deformed arm was out of its sling, gracefully moving about as he walked the length of the porch toward Jack. It was a queer and fantastic sight to be sure, but Jack had neither the time nor the inclination to wonder at the oddity. He waved and trotted up to the porch. Lucius did not return the wave, but just grimly nodded as he pushed off the rail and turned to the open cabin door. His serious mood suited Jack just fine, and he followed, his heart tickling in his chest.

As he passed through the doorway and into the cabin, Lucius stopped him, putting his long, thin hand to Jack's chest.

"You ready to go through with this? You better know for sure, because once we go, there ain't no turning back."

Lucius' face was as hard and serious as he had ever seen him. Clean bright sunlight streamed into the cabin from the window. The setting only served to make Jack's senses tingle even more. He looked into Lucius' face, staring into those eyes; the good eye yellowed and rimmed red, while the other sat in his skull like a dull stone. Jack's brows furrowed as he held the hard stare.

"I'm sure Lucius, let's just get on with it," he said.

Lucius' face sagged, and the doubt in his good eye was

plain. He whispered, "I've never done this boy. I don't know if it'll work."

"It *will* work. I trust you Lucius, please... I need your help." Lucius' eyes slid sideways to the small table in the middle of the room. Jack followed his glance to see an old bean tin sitting on the only table in the cabin. He moved past Lucius into the cabin. "What is that?"

"Patience." Lucius moved around to the opposite side of the table, motioning Jack to sit on the upright stump that served as a stool. Jack sat down, his heart fluttering a little more now as he reached for the can.

"Not so fast boy, we have to take precautions," Lucius said, and he moved over to the corner of the room to pick up a short coil of rope. He returned to Jack and motioned for him to lift his arms. Puzzled, he lifted his arms as Lucius explained, "In a few minutes you ain't going to be in your right mind. Even if I'm able to catch you, your body will keep on thinking' it's awake. If I don't tie you down, no telling where you'll wander off to, and you don't want that. Safer this way." *No,* Jack thought, *I don't want that.* Even as the thought came to him, he suddenly imagined what it must have been like for Abby, alone in a dark cornfield, scared out of her wits when she was taken. It was almost too much to bear that she was there even now, waiting for someone to save her. *Yes, she is alive,* he thought, *and waiting for me. I'm coming Abby.* As Lucius finished tying the rope around Jack, he reached up with his long arm and dropped the other end across the overhead rafter beam. He tied the rope around his own chest, and sat down. Even this small amount of precaution made Jack feel much better.

"Let's get started." They stared at each other across the table, the tin sitting like a stick of dynamite between them. Now that it had come to the moment, Jack found his heart beating in his chest like a bird in a cage, and his palms had started to sweat.

"What do I do?" he asked, a tremble in his voice betraying his fear. Lucius acted as if he had not heard the question, speaking in a voice as calm and smooth as if they were talking about the weather, "I picked these, just before they turned black. That's when they're the most potent, poison to man and beast. Sometimes people pick the wrong ones. They eat the poisonous ones by accident, only to wind up dead, or so sick they can't eat for a week. But I don't know any other way to put you in a right state of mind to cross over. I think you'll only need a bite or two, chewed up good, so they'll take full effect."

Jack swallowed hard, and reached out, dipping his trembling fingers into the tin and fishing out two thin mushrooms. They were small and soft, their smoky-brown caps looking like monk's cowls. He switched them to his left hand and started to reach back in for more, but Lucius waved him off and muttered, "Okay, those there'll do the trick..." He set the tin on the floor next to his feet.

"Last chance boy - if I'm wrong, this could kill you just like a damned dog." Jack was afraid if he listened to Lucius any longer, he would not be able to resist his fear, so he nodded, and tossed the handful of poison into his mouth. He started chewing, his face twisting at the raw, bland taste as he crushed the flesh with his teeth. The taste was unpleasant, probably made worse by fear, and he felt sour saliva running down his throat as he chewed. Lucius place both of his hands on the table, palms up, wiggling his fingers to indicate Jack should join hands with him. He couldn't help a small flinch as his left hand was grasped by Lucius' deformed right. It distracted him somewhat from chewing as he concentrated on the tactile senses of his hand, feeling the hard, bony hand that squeezed with a strong grip.

"Now look at me boy," Lucius said, "and keep looking at me, listen to what I'm saying." Jack did as he was told, still chewing. Whether it was the natural reaction of his body, or the fact his mind knew he was deliberately ingesting something toxic, he felt himself lurch with the first signs of nausea. He fought down the urge to spew out the mushroom mash he had made, and instead swallowed the whole of it down. His eyes were watering as he looked into Lucius' gaze.

"This eye," he said, and Jack knew what he meant. Focusing both eyes on the cataract, he stared at it. He had never noticed before, but the eye seemed to be swirling slowly and his brow furrowed as he swallowed again, willing himself to look at nothing but that blue-white eye.

"That's it Jack," Lucius said, his voice low and husky. "The eyes are windows to the soul, and if you look hard enough, you can see through the curtains." The nausea came over him again, this time more insistent, like a punch in the gut, and Jack could feel his insides twisting into painful knots. He grimaced, concentrating on keeping his lips shut tight and staring at the eye. Five minutes passed, then ten, and then it may have been an hour, but all the while Lucius kept up his whispered instructions, keeping his voice low and calm. Jack's head was swimming in dizzy confusion, and though his nausea had ebbed, the pain in his stomach got worse. He could no longer hear the words Lucius spoke, but they were a constant buzz in the background. The black face was a peripheral blur around the swirling blue magnet that now held complete control over him.

He had no idea how long this went on, but at last he was able to make out Lucius' words again, and the pain in his stomach was gone, "Alright, alright, calm down now, it's done."

As Jack began to gather his bearings, Lucius' face came into focus, then the wall of the cabin behind him, then the trees outside. He could tell something had changed though; there was an amber light illuminating the world now, and the air seemed slow and thick. A thrill of joy and fear passed through him; he had passed through the curtain.

30

SETTLING IN

THEY LEFT THE CABIN and Jack followed Lucius down a narrow worn path that ran away and into the forest. The cabin looked exactly as he remembered it, but the surrounding landscape had changed. It was still forested but the lay of the land was different, the humps and hills all switched around. It was hard to keep his bearings, and as the forest closed around them he tried to take note of their path. It was a very strange place to be; the hair on the back of his neck stood on end, and he had an intense sense of foreboding; they were not supposed to be here.

Although there was a breeze blowing, everything seemed to move in slow motion. The leaves of the trees slowly waved at them as they passed; a pinecone fell to the ground in a slow, drifting glide. In the strange light the shadows shifted differently. He had the sense he was catching movement in the corner of his eye, but when he turned to look, there was nothing there.

Lucius led, walking with a quick purposeful stride.

Neither turning his head left nor right, he stared straight ahead, his shoulders tense. They traveled through the honey-colored landscape at a good pace, moving through a wide valley before climbing a steep ridgeline and hiking the crest. Although Lucius moved with a punishing pace, Jack didn't feel the least bit tired. He didn't perspire, nor was he breathing hard. The climb up the ridge's slope might as well have been on flat ground. The temperature was also remarkable; almost as if there was no such thing. The sun shone, but there was no heat effect, nor did the air feel cold. The strangeness of this phenomenon helped distract him from the anxious fear that had gripped him since awakening here. It occurred to him that if anything happened to Lucius, he would be stuck. He doubted he could even find his way back to the cabin.

"Lucius," he hissed, "How much further?"

Lucius turned and put his finger to his lips for silence. "Not much, I can feel her nearby," he whispered.

Her, Jack thought. His mind still fought to grasp the reality of the entity Lucius was taking him to see. He only had a few more moments to think about it before Lucius finally pulled up short.

"There," he whispered, pointing with his good hand. It trembled, and Jack saw him staring wide-eyed at the being they had come to see.

"There she is, careful now boy, or we'll both be dead." Lucius' voice quavered, and Jack's heart started racing even faster as he turned to look at the creature which instilled such terror.

She was tall, probably over twelve feet, Jack reckoned, but a cloud of dust and leaves swirled around her, making it hard to see clearly. The sound of rushing air grew louder and it smelled like rain, the first thing he could remember smelling in this world. The hairs on the back of Jack's neck were standing on end, and he heard himself breathing fast and loud. *Calm down Jack,* he told himself as her erratic, zig-zagging stride turned in their direction. As she came on, he instinctively began to lay down for cover, but Lucius grabbed his arm in an iron grip and pulled Jack behind him, as he stood to face her. As she came nearer, the rush of wind became violent, and leaves and dirt blew into their faces.

The air felt heavy and wet, and Jack became aware of an insect buzz, like ten-thousand crickets screaming at each other. Squinting his eyes against the wind and debris, Jack could make out some details, and a more frightening apparition he had never seen. She was as dry and wrinkled as an old leather bag, not as with the softness of old age, but as though every last drop of water had been wrung from her skin before being stretched back over her skull. Her gray hair stuck out wildly, brittle and parched. The muscles, bones and sinew of her arms stood out in stark detail, conveying a terrible strength. Her hands were claws continually flexing and curling, as if looking for a neck to wring. She had no real clothing, but most of her form was wreathed in a dense mass of moss and brambles, as though she had strode heedless through briar patches, tearing up the vicious vines and pulling them along with her. All this Jack had seen in the space of a few heartbeats, but what captured his gaze and held it were her eyes. Black, unblinking pools which shone like liquid, but held no warmth at all. Looking into those eyes, Jack felt pathetically insignificant.

She drew up and stopped before them, turning her head this way and that. Now that it had come to the moment, Jack was too terrified to say anything. Lucius' head was bowed, and Jack quickly ducked his head to look at the ground, which was much better. Lucius started to speak, but he sounded so weak and small against the fury of the swirling wind that Jack couldn't hear him. Even as he strained to listen, the wind suddenly dropped to a whisper.

"...I'm beggin' you," Lucius finished.

"Lucius," she said in a loud rasp, a voice that threatened to make Jack turn and run, but he managed to stay where he was, clutching Lucius' arm and trembling. "Why have you brought this boy here? You should not have. You know I have no love for humans." This last was said with such menace a wave of heat washed over them, causing Lucius and Jack both to take a step back.

"Please Mother, you are the only one who can help us. Just hear the boy out. Please." There was no answer, and Jack wilted under her fierce stare.

"Why have you come?" she practically roared, her mouth opening wide and her hot breath blowing over him.

"M-my name is Jack, ma'am." Even to his own ears he sounded pathetic and small. He tried to make himself louder, and yelled back at her, "My sister is missing, the Goblins took her. Can you please help me find her?"

Her eyes glared at him for a moment, and Jack felt as if he were being weighed and measured. The inspection only lasted a moment before her lip curled in contempt as she growled back, "You do not know me child. You have no understanding if you believe the life of one human means anything to me. I am the Earth Mother boy, and I do the Creator's work. There is naught I can do for you."

"But ma'am, she's only five years old, and she's my only sister, and she needs me." Jack's voice cracked, and he felt the now-familiar tears welling up in his eyes. She stared at him, unblinking. The moment stretched, and Jack blinked his eyes against the tears as he withstood her gaze.

"Child," she whispered, "Thousands of humans die by my hand every day. I am the bringer of floods, fires, storms and earthquakes; disease, drought and pestilence. I am bound by the requirements of my role. It defines me and it is not in me to be merciful. Do you think only humans matter? All strive to live, but the strong survive and the weak die. Accept it boy, that is the way."

"Mother, his sister was taken by the Loki. They are not the Creator's work," said Lucius. Her brows furrowed as she frowned down at Jack. "This boy is strong Mother, but he can't fight them."

"He must," she hissed, staring at Lucius, "I am constrained; I cannot intervene. To do otherwise would be to compromise the Compact, which I cannot do. I will not fight this battle for you, child."

Jack heard the refusal from this powerful being that could bring Abby back. He couldn't help the anger that boiled up in him and he shouted back at her, "My sister is not weak, and she does not deserve to be turned into some creature!" He glared at her, his anger growing hot and he pointed at her, "You have to help me!"

An explosion of air knocked both Jack and Lucius to the ground, and Mother Nature roared a wordless scream of fury. The vines and brambles wrapping her body whipped through the air, slashing his face and arms as he tried to cover his head. Her voice was deep and monstrous as she thundered down at Jack, "Enough!" A moment stretched, the ground rumbling beneath them, then, "This was not wise, Lucius. Take him back and do not seek me out again." She turned and strode away, the ground vibrating with every step.

31

A CHANCE MEETING

JACK CLIMBED TO HIS FEET, brushing dirt and leaves out of his hair. He felt stunned to be so completely rejected. The disappointment was crushing.

"I'm sorry boy," Lucius said, the old black man's face a picture of regret and sorrow.

"Lucius, what did she mean? She said you knew what her answer would be. Why did we come here if you knew she wouldn't help?" But Lucius didn't answer, he stared into a line of trees and held up a hand for silence.

Lucius' attention had been captured by a figure standing under the eaves of a tall evergreen tree.

Jack rubbed his eyes and blinked several times, but the strange being still stood there in the odd golden light of this place, looking like something out of an old fairy tale. His face was fine-boned and sharp, eyes as black and shiny as oil, just like Mother's. The features were so striking Jack supposed the being might have been considered beautiful, but for the unsettling gaze he now found himself under. Altogether too old and knowing, those eyes bored into

Jack, eroding his innocence. It seemed if he stared back long enough, he could find every answer there, but the intensity of the gaze was too dangerous, too feral to get closer. The creature turned and took a few graceful steps to one side, maintaining eye contact with Jack. As it moved, a curly mane of golden hair slowly waved in the syrup-like breeze. He wore a shirt of mail, with shoulder-plate and arm greaves of a most ancient and decorative design. Although clearly of high quality once, it was rent and torn, and showing signs of long wear. In the amber light it was difficult to distinguish if it was made of silver or gold, but it seemed very thin and fine. There was also a leather pouch hanging on his hip from a strap across his chest, and a short sword on the other hip. Altogether, a fantastic looking figure, Jack thought.

"Lucius, well met," it said, nodding toward Lucius, finally breaking eye contact with Jack. Lucius returned a nod in greeting, a cautious look on his face.

"We came to see Mother," he said, taking a step forward, "but it warn't no help."

The creature frowned, shaking his head, "After all you've been through, I would have thought you knew better. In fact, I'm sure you did."

Lucius' skin was turned a dusky gold by the light, and with his elongated arm and cloudy blue eye Jack knew he was something more than human.

"I thought maybe she'd give a listen to the boy, but you're right, I should have known. Have you come for me?" asked Lucius. As he spoke, Jack could see his jaw clenching.

"Well, let's just say I've been keeping an eye out for you. What has kept you thus far? You know this is the ascendant season." As he spoke, the faerie's voice rose and fell, hypnotic in its meter, causing Jack to hang on every word, "and here you come, dragging a boy along in your wake. Bad form Lucius, truly."

"Then I guess we'd best be leaving," said Lucius, reaching out to gently pinch Jack's sleeve.

"No, no, don't leave just yet," it said, turning its face back to regard Jack. "Hello Jack."

Jack should have been surprised to hear his name, but after what he had already seen it barely caused him to flinch.

"Hello," answered Jack. He could sense the power in the creature's voice, and a small flutter of hope tickled his chest. Perhaps here he could find help, but before he could frame a question Lucius spoke.

"This is Blixt, Jack. He's the one I told you about."

"You're a very courageous boy, to come into this land with no one but Lucius to help you, or perhaps you're only ignorant?" he said, arching his brow. "I think maybe a little of both." A slow grin stole across the perfect face as Blixt looked from Jack to Lucius and back again.

"Lucius can tell you many things," he said, glancing at Lucius, "but his knowledge is only a small, rough part of the story. Neither of you comprehend the game."

"Please," said Jack, "I just want my sister returned. I need help."

"Ah, but that's the problem Jack. There is no help for you here. Lucius knows that better than anyone alive, and he should have told you. Neither Mother nor I can restore your sister to you. It is beyond our power. I am sorry." It stood still, looking at Jack curiously.

Jack was bewildered, *Why would Lucius bring me here? Why couldn't they help him?* Growing desperate and angry, he looked at Lucius and back at the creature. "Why not? I don't believe you, you're lying!"

"Am I? Am I, Lucius?" Blixt arched his eyebrows and sighed, "Perhaps you're not asking the right questions, boy."

Jack was confused, his mind racing, *What do I do?* Something was going on here, perhaps he was being tested somehow. *Ask the right questions? Think, Jack, think.*

"All right then," he said, "who *can* help me?"

The creature smiled and winked, "You're catching on now Jack."

Blixt motioned Jack to sit down, and folded himself into a sitting position on the ground. Lucius sat next to Jack, his deformed arm stretching across both knees. Once settled, the creature began, "Where should I start? I suppose at the beginning, but that's far too long a story." Blixt cocked his head as if listening, "There's not much time, but I will tell you what I can."

"Did you know once there was no such thing as winter? When the world was formed, there were only the spring, summer and fall cycles, a never-ending circle of life. No, winter is the result of this nasty little situation you've stumbled into, but where was I? Ah yes, the Creator established natural laws to regulate the earth, and created creatures whose purpose it was to preserve and maintain order." Blixt paused, "That was our charge. We are the Ba'ath. In our language it means 'The Faithful.' You humans have given us many names – sprite, pixy, faerie, elf, even demon or angel. In the beginning, we mixed with humans freely, befriending them and in some cases living amongst them. It was a golden age, no aging, death, or violence. Over time however, a chasm grew between us. Trust eroded on both sides and even the Ba'ath that loved and admired the humans did not feel welcome amongst them anymore."

"In the wars that followed, many horrible things happened. I was there to see it, and I remember it clearly."

"Moreover, the magic of the Ba'ath was brought to bear in these conflicts. As a sign of contempt, some of the Ba'ath used their magic to transfigure humans into hideous creatures, who were forced into service. You may have heard of them as trolls, goblins, vampires, werewolves, and more. Your sister wasn't just taken Jack, she has been turned."

Jack's breath caught in his throat. After hearing the story of Isreal, he was afraid of hearing those words, but in his heart he couldn't believe Abby had been transformed. The creature Lucius had pulled from the water was too hideous and ugly to contain the innocent spirit of his sister. He believed Blixt however, and that scared him more than anything else that had happened thus far.

Blixt lowered his eyes and said, "The only one who can return your sister is the one who turned her. In her case, it will require the destruction of the spell-caster."

In spite of his dread, Jack asked, "I have to kill someone to get Abby back? Who? Where is this person?"

"I didn't say 'kill' Jack. Your true challenge will be in finding him. I cannot help you in that task, but perhaps this can." He lifted the flap on his pouch and drew out a small book. It seemed very old, and was bound in dark leather, worn slick and shiny through years of handling.

"This book was written by a man named Thomas More. I wouldn't be surprised if you've heard of him. He was a very dear friend of mine, and we spent many nights on his roof gazing at the stars through a looking glass. He was the greatest mind of his age, until that fat, stupid king lopped his head off. I laid a curse on the king that took his children, spoiled his seed, and made him swell like a pustule until he died in agony with poison coursing through his veins."

Jack flinched at that, but Blixt held the book out to him. "Read his words. The Loki have your sister Jack. I do not know if it is possible to recover her, but if you find her, listen to Lucius, he will know what to do until the spell can be broken. Do you understand?"

Blixt raised his head suddenly and looking at the trees behind him. He stood, "And unfortunately, it seems we have run out of time."

Jack took the book as Blixt stepped back and drew his sword. "Now you must go. Lucius, quickly, it is almost too late. If they find you unprepared…"

Lucius grabbed Jack's hand with his goblin hand and pulled him into a run. They raced away from the trees, running as fast as Jack's legs could go.

"Lucius! What's happening?" Jack shouted as the wind began to swirl around them.

"Just run, run like hell!" Lucius yelled, pulling Jack on toward a shimmer that had appeared in the air. Jack saw Blixt leap into the air, sword poised to strike, as several dark figures burst out of the trees. They were moving impossibly fast, and even as Jack watched two of them ran past Blixt and raced over the ground toward the escaping fugitives. The space between them shrank so rapidly Jack could see their faces, Blixt-like perfection, but distorted now with a fearful hatred and fury. Jack screamed, pushing his legs even faster now. The shimmering air was just before them, and Jack heard a shout of rage and a clash of steel as he and Lucius ran headlong into the curtain of wavering light.

Jack awoke to a frantic scrabbling and banging. He opened his eyes to find himself lying on his side on the floor of Lucius' cabin, entangled in the rope tied around his chest. His stomach had reacted violently to the mushrooms, and a puddle of vomit lay in front of him while his head pounded. He rolled onto his back and struggled to sit up. Though his head swam, he could see Lucius had turned up the lamps and was slamming the shutters of the cabin closed. He had a length of iron chain wrapped around his good hand, and he used it like a whip to flail at something scrabbling at the windowsill as he tried to slam the shutters. There was a squeal of pain, and Jack heard a few cackling laughs outside. After that, the only sound was Lucius breathing like a bellows. Jack pulled himself to his feet and stumbled over to him. That was when he noticed the blood. Lucius was soaked in blood on his right side from the waist down, and was half-slumped in the chair gasping.

"What happened!?" he asked frantically.

"My leg," Lucius replied, "Help me onto the bed." He stood wincing, slung his left arm around Jack's shoulders and hopped over to the bed. He rolled into the cot, hissing and holding his leg up. Now Jack could see Lucius' trousers were slit and there was a deep gash in his flesh from the outer thigh around to the back of his leg.

"What can I do?" he asked.

"Just get me some water, and start tearing some rags to bind this with." Lucius gasped.

Jack hurried to do as he was told. As he did, he noticed it was dark outside. That didn't make any sense to him, because it seemed like they had only been gone a short time, an hour at most. Yet, from their early morning departure, it appeared that at least half a day had passed in the cabin. The inconsistency was in the back of his mind as he took Lucius the water and bandages. Jack helped him wash and bandage his leg, wrapping it tightly, then settling him comfortably on the cot.

"You're lucky Lucius, they came that close to taking off your leg," Jack said, holding up his thumb and index finger in illustration.

"Lucky hell, they would have had my leg, except Blixt spoiled their stroke."

The speed and ferocity of the attack of the Ba'ath still shook Jack, and he asked Lucius, "Do you think Blixt survived?"

"Yeah, but that's not for us to worry about right now. You got the book?"

The book was lying on the floor where he awakened. For a moment after coming to, he thought he'd been hallucinating, but incredibly, there was the book. He retrieved it and carried it over to Lucius, handing it to him as he pulled the chair over to the bed and sat down. Lucius held the book in the palm of his goblin hand, and had opened it, looking the pages over with hungry interest. Jack watched him for a few minutes, then he asked, "Lucius, what did he mean when he said you knew better than anyone they couldn't help?"

Lucius continued to stare at the pages, but Jack saw his jaw muscles working. An awkward silence hung in the air for a moment before he stated flatly, "I can't read." Jack blinked, but Lucius went on, "Blixt wanted to give me this book once, but I didn't take it. I didn't figure it would do me any good because I couldn't read."

"I'm confused Lucius, why did we go over if they weren't going to help us?"

"I really didn't know what would happen. You can never tell what Mother will do. You didn't see her at her best either; it would have been much better if we had gone over in the Spring. The reason I should have known was because they didn't help me when I asked them about Isreal, and I asked plenty of times."

"So there's no help for us?" Jack asked.

"Like I said, Blixt gave me this book before, but I couldn't do anything with it. Now, maybe we can figure out what we have to do to get Abigail back," Lucius finished, thumping his finger on the book for emphasis.

"Yes!" Jack said excitedly, "and maybe we can find Isreal too!"

Lucius looked back down at the book, "We'll see."

32

BOOK OF MORE

IN FACT, JACK HAD HEARD of Sir Thomas More. He was a noted 16th century intellect, knowledgeable in a wide variety of subjects during his lifetime, a virtual Da Vinci. Astronomy, medicine, law, and religion were among the many academic studies to which he contributed, and his gifts had brought him considerable fame and influence. Fate, however, had put him within the orbit of King Henry VIII, which was always a very dangerous place to be. Even more so for those who were closest to him, and Sir Thomas More had been one of those. In fact, it was King Henry who knighted More. He was the king's friend, advisor, and confidant, but he was also a courageous man of conviction. This was what ultimately doomed him.

King Henry demanded More's support for his forced divorce of Catherine of Aragon, and declaration as head of the Church of England, thereby severing ties with Rome. Sir Thomas More, knowing it would mean his death, refused to support Henry's pride and ambition. Henry pleaded with his friend, begged him to reconsider, but resigned to his fate, More refused to abandon his principles. Enraged at the rejection, King Henry VIII declared him a traitor to the crown, and ordered his head chopped off.

The Headsman carried out the execution in the courtyard of the Tower of London in 1535, severing the head and quartering his body. The parts were sent to all regions of the kingdom as a warning of what happened to those who defied King Henry VIII.

Thus it was that King Henry incurred the Ba'ath's wrath, Blixt in particular. His curse prevented Henry from fathering a male heir, and with no one except a daughter to inherit his kingdom, he died in swollen agony from a blood sickness no physician could alleviate.

Blixt had found in Sir Thomas More one of those rare humans who possessed the gifts of wisdom, courage, and compassion. They had spent many nights on More's rooftop, surveying the stars, discussing the composition of the universe and the meaning of life. In fact, of all the humans Blixt had known throughout the millennia, Sir Thomas More came the closest to being a friend in the truest sense of the word. Blixt had revealed many things to him and ever the tedious academic, More had written them all down. He completed three books detailing the various aspects of the Ba'ath/Human drama, but only one of those had survived. Blixt had rescued the one, but the other two had vanished or been burned with many of More's other writings.

Of course, Jack didn't know that part of the story, but he

marveled at the ancient little book on the table before him. For such an old relic it was in remarkably good shape, the pages appearing fresh and crisp. It did not occur to him the book's pristine condition was undoubtedly due to being kept on the other side all these years.

The book was written in a neat, flowing script, with very few defects, but the language was of such an archaic style Jack struggled to make sense of it.

In the course of this conflict betwixt the Ba'ath, magic was brought to bear on the creatures of the earth. In many cases these poor beasts were transformed in body and mind, to act as agents of the divine. The Sprite, for example, is but a mouse or shrew, transformed and gifted with some small measure of knowledge. Although possessed of free will of a sort, these mutations are subject to use by the Ba'ath at any moment. Watchers, Companions, Wards, and Hunters all perform their designed purpose...

There were numerous notes in the margins, and sketches covered the corners or sometimes a whole page. Lucius looked over Jack's shoulder as he flipped through the pages. A sketch of a warty, vicious-looking Goblin took the first half of a page, with a description underneath.

These are the children of Man, enslaved by black magic to serve the Ba'ath. Their powers are considerable; they have superior strength, may deceive with their voices, vanish, turn to stone, or lay a compulsion upon the unwary with their gaze.

They steal other children. Very cunning and dangerous...

Jack turned the page. The narrative went on, describing other creatures and aspects of their abilities and appearance. As he turned to the last page, a black hole of ink appeared. The lines of More's pen had scratched an impenetrable bird's nest on the paper, except for two white points. On the inside of the back cover of the book was More's final inscription.

Oh, my God. This is the Abomination. I have seen the Walking Death with my own eyes. The Wight is the supreme agent of evil, transfigured from a rotting, stinking corpse. I myself fell under its gaze and would have been taken but for Micah, who destroyed the creature. With the strength of many men, its' skin is the purple-black of putrid corruption, terror of the grave. Only complete destruction of the corpse can prevent the relentless attack. A severed hand will continue to grip and choke, or drag itself back to the body to be rejoined through dark magic. Because the flesh is dead, it does not fear the flame as do other mutations, although it shuns the clean light of the sun. It is the Wight who is given the power to cast the spell of transformation. It is this ghoul, who with gross violation, transforms the child into the monster.

Jack finished reading the passage out loud, then turned to look at Lucius. "Is that it? Is this what we're looking for?"

Lucius breathed hard, staring at the page with the eyes, "Yes, that's it. I haven't seen that face in so long I almost forgot. All these years, I thought it was a Ba'ath that turned Israel that night. Now I understand."

33

WRATH

Aʙɪɢᴀɪʟ sᴀᴛ ᴏɴ ᴛʜᴇ ʙᴀɴᴋ of the slow moving stream. It was late afternoon and a trio of ducks floated by, quietly dabbling as they paddled their way around the next bend in the bank. As they disappeared she stood, brushing the leaves and grass off her dress. The hem had gotten very dirty, and Mother would be upset it was likely ruined. There was nothing she could do about it though, because she was lost in these woodlands, waiting for someone to come find her. She turned away from the water and started through the forest.

Abigail had only gone a few steps when she saw a man moving through a stand of trees toward her. He was close enough for her to recognize her father, and a huge smile creased her face as she called out, "Thomas!"

"Thomas. Thomas, wake up." His eyes fluttered open with a start, the excited tickle in his chest now a confused alarm. Elizabeth lay on her side, shaking his shoulder where he was slumped in the chair by the bed. He quickly regained his wits and patted Elizabeth's hand, leaning in to rest his forehead against hers. It only took a second, by some emotive connection, for him to feel the questions building in her, threatening to come out in hysteria if he didn't say something. Fortunately, he had already worked that out.

"We haven't found Abby yet, but wait..." he cautioned as he saw the despair in her face, "that may be good news." Her brows furrowed, but she said nothing and Thomas was just glad she was holding up.

"There are over a hundred men and dogs out there scouring every inch of the area around the Plunkett's farm and beyond. They have plenty of incentive to keep at it, but thus far there hasn't been any trace of her."

"Thomas, how is this good news?" she began.

"Don't you see? If something terrible had happened to her, there would have been something. Blood, clothing, a shoe; something. Easily found by now, but there's nothing. It's as if she just vanished into thin air."

Elizabeth glared at him with a raised eyebrow, "Yes?"

"Since we can be sure *that* didn't happen, it stands to reason she was taken by someone, but what would anyone want with a child? Our child?" He let her work it out by herself, watching the tumblers of logic falling into place.

"Ransom?" she whispered, the possibility dawning on her.

"Yes, of course! Why else? We have no enemies here, and it would be a quick and harmless way for some group of thugs to reap a hefty reward. This is nothing more than that," he finished.

"Nothing more than that!?" she exclaimed. "They have our child, Thomas! Whoever 'they' are!"

Thomas made shushing gestures, trying to keep her calm, "Yes, yes dear, but don't you see? It's really in their best interests if she is kept safe and sound. Don't worry, I have a plan. You trust me don't you?"

Elizabeth's eyes teared up and her shoulders sagged, "Oh, of course I do. Please, find her and bring her home, right away."

"I will. Now you stay here, keep your strength and spirits up. I will find Abby," he said, smiling as he stood stiffly. As he walked out of the door, he turned back again, "Darling, nothing to worry about, but you should know I've had a falling out with Reverend Fetch and the Judge. I would much prefer it if neither of them were to set foot in this house while I am away."

"Yes, of course," she nodded, and watched as he left the room.

Thomas went downstairs and left through the kitchen, grabbing a sausage as he passed. He momentarily wondered where Jack might be, but wasn't concerned about him at present. Out in the barn, Clive and Mr. French were already waiting with the horses saddled. Thomas was glad to see both men were armed.

"Mr. French, send word to the mine; every able-bodied man is to meet me on Main Street in front of the office right away. Send runners to the camp and also to the locals. Be quick about it, I'll see you there."

"Yes sir," answered Mr. French, and with a cluck he

turned the horse and put his heels to its flanks, clopping out of the gate and down the road.

Thomas and Clive mounted their horses and followed in French's wake, thudding their way down the dirt lane until they reached the outskirts of Cobbs. They reined up at the mining office and went inside.

"Clive, watch the door please, give me a moment."

"Yes sir," said Clive, closing the door behind him as he stood on the boardwalk with his hands clasped in front.

Thomas walked to the rear area of the office to the floor safe that sat underneath the desk there. He quickly dialed the combination and the door swung smoothly open. Inside, bundles of bills were stacked in rows across the back wall of the safe. This was the payroll, operating funds and profits from his mining operations. There was almost $40,000 in cash in the safe, and Thomas was about to put it to good use.

He pulled the bills out and stacked them on the desk, making two large stacks he could easily carry.

Pacing the floor an hour later, he finally judged there were enough men outside to begin with. Gathering the bills in both hands, he opened the door and walked outside. The crowd ceased buzzing and an expectant silence fell. Handing one of the stacks to Mr. French standing beside him, he turned to address the men.

"By now, I expect you all know my daughter Abigail is missing. I appreciate those of you who have been helping look for her, but she has not yet been found." A smaller group gathered down the street toward the church, watching his presentation.

"Until she is recovered, the mines are closed," he yelled, speaking loud enough for all of them to hear. A general mumbling coursed through the crowd, and he continued, "But there will still be plenty of work for any man who is willing to help find my daughter. Please see Mr. Dalby who will be assigning your duties."

"I am also doubling the reward; $10,000 to the man who finds her!" Thomas stuck the thick stack of bills into the air for emphasis, starting another excited buzz. He turned to Mr. French, "Mr. French, a word please." He turned and walked back into the office.

They walked back to the safe, where Thomas deposited the cash he carried. Mr. French started to hand over the stack Thomas had pushed into his hands outside, but he waved it away, "No, you're going to need that."

"Yes sir," Mr. French said in his thick brogue, "what's the plan?"

Thomas told him about Jack's story, the scene at the church, and his suspicions about a ransom plot. Mr. French nodded his head in agreement when Thomas said, "It's time to put some pressure on whoever is behind this."

"Go on, sir."

"I suspect you know something about rough work Mr. French, am I right?"

"I've been in a spot a time or two, sir, always managed to come out standing up," answered the Irishman.

"Good man. I want you to hand-pick ten or fifteen men; hard men, handy with their guns. I want this whole valley shut down. Deputize them under whatever means necessary, but I want them on horseback and armed at all times. No one will leave this place, and no one enters until my daughter is found. No unnecessary violence, but see they follow their orders strictly, and allow no one to escape."

"I understand, sir, I already have a good crew of men in mind. What do you want me to do with this?" he asked, lifting the stack of cash.

"Make a good accounting, but use whatever is necessary to keep them properly motivated, and if the opportunity arises, to pay for information leading to Abigail."

"Yes sir. Not to worry Mr. Rutherford, I know how to handle this mess." Mr. French rose and strode out of the office. Thomas' heart raced a little at what he had just done. He had just placed his own martial law on the town of Cobbs. Depending on how things turned out, there would be hell to pay, but for now, he couldn't care less.

Within two hours, all access roads in or out of Cobbs had been blocked off and were manned by at least two armed sentries. Any creek large enough to float a canoe was patrolled, and a curfew had been set. The tension was high as French's men, marked with black armbands made their presence known throughout the town and the nearby homesteads. They brought news of the reward, the travel restrictions, and offers of cash for information to every person in the area. There were a few shouted arguments and scuffles with the local people, but nothing deadly, and by nightfall, the entire region was in Thomas' grip.

34

THE LAIR

IT SEEMED THEY HAD BEEN trekking through the forest for at least a half hour before Lucius held up his hand for a halt. They were headed to the backside of the mines, the other side of the mountain. Jack was just glad they were finally looking for Abby, and he could barely contain his eagerness.

Lucius had told him the plan back in the cabin.

"I don't know exactly where they are, but I got a pretty good idea," Lucius had said. He suspected the trouble at the mines was more than just out-of-hand mischief, that there was a purpose in the activity.

"Seems to me they're trying pretty hard to scare the miners out; now why would that be? I'm thinking it's because some of the digging is getting too close to something they need."

Jack nodded his agreement.

"So, let's head around that way and see what we can find."

On Lucius' instructions Jack had grabbed his rifle when

he'd left the house, and he also carried a six-foot length of chain and a pack with rags, matches and oil. He didn't know what to expect from this evening but he had placed all his faith in Lucius, and now he would see it through.

"Alright then, now we're getting to the dangerous part. From this point forward we need to be real quiet, as quiet as you can be, ok?" Jack nodded and Lucius continued, "I got no idea how many might be here and we're going to have to leave fast. Now, what are you going to do if we get separated?"

"Find the nearest evergreen and claim sanctuary," Jack answered. *Thin protection*, he thought, but what choice did he have? They readjusted their gear and started off again down the game trail.

Dusk set in and an ominous feeling was in the air. The forest was completely silent; no insects or birds, just a slight swishing of wind in the treetops, and even that was embarrassed and tentative. Lucius seemed to dissolve into the grayness that fell over them. He wore a charcoal-dyed linen cloak, and appeared to be a stalking shadow, barely visible, and only if he kept moving. When he was still he virtually disappeared.

Except for the occasional snapped twig or crunching leaf, they moved quietly, wending their way through the trees toward the looming dark mass that was the mountain. Lucius didn't hesitate, but walked confidently, as if there were a road sign pointing the way. Jack had gotten into a rhythm of placing his heel and rolling onto the ball of his foot, stopping when pressure told him he had stepped on something that might make noise. He was so focused on being stealthy he almost ran into Lucius who had stopped to kneel down on the trail, which started to climb upward.

"Just like I thought, this is it," he whispered. "They're up there. You follow me on up, and I'll tell you where to wait for me." Jack nodded and they moved forward once more.

The trail got steeper, until they were pulling themselves from tree to rock, the occasional low clatter of pebbles or gear making them wince. A black crevice in the mountain rose in front of them and Jack knew they had arrived.

Lucius took Jack's pack and quickly wrapped the rags around the ends of two long sticks, and soaked them with the oil. He took another rag and stuffed most of it into the bottle of oil itself. Lucius took one of the torches and the oil bottle, leaving the other torch with Jack. He positioned Jack just inside the cleft, and gave him his final instructions, "Once I leave here, count to one-hundred, then light your torch and fire one shot into the air, understand?" Jack nodded at the hooded shadow. "Don't let them get near you boy. Keep waving that torch in front of this opening, and that should keep them away from you. I will bind Abby and bring her out."

"How will you know which one is Abby?" he asked.

"Don't worry," he said, tapping his temple next to his goblin eye, "I'll know. Now, be brave and we'll have her out in just a few minutes." With that, Lucius turned and disappeared into the breach with a soft clink as he gathered his chain.

For a second or two, Jack just knelt there watching the blackness where Lucius had disappeared. He was utterly alone and fear started to creep in. He looked around for an evergreen, but in the darkness he couldn't tell one tree from another. *Be brave*, he told himself, and started to count.

As he reached seventy, he groped around in his pack for a match, and had a moment of panic when none came to hand before remembering Lucius had set them out on the rock near the torch. He scrabbled over the ledge until he found one and held it ready to strike. At one-hundred, he scraped the match cross the stone, igniting a bright bloom of fire in the darkness that surrounded him. He brought the match to the torch, which ignited with a *whoosh!* and threw light and shadows out in every direction. The light did little to illuminate the passageway however, and Jack felt more exposed than ever. Picking up his rifle, he levered a shell with one hand and fired a crisp, loud shot into the night sky.

For a moment, nothing happened. Jack stood there bathed in the blue-yellow light from the torch and listened, although the pounding of his heart made it difficult to hear anything else at all. A faint screech wafted out of the passage. He stared but heard nothing else, and anxiety for Abby and Lucius made him take a step into the cave. He held the shaking torch out in front as he took one step, then another, further into the blackness. The walls were close on either side, and he was almost obliged to turn sideways to get through. Another screech, followed by a bellowing and a crash came through the air. He couldn't see anything though, and Jack stepped in another ten feet. The hand holding the torch shook, but he remembered to chamber another shell in the rifle as he stumbled over broken rock.

Suddenly, the screeching turned much louder. Jack realized a few bends in the passage had muffled the sounds, and the goblins were coming his way! A slight flicker of light appeared on the wall in front of him, and the sound of clattering rocks and slapping feet made his heart race even faster. As he stood with the torch poking out in front of him, a trio of creatures came scrambling around the corner!

The goblin in front screamed and threw itself down onto the rocks almost at Jack's feet. The other two leapt high into the cleft and using both sides ran right past him, screeching as they passed overhead, and continued out of the cave mouth. Jack swung the torch over his head and down, trying to keep them at bay. Now he had goblins in front and behind him, and things seemed to be going downhill fast. The goblin on the ground in front of him leapt up and ran back the way it had come, shrieking the whole way.

His eyes wide as dinner plates, Jack quickly backed out of the cavern, swishing the torch back and forth.

The bellowing got louder. Jack wondered if he should go back in to help Lucius when a rock cracked into the wall next to his head, a spray of pebbles falling into his hair. Several pairs of faintly glowing eyes spread out through the forest. A second rock was better thrown, and a sharp rap on the side of his head caused him to clap his torch hand to his scalp in pain.

"Ahhh!," he yelled, pivoting to fire the rifle one-handed from the waist in their general direction. The chain draped across the back of his neck clinked as he swung, and the hoots and caws of the goblins seemed everywhere.

The noise behind him rose into a crescendo, and he turned to see Lucius running toward him with his lit torch. A multitude of shadows boiled behind him. "Move, Jack, let's go!"

Jack turned and ran out of the cave, but misjudged how steep the trail was and promptly fell down the slope, rifle, chain and torch all clacking and bouncing as he tumbled. Sprawled in the leaves, Jack reached out to pick up his torch when a goblin grabbed his wrist, and with a vicious snap, bit down on his forearm. He screamed and kicked at the monster, but it was horribly strong. Its eyes glared at him, then disappeared in a shower of sparks as Lucius brained the beast with his torch. The goblin instantly caught the flame and shrieked as it fled, a fiery comet flying through the trees in agony.

"Up Jack, we can't stop!" Lucius said, and his voice was labored. He held a limp and unprotesting goblin on his back, slung there by the chain he had secured around its neck. He held his torch and the end of the chain in his goblin hand, but his left arm hung limply and Jack knew something was wrong.

He leapt to his feet, scooped up his rifle and torch and scooted down the trail ahead of Lucius as fast as he could go. Dark figures ran past him on either side, and rocks and missiles flew past his head. The screeching was all around them now. Jack had no idea where he was going, he just wanted to survive.

"Here! Jack, here, with me!" Lucius yelled, and Jack screeched to a halt, running back to Lucius, who stumbled off to one side. Together they crashed through the brush, falling to the ground, and Lucius flung one hand into the air crying, "*Dun' na mehr ich va!*"

A thunderclap of silence followed, and Jack lay on his back, pointing his rifle behind them, panting and looking for a target.

"NO! Don't shoot, don't shoot. We're safe now." Lucius lay on his side, wheezing. The goblin he had brought along flopped onto the ground, unmoving, apparently lifeless. It was then he noticed the soft carpet of pine needles they had landed on; an evergreen – they had made it to sanctuary.

35

TIME TO HEAL

OUTSIDE THE BOUGHS of the tree, a dozen or more eyes glared at the pair, coming as close as possible without violating the boundary of the pine. They growled and screamed at Jack, slapping the ground and breaking sticks in frustration.

"Put your gun down Jack, we are protected," Lucius panted.

The goblins stayed outside the protective area of the pine tree for some time, taunting them, but it was clear their quarry wouldn't be leaving anytime soon. They faded back into the forest, although Jack was certain they were still watching them.

He could hardly believe his eyes. Was the creature lying motionless amongst the pine needles Abigail, magically transformed into a monster? He shuddered as he bent down again to check the proof. The glint of a deep red stone on the flabby, warty green earlobe was all he needed to see. Abby's birthstone was a garnet, and their mother had given her the earrings for her fifth birthday.

Abby had rarely taken them out since, and had they not been there Jack could have never been convinced. Perhaps he should have felt a greater sense of elation at having rescued her, but in her present condition, it was difficult. Her jowls were sagging open and the jagged teeth and black tongue made him cringe as he studied her. The chain around her neck was not very tight, but Lucius had assured him she would not awaken.

They were lucky to have escaped with their lives. Besides a number of scratches he had received tearing through thorns and sharp limbs in their flight, blood slowly dripped down his neck from the scalp wound, and his left forearm burned from the bite he had taken. He saw Lucius slowly turning so he could lie down under the pine boughs. His wounds were far worse than Jack's; a pointed stick protruded from his right side and his breathing was labored, while his left arm was obviously broken below the elbow.

Jack knelt by Lucius as he rolled onto his back, wincing in pain.

"What can I do? Should I try to get back and fetch Dr. Keene?" he asked.

Lucius eyes were squinted tight, and he blinked a few times before answering, "No time, I have to go over now Jack. I can fix this if I can get to the other side." He hissed again, and a tear slid out of the corner of his eye. "First, though, I need you to get this stick out, understand?" Jack nodded and he continued, "Do it fast, then. Stay here, and don't worry, I'll be back soon."

Lucius gripped the stick at the base with his goblin hand, and Jack reached over to grasp it with both of his. It was wet and slippery with blood, and his hands were trembling, so Jack gripped it as hard as he could. With a last look at Lucius, Jack squeezed his eyes shut and pulled with all his strength, ripping the stick out in one smooth motion. He heard Lucius gasp, and Jack opened his eyes to see him covering the wound with his hand, his face showing the horrible pain. Lucius seemed to convulse, and a trickle of blood ran out of his mouth while his wide eyes stared upwards. Jack stood there with the bloody stick, not knowing what to do. He watched as Lucius' muscles unclenched and he slowly collapsed, his eyes closing. Jack couldn't tell if he was breathing; he didn't think he was.

Lucius' face and body were so deathly still, he seemed almost a mannequin instead of the living, breathing being he had been only moments before. Then he witnessed a miracle.

The inflammation around the bloody hole in Lucius' side eased and the hole itself began to close! The awkward bend in his left forearm straightened and the skin over his face seemed to become tighter and smoother. He still didn't seem alive; in fact, the rubber-like quality of Lucius' face and body was disturbingly inanimate. There was nothing he could do at this point however, so he retreated closer to Abigail to sit and wait.

He laid there staring out into the night, gripping his rifle and occasionally seeing the pale blue luminescence of goblin eyes. Once he heard something running through the trees, sprinting at full speed. The hairs on the back of his neck stood on end, but whatever it was flashed through the area without even slowing down and thrashed off into the darkness. He heard it again a few minutes later, followed by complete silence.

36

HARSH DISCIPLINE

BAEL'S HEAD SNAPPED UP, staring into the copper sun, black eyes reflecting the amber light. The spells surrounding the grotto jangled and bounced like a spider's web with a caught fly. He leapt to his feet, and in a flash of dark vapor, vanished.

He reappeared in the grotto, striding through the chamber, hands flexing, arcane spells at the ready. There was chaos in the room, as goblins shrieked and gabbled, pulling their hair and scratching at each other. Some screeched even louder at his arrival, while others whimpered and slunk to escape his view.

"Enough!" he shouted, "Utha! Come!" He peered around, looking for the Goblin King.

In every goblin clan, the Ba'ath appoint one to be the king. Partially in mockery of the human practice, but also as a matter of practicality in delegating orders. The king has privileges and authority of course, but he is also held responsible for the clan's failures, and clearly, a little discipline was needed here.

A goblin stumbled out of the darkness of the cavern and into the grotto. He wore a beaded necklace and a silver hoop in one ear. Rings of various qualities were on every finger of his hands. Utha had ruled this clan for close to forty years, but had been Turned many years before that. His skin was a dark, sooty green, with warty, fleshy bumps all over, and he kept a menacing snarl on his face to show his ferociousness. Not now though; he shuffled towards Bael, eyes downcast and hands trembling.

"My Lord," he croaked, "it was Lucius, he attacked us here within our chambers. He brought fire, and he had another with him, the boy Jack."

"Fool!" Bael spat, and struck the goblin a hard blow across the face, sending him rolling across the floor. Utha sprawled in the dirt, stunned, but Bael walked over and kicked him in the ribs, "Why was he here Utha? Who is this boy?"

Utha grunted, and raised himself to his knees. "He came in by stealth, Lord! Crept in here like a thief, he did. We were working on the chamber, but he laid upon us with fire and iron. As for his purpose, the boy's sister was taken a few days ago, and they meant to steal her back away from us."

Bael grabbed a handful of Utha's greasy hair. "And were they successful?" he asked, shaking Utha like a rag doll.

"Y-yes Lord... but we still have them! They are just outside, they claimed sanctuary!" Utha answered, his dead fish eyes rolling in their sockets. Bael enjoyed his fear, and wanted to ensure those watching saw it as well. "And how many others did you lose?" he growled.

"I think only two Lord," Utha said, a thin smile creasing his face. If he thought this news would be pleasing to Bael, he was mistaken.

"Two!" Bael flung Utha to one side, bouncing him off the chamber wall to sprawl in the dirt again. "You have failed me Utha. Lucius should have already been dead, and now he has robbed me of three goblins in one night! This chamber was not to be violated!" He held out one hand and a small ball of blue flame roiled there, crackling with energy.

"No, Lord! Please! I will kill Lucius and get the girl back!" but Bael flung the ball, and it streaked across to thump into Utha's chest. The eldritch flames quickly enveloped him as he shrieked and rolled on the ground, heels and hands beating and clawing at the earth.

Bael summoned the Wight. It would take the Wight a few moments to arrive, so until then he would watch his victim and enjoy his suffering. The whooshing sound of the flames mixed with Utha's grunts and agonized howls. The other goblins in the chamber had drawn back from Utha as far as possible, some of them whimpering in fear, others snickering and pointing.

Some minutes passed. Utha was reduced to squirming in one spot on the ground, making pitiful mewling noises. The Wight entered the chamber at a run, slowing to a walk then stopping before Bael. He didn't even glance down at the Goblin King writhing in flames and misery.

The animus had lost the power of speech long ago, so it simply stood staring at Bael, black smoke smoldering from its head and shoulders. Humans called them wights, liches, or ghouls, but by whatever name, it was the reanimated corpse of a human, imbued with dark magic and evil purpose. It did not breathe, eat or sleep. It had enormous strength, and it simply did what it was told, which made it such a useful tool. It was the wight Bael had given the power to cast the turning spell, and when the goblins stole a child, the monster was there to do its evil. This one had been dead a long time, and despite the preserving effect of magic, flesh sloughed off parts of the skeletal frame. The lips were dessicated and drawn back from the teeth, showing a perpetual and frightening grin. Clumps of frizzy moldering hair still clung to the scalp, and its' entire face was purplish-green, marbled with blue veins of corruption.

With a wave of his hand, Bael snuffed the flames wreathing Utha. The magical blue flames burned hot, and the pain was horrific, but it caused no damage. Bael needed every goblin he could get. The last echoes of Utha's screams faded as he lay panting and crying on the floor, but he quickly got to his knees when he realized the Ba'ath addressed him.

"You say Lucius and this boy are in sanctuary outside?"

"Y-yes Lord, and Lucius was badly wounded by my warriors!" boasted Utha, but Bael knew the Goblin King would say anything to save his own skin at this point.

"I've had enough of that man's interference. You," he

said, motioning to a goblin standing meekly back against the wall, "take the wight to Lucius' cabin. Wait for him to return." He commanded the wight, "When Lucius returns, turn him if you can, kill him if you must. Turn the boy as well." The ghoul's pale blue eyes flared before it turned and left the chamber.

Bael would leave Utha as king, for now. The torture would serve as a warning, and the humiliation would certainly result in brutal reprimands for his subjects. There would be no further breaches in security.

"You will not survive another failure Utha, do you understand?"

The Goblin King nodded his head quickly, "Yes, Lord!"

"Finish the preparations for this chamber, and ensure there are no more intrusions." Bael vanished in a puff of black smoke.

Utha's, "Yes, Lord..." fell into a silent chamber, and the snarl returned to his face as he looked around for his own victim.

Clinging to the ceiling unseen amongst the stalactites, enchanted camouflage aiding its escape, the Watcher crept out of the chamber.

37

MALICE

Bᴀᴇʟ ʀᴇᴀᴘᴘᴇᴀʀᴇᴅ ɪɴ ᴛʜᴇ ʙʟᴀᴄᴋ of the night, a puff of dark smoke amongst the trees. He sensed the scattered goblins in the area, and knew exactly where Lucius would be. He wanted to see this boy for himself.

He walked like death itself, gliding and silent. He saw the pine tree ahead, and saw the forms lying on the ground beneath its boughs. Of course, the darkness was no impediment to his sight, and he could clearly see Lucius had passed over. Perhaps he would find him there. He also saw the goblin Lucius had stolen from him, as well as this "Jack" boy. The stupid little monkey sat terrified, eyes searching the night, the barrel of his rifle stuck out like a pike.

Bael hated Lucius. Hated him more than any other human he had ever known. He had escaped from being Turned all those years ago and Bael had yet to set that score right, but then, he had never really made it a priority. It was beneath him to chase after this fly, and so, the wight would finish him once and for all. Perhaps this boy would be enough to distract Lucius, and give the wight the best time and opportunity to strike.

As for the boy, he cared not at all. There appeared to be nothing special about him; he was a little old for Turning, but whatever happened, he would be killed in the end. No, he thought to himself, I will leave Lucius alone tonight. No need to get his guard up and spoil the wight's hunting. That thought caused him to smile, and he puffed out of sight.

As the Ba'ath vanished, his goblin ran down the track, leading the way for the wight. The two creatures hurried through the forest on their master's bidding. Lucius' cabin was well-known to all the goblins. They haunted him relentlessly, just as he hunted them. They threw rocks through his widows, taunted him at odd hours of the night. All the same, they were terrified of him. He was old and wise to their tricks. He had hunted and captured many goblins, and was a vicious fighter when cornered. They had never been able to catch him unaware.

Usually Lucius protected his cabin with the hated steel or irons chains, draping the thresholds with them, making it too dangerous for a goblin to attempt to enter.

The wight, however, did not share this weakness. While it did not like the bite of metal, it was no barrier for the monster.

Presently the cabin came into view, and the goblin tentatively approached the door. Lucius was known for his cunning tricks too, and more than one goblin had ended up snared.

"There," the goblin croaked, pointing to the door, "inside. Wait for Lucius inside. Kill him!" it cackled, taking pleasure in repeating the Master's order, as if the wight acted at his command.

The wight's serpent gaze slid from the goblin to the cabin. Ignoring the little goblin's gabbling, it walked purposefully up the steps and pushed the door open, then disappeared into the shadows.

38

CHAOS IN COBBS

MR. FRENCH HAD BEEN very generous in the pay he offered to Mr. Rutherford's armed deputies. That's what they were calling themselves anyway, and they all wore black armbands and pistols.

Hank had lived in Cobbs all his life, but he had no qualms about offering his gun to Mr. French. Many of the people in Cobbs considered him a pathetic drunk anyway, and besides, he had his own motivation to find the Rutherford girl. His son had disappeared over ten years ago, and it almost destroyed him. The sorrow and despair had driven him to drink. He was useless to everyone around him for awhile, including his wife, who was just as distraught as he. She needed him then, but he just couldn't be there for her, so she left. After that, what was there to do but drink?

Here though, was a chance for Hank to gain back a little bit of what he had lost. If he could help find the girl, it would be just a little like finding his son, and he could spare the Rutherford's the pain he still endured. That would be something he could feel good about, and he hadn't felt good about anything in a very long time.

Hank had been on his horse since before supper. He and his assigned partner, a miner from Tennessee named Paul Hattaway, were supposed to be making rounds, watching for people traveling at night, and anyone trying to sneak out of the boundaries set by Mr. Rutherford.

Hattaway had wanted to stop and get his dinner from his wife at the miner's camp, inviting Hank to join them, but he declined, saying he was going to stop in and see a friend for his meal. He told Hattaway he would be back for him in a little while, and headed his horse upstream.

It was late for a house call, but Lucius seemed to always be awake, and Hank didn't think he would mind a visitor. He cantered his horse down the track leading into the forest. Lucius was really the only one who used it with regularity, so it wasn't a very wide track, and the bushes and trees grew close on either side. The moon had risen, casting enough pale light over the landscape for him to see, but even so, Hank felt a little uneasy riding through the menace of the trees.

It was only a short ride before Lucius' cabin came into view. The clearing around the place allowed a wide apron of moonlight, reassuring him as the shadows retreated. There were no lights inside however, and as he reined up he could see the front door standing open.

That was queer, because Hank knew Lucius took care to always leave his place closed. He had this strange habit of stringing chains everywhere, which Hank supposed was some superstitious mumbo-jumbo. *So why*, he wondered, *is his door standing open?*

Ah hell, he thought, *I bet a raccoon pushed it open and is going through his larder right now.* He smiled to himself and dismounted. He didn't bother hitching his horse. It wasn't going to wander off at night, and he walked up the steps and into the cabin, calling for Lucius.

It wasn't as dark inside as he thought it would be, because besides the door, moonlight also slanted in between the shutters. There was just enough light to make out the objects in the room, and he started when he saw a figure standing in the back corner of the cabin.

"Whoa! You scared the bejeezus out of me! Sorry to come out so late..." he paused as the figure took a step toward him. A heartbeat of doubt; "Lucius?" he said, his hand drifting toward his pistol. The man took another step and Hank drew on him. He held his other hand out, signaling the man to halt. He was on the verge of warning the man he was going to shoot when he noted the eyes. Two pale blue points, barely noticeable, seemed to float in the dark silhouette of the man's head.

Hank fired, snapping off two quick shots from the hip, but he must have missed, because the figure hissed and hurled itself at him. Hank yelled as he fired off one more round before the thing reached for him. A cold, heavy hand struck his arm aside, while another slapped him with a stunning blow across the face. Even as he fell to the floor, Hank registered the fiery traces of nails across his skin.

Although it was a crushing blow, Hank was a strong, wiry man, toughened by years of hardship and work. He had somehow retained his pistol, and as he landed on his back he brought it around to face his attacker. The thing fell upon him at once, but he kicked his left foot upwards, hard, and felt it bury itself in the figure's gut. It was a satisfying blow, but the weird berserker hardly seemed to notice, a mere pause in its attack. It reached out for him, like a jilted lover pleading for one more embrace. Hank fired again, and this time he knew he had struck true, right through the chest. Incredibly, the thing barely flinched, and with a wild swing smacked Hank's legs out of its way. It dropped onto him and with horrible strength began to pummel him about the head and shoulders. Hank tried to defend himself, holding his hands up on either side of his head, but it was too strong, and he knew he was going to die if he couldn't get away.

With all the strength he had left, Hank brought his knee up hard into his assailant's back, knocking it forward and over him. He rolled toward the door and onto his feet, his head swimming as he tried to focus his eyes on the maniac. He knew he only had two shots left, and he had to make them count. The thing stood back up and stepped toward him again. Hank yelled at it and drew his knife with his left hand. He circled around the room, putting the table between them as he tried to make out the face behind those eyes.

The silhouette grabbed the edge of the table and with seemingly little effort flung it across the bed to splinter against the wall. Hank fired directly at the eyes this time and saw the head snap back, but then it rushed at him again. He had no time for thought, firing his last shot point-blank into the creature's breast, and then he was fighting for his life.

He twisted every way he could, trying to avoid the vicious slashes and heavy hands as they began beating the life out of him. He flailed at the creature with his knife, a long deadly blade which had served him well in the war. He slashed and stabbed, trying to puncture the heart, sever tendons, cut arteries. The only reaction he could sense was when he stabbed into the creature; then it would hiss and grab his wrist in a crushing vise and wrench the knife out.

The thing cracked his jaw, and Hank felt himself sliding toward unconsciousness. A fist like a sledgehammer thumped into his ribs before it picked him off the ground and slung him across the room. He crashed into the larder, but this put him close to the door and Hank scurried on hands and knees out onto the porch. He tried to stand to make a run for it; his horse stood in the moonlight, nervously stepping away from the violence. His legs were just too wobbly though, and he fell back to his knees. He had missed his chance, and the creature grabbed him from behind. He made a vicious stab backwards, feeling the knife plunge in and scrape against bone before it was knocked away, glinting as it spun out into the moonlit yard. A mighty blow thundered against his head, nearly breaking his neck, and he tumbled down into the grass like a dead thing.

As he flopped onto his back, blackness crowded around the edges of his vision, and he dumbly gazed at the moon. He gasped as his hair was gripped with a brutal strength that threatened to scalp him, but he couldn't even raise a hand in defense.

The thing squatted over him and he was pulled by the hair into a sitting position as if he were a child. He stared into the wight's face for the first time, and screamed in terror at the corrupt, grave-dead creature that held him. But the scream was choked off as soon as it began, as the ghoul darted a long, thick black tongue out, forcing it down his throat.

The horse's hoofbeats faded away as Hank choked and gurgled in the wight's embrace.

39

AIDING A FRIEND

JACK HADN'T REALIZED he had dozed off until he was awakened by Lucius' voice, "Hey boy, here, why don't you lay down for awhile?"

Jack's eyes popped open to see Lucius standing next to him. The sky had just started to lighten with the coming dawn, so Jack could see him clearly. His wounds appeared to be completely healed; not even a scar remained to indicate the skin had ever been broken. The perfection of his flesh made him look years younger, and he smiled at the look on Jack's face.

"Yeah, I know, it's a mystery to me too, but now you understand how I've lived so long." He pushed Jack back to lie down, "And now you need rest a lot more than I do. I'll keep watch, and you sleep awhile longer."

Jack nodded, and laid his rifle down alongside him as he fell back amongst the pine needles. As he drifted off again, he flung his arm unconsciously over Abigail's goblin form, protective of his prize.

It seemed mere minutes later he was nudged awake by

Lucius. "Wake up boy, we got to get moving."

Jack winced as he slowly sat up. The sun had fully risen, but it was still early in the day, not more than nine o'clock he judged. His injuries from the previous night stung and burned in earnest now, and he envied Lucius' special ability to heal.

The goblin that was Abigail still lay where it had the night before, not a twitch or breath to indicate she was even alive. How strange to him to think all he had to do was take the chain off and she would spring to life as a rabid, snarling monster.

Jack climbed to his feet and brushed the needles from his clothes, while Lucius collected their gear. He handed Jack his rifle, and leaned over to hoist Abigail onto his back. She hung over his shoulder again, and to Jack it seemed her own weight must be choking her, but Lucius reassured him, "Don't worry, this doesn't hurt her."

They started back down the track towards Lucius' cabin. It was a nice temperate morning, but Jack's scalp stung, and the bite to his forearm was hot to the touch, so he wasn't feeling his best as they walked along. Abigail's feet swung back and forth as she hung off Lucius' back, but otherwise she made no sound. Lucius stepped it out, and after a quick thirty-minute trek, the clearing came into view.

Even from a distance Jack could tell something was odd, and Lucius said, "Well, looks like they've been at the cabin. Can't tell you how many times I've had to replace shutters and such. Seems they got the front door open this time though."

The dark rectangle of the doorway grew larger with every step, and by the time they entered the clearing proper, Jack could see the tangle of furniture and splinters inside.

Lucius stopped in front of him and slid Abigail off his back to lie on the ground. Jack moved to one side as Lucius stooped down to pick something up; it was a deadly-looking knife, with a deer-antler handle and a six-inch single edge blade.

"This is Hank's," he said, looking toward the cabin. Lucius left Abigail lying and walked up the steps and inside, with Jack behind. They spread out to either side of the doorway, staring at the mess they found. The once-solid table was broken into several pieces, and the larder was cracked and spilled open. Occasional drops of blood were sprinkled here and there.

"Lucius," Jack said, pointing at a pistol lying next to the overturned stool.

Lucius walked over and picked up the pistol, swinging the cylinder open and dumping the empty casings into his hand. All six had been fired.

"Hell, this ain't good," Lucius said, shaking his head. "Looks like a full-blown scrape, and he got hurt. We need to go check on him. Here, let's get her inside…"

They brought Abigail into the cabin, where Lucius took a few minutes to swath her in a mess of chains, then covered her with a blanket and pushed her under the bed. They picked up the splinters of broken furniture and tossed them under the bed as well before walking out of the cabin, pulling the door closed behind them.

It was almost two miles to Hank's house, and by the time they got near it was almost mid-day. Heavy grey clouds had started scudding across the sky though, and the pall made it seem later.

As they walked, Lucius told Jack Hank's family had lived in Cobbs for a very long time and their house was one of the first homesteads built in this area. They had built the house back on the property a bit, surrounded by acres of land on all sides. Hank was the only one left in his family though, and it was apparently beyond his ability to maintain the home in good repair. The house had once been painted white, but the layers had long-since cracked and now brittle chips curled away, exposing the gray, weathered wood. Waist-high grass and vegetation grew haphazardly, making the place look forlorn and abandoned.

They walked up the rough lane toward the residence.

"Lucius..." Jack said, pointing toward the house. Again, the front door stood wide open, the dark interior threatening and silent.

"I see it," Lucius answered, "that don't mean nothing, he may not even be here." He led the way quietly up the porch steps, pausing when a board creaked underfoot. They strained their ears listening, but no sounds came from the old house. Together they eased through the doorway. Except for a few furnishings, the front room was empty. There was an odd smell though, and the air seemed hazy.

"We got trouble boy," Lucius whispered, letting out his chain. He moved toward the doorway leading further into the house and the lazy drifts of vapor hanging there. He pointed to an oil lamp on a table between a pair of chairs, "Light that lamp, quick now!"

Jack hurried over to the table and pulled open the drawer where he found a handful of matches. He struck one and lit the lamp wick, all the while nervously glancing at the opening.

"Now, stay close to me," Lucius said, moving toward the door. Jack followed, trying to hold the lamp high enough for the light to reach ahead of them. Passing through the doorway he found himself squinting to see through the cloudy haze.

"Oh hell," he heard Lucius whisper, and Jack stepped to the side to see a thick figure sitting in a rocking chair. The man appeared to be smoldering, smoke wisping off his head and shoulders. The face was criss-crossed with thin blue and green veins, while thorny projections jutted off the scalp and neck. Fleshy nodules stood out in odd places, and the fingers of the hands seemed impossibly long. The eyes were closed, but a painful grimace twisted the face.

"Hank. Hank, can you hear me?" Lucius said. Horror-stricken, Jack could only stare open-mouthed as Hank's eyes snapped open. Except for the tiny pinprick of the pupil, they were entirely red, as if every blood vessel had burst. His nostril's flared and his mouth opened to make a loud, high-pitched whine. It was a maniacal screech that made the hair on the back of Jack's neck stand up.

"I'm going to try to bind him," Lucius whispered toward Jack. He took another step, letting the chain hang from his goblin hand, "Hank! Listen, we can help you!" Hank's noise subsided to a gasp, and he stared at Lucius with malevolent hatred. The long fingers curled and flexed, creaking like a rope being pulled tight.

"Easy now, remember me? We're friends Hank..." he eased another step closer while Jack's heart thumped fast and hard. Suddenly, quicker than a snake, Lucius whipped the chain out in a sidearm motion with his goblin arm. It gave him enough reach that the chain struck the left side of Hank's neck and wrapped around. Lucius was already moving, reaching in with his other hand to secure the chain around Hank's neck, but the long fingers shot up and closed around Lucius' wrist. At the same time Hank let out a furious bellow and twisted up and out of the chair, dragging Lucius with him. Hank rushed toward the wall, slamming Lucius into it and pushing against him. His other hand scrabbled at the chain encircling his neck, but Lucius held on tight, his hands gripping both ends of the chain. Hank let out another screech as he and Lucius thrashed around the room, splintering the rocking chair in the process. Jack could only hop around, looking for an opportunity to help. He set the oil lamp down and held his rifle at the ready in case he got an opportunity to shoot, although he wasn't even sure he could shoot Hank if it came to that.

In his transformed state, Hank was obviously much stronger than Lucius, throwing him around with ease, but Lucius countered Hank's advantage by staying in close. He had closed the chain loop around Hank's neck, and held on, even as Hank smashed him against the walls and furniture. The iron didn't incapacitate Hank in the same way as the goblins, but it was clearly having an effect. He kept clawing at the chain, but the longer the fight went on, the more feeble his efforts, until he finally sank to the floor. Hank fell sideways and rolled onto his back, moaning and pawing at his neck. Lucius was also winded, but he pulled himself on top of Hank and cinched the chain down tighter, until Jack thought he must be trying to choke him to death.

"Hank! Stop fighting me and listen!" Hank stopped fidgeting for a moment and became still, as if listening to something far away.

"L-Lu..ci..us?" he croaked, long-fingered hands relaxing and falling to his sides. His eyes seemed to focus on Lucius.

"What happened to you? Who did this?" Lucius leaned down to stare closely into Hank's eyes. Hank returned the stare, his mouth working as he tried to form words.

"D-Dead... cold...," he choked, clearly struggling to keep control. One hand flopped onto his chest, scratching at the chain, "P-Please... burns..."

"I know Hank, but you need to keep it on so I can help you."

"No, you... can't. Kill me, Kill me," he panted, eyes rolling around in a panic. His feet began kicking, heels drumming on the floor.

"Hank, stop it, look at me!" Lucius yelled. But the sentience in Hank's eyes had passed, and his face was twisted in agony, terrible to see. Lucius stood up and backed away from him, watching as he thrashed and writhed on the floor.

"Give me the lamp boy," he said, holding his hand out to Jack but still staring at the creature that had been Hank. Jack handed Lucius the lamp. "Go outside, now. I'll be right out." Jack stared at him for a moment, incredulous understanding dawning in his brain. With one last look at Hank he turned and hurried out of the house. He quickly trotted out into the yard, looking back toward the doorway. The sound of Lucius' voice drifted out to him, but he couldn't hear the words. Then the sound of breaking glass and the frenzied screeching began, louder and far more frantic than before. Jack put his hands over his ears and watched as smoke began drifting out of the doorway. After a few moments, the screeching stopped. Then Lucius walked out and down the porch steps.

Without a word he started back down the lane. Jack turned to hurry behind him, looking back one last time to see orange lights flickering in the windows and smoke escaping the house.

They walked on for a few minutes without talking, but finally Jack couldn't stand it any longer and asked, "What did they do to him?"

"They turned him. That's what happens when they don't use children. In the old folk's tales they were called trolls."

"Why didn't your chain put him to sleep?" Jack asked.

"I don't know, that was the first one I've ever seen, but Blixt told me they were uncontrollable, crazy."

"But he talked to you, he recognized you."

"He must have been turned only a short while before we got there. Otherwise, I don't believe he would have known me."

40

CONSPIRACY

SINCE THOMAS ORDERED Mr. French to gather his men and lock down the area, several of the locals had protested vehemently to him of the blockade of the town. He did his best to assure them the men were only trying to help find his daughter, and did not intend to frighten or inconvenience anyone. Of course, in reality, he didn't care if they dragged every single person out of their homes kicking and screaming if that was what had to be done. Truth be told, his confidence had begun to crumble, and panic gnawed at his insides. His ransom theory had sounded completely reasonable, except there had been no attempt by kidnappers to contact him. Now he was truly worried.

He had returned home a few times to eat or take a quick nap, and each time Elizabeth had thrown a series of questions at him. He gave her his most confident, knowing look, arching one eyebrow and tapping his temple as if he knew the secret to the whole affair, and he would reassure her, "Don't worry Dear, I have it all quite well in hand..." How foolish and impotent he felt now, and he had resolved not to return to the house until he must, when hope of Abigail's return was either realized, or dashed once and for all.

Sitting in the office, head in his hands, his thoughts were disturbed by a tapping on the window. He leaned around the doorway to see who was there, and was surprised to see Emma James. She wore a worried, pained look, as if she might break into tears at any moment and his heart skipped a beat. Was she bringing some terrible news?

He stood and walked quickly to the door, pulling it open, "Yes, Mrs. James?"

She looked up the street toward the saloon, then back at Thomas before pushing into the office.

"Mr. Rutherford, we need to talk." She wrung her hands, her nervousness and anxiety apparent.

"Indeed, but I can tell you the only subject I'm of a mind to discuss at the moment is the whereabouts of my daughter."

"Of course," she said, "that is why I have come, to help in any way I can. You need to know what you are up against."

"So, you know what I'm up against, do you?" His expression darkened and he firmly shut the door. Perhaps he was about to hear the ransom demand he had been expecting all along.

"I do. You see, Cobbs has a long history of losing children," she looked him directly in the eyes, "including

270

mine."

That was unexpected, and his head swam as he motioned for her to sit down, "Alright then Mrs. James, how can you help me?"

"Your daughter was taken, Mr. Rutherford."

"I guessed as much, and am prepared to do whatever is necessary to secure her safe return as soon as I hear the kidnapper's demands."

"No, no, you don't understand. There will be no ransom."

A chill ran down his spine, and Thomas sat very still, "What do you mean?"

"Whoever took your Abigail is not interested in your money, sir."

He blinked. "Well then, what do they want, the mine? They can have it."

"Children are a precious thing in this town Mr. Rutherford. More precious than diamonds or gold, or anything else you can dig out of the ground. My own daughter, Julianna, was taken four years ago. Almost every family in Cobbs has been afflicted by the loss of a child, some families several times."

Alarmed now, Thomas still wasn't sure if this woman was a threat to Abigail or not. "Who is responsible for these kidnappings?"

Her shoulders sagged, and she sighed, "I don't know. Children have been disappearing for years and it's always blamed on some animal; wolves, mountain lions, or some other nonsense. We've tried to take precautions, but every year a few children vanish in the middle of the night. Some years it is only one, while in the worst of times, as many as nine young ones were taken."

She looked down at her hands, "We were desperate to save them. We thought if we could placate whatever wanted our children, perhaps more of them would survive. We tried leaving our animals out, offerings of every sort left on the front step, prayers at the church went on almost daily. All of it ignored. The children continued to vanish, no violence apparent, only an open window shutter, or the front door standing open. Eventually we came to the conclusion there was only one way to treat with the menace."

"What are you talking about? Will you just tell me plainly what is going on?"

"A lottery, Mr. Rutherford," she said, "a lottery to see whose child would be offered as a sacrifice."

Thomas could only sit stunned as she continued, "We drew a name each year at harvest time, to see which child would be offered, so that others may live. Julianna was the last child offered through the lottery." Tears swam in her eyes, and she sobbed a little as she continued, "The lottery was stopped because more children started disappearing again. Apparently one child per year would not suffice."

"The Fox Hunt," he said, realization dawning. "My daughter's name was picked as a sacrifice?"

Emma nodded her head, "Except I believe she was selected, there was no lottery."

Thomas stared at her incredulously for a heartbeat before the anger welled up in him. "Bastards!" he shouted, slamming his hand down on the table between them. He grabbed her by the arm, hauled them both to their feet and shouted, "Enough of this! Where is my daughter and who has taken her!?"

"I don't know! I didn't know they were planning this, I swear! There must have been some who knew, but I am not one of them. After she was taken though, I knew what had happened."

She stared directly into his eyes, and Thomas knew she told the truth. "You're hurting me," she whispered. He released her, and took a step back.

"I cannot give you any hope of recovering your daughter. None of our children have ever been returned, but you still have your son to consider. I am begging you to gather your family and leave Cobbs, tonight if possible."

Thomas shook his head, "If that is the only help you can give me, then I'm afraid you have wasted your time. I will not leave this place without my daughter."

She wrung her hands again and nodded, "I thought as much, but I wanted to warn you. God be with you Mr. Rutherford." Thomas opened the door for her as she walked out and down the boardwalk.

41

PROTECTION

JACK WATCHED AS LUCIUS knocked away the splinters of broken furniture that had hidden Abigail from casual view under the bed. He still breathed hard from practically running after Lucius on the return from Hank's house. They had traveled overland quickly, although Lucius never explained his urgency to Jack. He thought again about trying to find Eli, but what could he tell him to make him believe? Of course, once he saw Abigail, he would have little choice but to believe. Lucius didn't want to detour to find Eli though, so they just rushed back to his cabin.

Lucius grabbed a few strands of chain and dragged Abigail's limp form out.

"What are you doing?" Jack asked.

"I don't know what is going on here boy, but if they are willing to do things like what they did to Hank, then we're in trouble." He looked down at Abigail, "We're not going to have time to take her to the pool to hide her," Lucius said. "If we don't want to lose her again, we need some help. We need Blixt."

Jack nodded numbly, watching as Lucius unwrapped the blanket from around Abigail's goblin form, and unwound all but one strand of chain around her neck.

Lucius stood and walked over to the box that served as his larder. The wooden slats were broken and flour seeped through the cracks, but he paid no mind to that as he slid it along the wall and out of his way. He reached down to tug at a nail protruding from a board in the floor, and to Jack's surprise, the entire slat lifted right out of the floor.

He couldn't help but try to peer over Lucius' shoulder as he reached down into the dark space. He drew out a small dusty wooden box, perhaps a foot long. There was nothing remarkable about the box; it didn't even have a lock on it. Just a small clasp which Lucius thumbed open, before raising the lid. Clattering around inside were two exquisitely beautiful items.

The first was a stone, about as big as Jack's thumb. It was multicolored and polished to a smooth, brilliant finish. The closest thing to it Jack had ever seen was an opal, except this stone seemed primarily champagne and blue, instead of pink and green. Lucius left that in the box however, and took out the other item.

It was a small golden flute, only about four inches long, but it seemed very heavily made, with rolled edges and a fine, supremely detailed filigree rolling all over the surface. It was clearly a priceless artifact, and Jack wondered that Lucius, in his poor cabin, possessed such a treasure at all.

Setting the box on the stove top, Lucius held the flute up for Jack to see. "Blixt gave this to me a long time ago and told me he would hear if I blew it. I've never used it though, so I don't know what will happen. Maybe you should stand back out of the way."

Jack scuttled to the corner and took cover behind the stove, as if the flute were a stick of dynamite.

With a glance at Jack, Lucius drew a breath and put the flute to his lips. As he blew, the flute released a trill, but in a pitch and tone unlike any either of them had ever heard. It was as if several flutes of different qualities were being sounded at the same time, but in perfect harmony, and even though the pitch was high, there was a rumble to the note as well. Jack's vision seemed to vibrate for a moment, and a thin fall of dust drifted down from the rafters before complete silence fell.

The darkening clouds outside made the interior of the cabin gloomy and shadow-filled. The silence stretched on for several moments when suddenly, the air inside the cabin popped with a silent explosion of air, and there stood Blixt, black vapor wafting off his shoulders.

An alert look was on his face and his hand was on the hilt of his sword, as he took in the scene before him.

"Lucius," he nodded, "this is unexpected. I had begun to think you had discarded my gift. After all, it's been more than a century..."

That incredible statement flew past Jack as Lucius replied, "I don't know what is going on out there, but we need your help."

Blixt smiled, "At last. Come with me then, and leave the things of this world behind for a bit."

Lucius shook his head, "You know that's not what I meant. We found his sister," Lucius said, pointing down at the goblin lying on the floor, "and we need to hide her. Will you do this for me?"

With a frown, Blixt walked around the goblin. "Why should I? You rebuff every attempt I make at friendship. I have offered to help you so many times in the past, and yet, you still mistrust me."

"If I didn't trust you I wouldn't have called you," Lucius said in a quiet voice, "but sometimes we don't see things the same way." He turned toward Jack, "See, I told you it wouldn't do any good, he isn't going to help us."

"Of course I will help," Blixt said, "but I am limited in what I can do at this time."

Jack saw Lucius wink before turning back to face Blixt.

"I wanted to thank you for the book. Now I know what I'm looking for." Lucius told Blixt about the circumstances of Hank's death, but Blixt simply listened without comment. "I'm going to destroy that damned monster, but I can't hunt it and guard her at the same time. I don't have time to hide her, but I know you can," motioning again toward Abigail's lifeless form.

"Very well Lucius. As a token of my great affection for you, I will do this thing." Blixt extended his palm toward Abigail and said, *"Gelga sin, ba fernum..."*

As he finished the incantation, Abigail started to shrink,

her body collapsing and shriveling like a hot air balloon.

"What are you doing to her?" Jack yelled.

Blixt ignored him, telling Lucius, "But once again, you are in my debt." Smiling, he turned back to Jack, making a strange motion with his hand before winking in an overt, obvious imitation of Lucius and vanishing in a smoky implosion.

It was astonishing to watch, but within the space of a few heartbeats, Abigail's goblin form had shrunken to an object Jack could easily hold in his hand. The chain had been left behind however, and Lucius bent down to pick the item up; it was a walnut. He held it out to Jack and dropped it in his outstretched hand.

Jack handled the walnut as if it were an egg, and much to his surprise, felt it lurch in his hand. There was definitely movement inside the shell. Holding it between his finger and thumb, he held it to his ear, and his eyes went wide as he heard the tiny sounds of a beast enraged. Apparently Abigail was awake, and furious at being locked inside this prison.

"Don't worry Abby, we are going to turn you back, just be patient," he said, whispering to the walnut. The only response was a renewed burst of anger from the creature inside.

"Well," said Lucius smiling, "I can think of a thousand places to hide a walnut, but this one will do." He opened the wooden box and motioned for Jack to put the walnut inside. He did so, nestling it in a corner. Lucius took out the gemstone, replaced the flute and closed the lid.

"You know where this box is boy, so if anything happens to me, you come get it and call Blixt, ok?" Jack nodded his head. Lucius stuck the gemstone down deep into his pocket, then stashed the box in its space under the floor and replaced the plank. As he slid the larder back into place over the plank, Lucius pulled the lid off and fished out a handful of salted pork and some hardtack.

"Here, you need to get something inside you," he said, handing most of it to Jack. Lucius crammed a chaw of meat into his mouth, chewing as he continued.

"Now, our problem is, we have to find the thing that attacked Hank. I believe this devil turned your sister, and many others besides." He shook his head, "I don't know though, I've been all over this area, and I can't think of one place to start looking."

"Perhaps it's back in the goblin cave?" Jack suggested, biting off a piece of the thick, crunchy hardtack, and a strip of the salt pork. With everything going on, he wasn't very hungry at the moment and stuffed the rest of it into his pocket.

"Maybe, but this thing has been taking children for years, and the work in that cave seemed recent to me."

"Where else could we look, the mines?"

"No, no, too many people coming and going. When I was inside that cavern, it had been widened out pretty good. I think the trouble at the mines was meant to run us out of there because our digging was getting too close to theirs." Lucius sat on top of the larder, "It could be anywhere else though."

"Could it hide in Lumis? The book said goblins could vanish or turn to stone, maybe the wight can too."

"Maybe, but I don't think so. I don't believe it would survive there long at all, but it's been here for many years. No, it hides around here somewhere. It could lay at the bottom of a pool, or any other hole it finds."

Jack thought again about the book, ...*transfigured from a rotting, stinking corpse*... "If it's dead, maybe a cemetery?"

"The only cemetery around here is the one in town, and folks would have noticed if a grave was dug up every once in awhile."

"That's true..." he thought, recalling there were no mausoleums in the cemetery either. "In that case, where else could it hide? Perhaps a tomb?"

"There ain't no tombs around here I know of," Lucius said, furrowing his brow, "the closest thing might be a cave, but I've been all over this mountain in the last thirty years, and I don't recall ever finding such a place."

That's when it occurred to Jack, he knew of such a place. "Lucius, I think I know where it is..."

42

PREPARATIONS

THE CHAMBER WAS CROWDED with goblins, each of them working slavishly to complete their master's final preparations. To stop for even a moment would have invited horrible punishment, which had already been demonstrated on Utha. Their master watched.

Bael sat cross-legged on the island in the center of the grotto. From his position he ordered the work, directing goblins to clear away rubble and re-align the rune stones. Utha ran about with a knotted rope, striking and cursing at his subjects in a frenzy of energy to please Bael.

By the terms of the Compact, the solstice had marked the transfer of power, with Bael's faction assuming leadership. Although Micah was bound to obey the articles, his presence in the area today was a bad omen. Bael was not willing to risk hundreds of years of study and planning to be denied now, and a sense of urgency drove him to push the goblins to finish their work. The last several years had been the worst, having to keep his experiments secret, even from his fellow Ba'ath. The slightest whisper of his activities could have destroyed his opportunity.

Even at this point, Bael's accomplices could not guess, would not even dare to consider, the true intent of his plan, most especially Samael. It had taken him centuries to gain their loyalty and confidence, and if he had tried to explain his ultimate goal in the beginning, they would have deserted him immediately. He must demonstrate his newfound power, show them he could achieve his goals; nothing guaranteed loyalty like success.

It appeared everything was in order, and the others would be here soon to witness his power.

"Utha! Enough, get them into their places."

"Yes Lord!" The goblin king laid into his minions with renewed zeal, lashing the goblins into their places. The precision of their placement for these incantations was vital, and Bael himself had directed the excavation of shallow holes for the goblins to stand in, so there would be no chance of them disrupting the spell by stepping out of place. As they took their places, the lines of power became clear, the formation taking on the appearance of a spider web, radiating out from the island pool.

As the last goblin fell into line, Bael's confederates began to arrive. Dark smoke wafted through the chamber as one by one, they popped into existence. Pahn, Urba and Fale, followed by Azel and lastly, Grim. Samael was conspicuously absent, but that was no matter, in fact, Bael had counted on it; he would be the subject of this demonstration.

"Friends," he smiled, "welcome. Please, take your places." Seven daises were positioned around the outside of the spider-web design, and the newcomers found their respective platforms. The only open positions were his and Samael's.

Bael reached over and picked up the small golden bowl before smoothly standing, and walking down to the water's edge. He scooped a small amount of water into the bowl and turned to the newly-grown tree. He sat the bowl on the ground in front of the tree, waded across the knee-deep pool and stepped onto his dais. As he turned to face the island, Bael could sense the consternation in the others, wondering what Samael's absence portended. He smiled inwardly, *I will answer that question right now...*

Without preamble, before anyone could lose their nerve, Bael raised his hand and cast the spell, "*Il nath tor da braukin fer!*" Four dozen goblins instantly lurched into raspy voice, repeating the refrain. Blue arcs of energy and power sparked intermittently through the formation.

The golden bowl seemed to illuminate slightly, and a light steam began to rise from it. The goblin's song grew in volume, while the mist grew thicker and thicker, becoming darker by the second, until there was a small, roiling black cloud obscuring the island.

A leather boot stepped out of the cloud, and Bael watched as Samael took another step forward and the cloud dissipated. He didn't even need to look around to see the surprise in his fellow's faces. They had no idea he had gained the power to summon them at will. Anger pulsed in Samael's eyes and both hands were at the ready to cast his own spell. Here was the test. Bael was ready.

"I was beginning to worry..." he began.

Samael extended his palm toward Bael and shouted, "*Tor bre...*" but Bael intercepted him, flashing fingers, "*Il Nazim!*"

The goblins were still in full voice, and Samael seized up, his arms retracting to curl at the joints and plaster themselves against his sides. His face registered the shock of being interrupted mid-spell, but his voice was no longer his to command. His balance likewise compromised, Samael's body turned in a slow circle, before starting a ponderous fall to crash to the earth with a clatter of armor.

Bael made a motion which cut off the goblin's chant, and as the last echoes fled the chamber, a profound silence fell. He allowed a dramatic pause, to let the impact of his capture of Samael sink in. Samael was one of the stronger Ba'ath, and to see him handled so easily was a shock to the rest. *Well, there is more to come*, thought Bael.

He reached down to pull the leather bag at his waist open, the one containing the fingers of his coalition.

"Have you forgotten your commitment to this fraternity so soon? So easily? I'm sorry, but I have your word, and I mean to hold you to it." He turned the bag over, tumbling the fingers out onto the dais. They wiggled ineffectually on the stone like blind worms.

"I will have you in your proper place," said Bael, using a simple levitation spell to lift Samael and send him floating over to the dais reserved for him.

"Very good. Now that we are all here, it is time to send for Mother. It is time to ask her to break the Compact. We have the majority, we have the right, and now it is our time." Looking around at his fellow Ba'ath, he saw that, for the moment, he still had them. Had any of them known what he was about to attempt next, they would have fled en masse from the chamber. He couldn't allow that to happen, because he still needed all of them. If he could take the chance, he would explain his plan to them. Why break the Compact? The only thing that would accomplish is to remove the restriction of using their magic directly against humans, and initiate renewed conflict between the Ba'ath. No, he had grander plans than just a return to the ancient days, and he had already proven it could be done. He could barely contain the glee he felt at the ease of capturing Samael, only a flicker of the power available to him through this arcane power grid. He was capable of so much more, and he was ready to reveal the extent of his power to his brethren. Bael was going to capture Mother Nature.

43

NOW THE CHASE

JACK'S DESCRIPTION OF WHERE he thought the wight was hiding sent Lucius into an excited frenzy of preparation. He pushed a four-foot length of chain into Jack's hands, and took one for himself. Jack also noticed he had stuck Hank's knife through his belt. Lucius quickly restrung chains across his doorway, and pulled it shut as they left the cabin. The day had waned away, and the dark clouds that had been threatening all day started to release small patters of rain. It would be dark soon, so Lucius lit a lantern and the pair were off, striding down the path.

Jack soon realized they were headed toward the mine. Perhaps Lucius had misunderstood, "Lucius, this isn't the way..."

"I know boy, but I need to get something first."

Jack nodded and they hiked on. A short time later they were trudging up the slope to the mine. Jack was breathing hard with effort by the time they walked onto the apron in front of the mouth of the mine, and darkness was falling fast. There was no one around, and the lamps hung around the site were unlit.

Lucius stopped just inside the mouth of the mine, "Here, you hold this," he said, thrusting the light into Jack's hands. "I'll be right back." He turned and in three strides had disappeared into the blackness.

He was only gone moments before he returned, a small bundle in his left hand, wrapped in an oilskin. "Here, I'll carry the lantern now. Let's go."

They started back down the mountain, and took the well-worn path which led off the main road, heading toward the miner's camp. Full darkness had fallen now, and the only light available was the lantern, and the not-too-distant specks of light from the camp. The rain had also started to fall a little heavier now, although it still wasn't a true rainstorm. They wound their way down to the camp, but when they reached the outer edge, they headed around to the west. They were making no effort to hide their presence though, and dogs barked as they walked past the various shelters the miners had erected for themselves and their families. They skirted a number of open tents, the people inside staring out with shining eyes and worn expressions. Jack nodded a few greetings, but for the most part, just kept his head down and followed in Lucius' wake.

As they rounded the edge of the camp, they came to the bank of the stream running through it. Although the rain had only been falling a short time, the stream was already gurgling and the current a little stronger than normal. It was not yet a rushing muddy mess however, and Lucius and Jack turned to follow the bank northwest into the forest.

They left the comforting yellow lights of the camp behind as they entered under the eaves of a great oak, and then a profusion of trees and vegetation closed in on all sides as they stepped further into the darkness. Many trees were starting to shed their leaves, carpeting the forest floor, but there were still plenty left on the branches, however, and the rain was all but stopped by the canopy of overlapping cover. After moving along the path for another ten minutes or so, Lucius stopped under the branches of a tall pine. Setting the lantern on the carpet of needles, he got down on his knees and motioned for Jack to do the same. Once Jack had done so, Lucius took the oilskin bundle and laid it on the ground between them.

"The book said we had to completely destroy this thing to kill it," he said, as he un-wrapped the object. "I believe this will do the job." He held up two sticks of dynamite, bound together with twine, their fuses twisted together. Matches were also in the oilskin wrap, and Lucius held one up as he explained.

"Once we get inside the cave, we're going to have to find it, try to block it in somehow, and then blow it all to hell."

Jack nodded, "What do you want me to do?"

"I need you to be ready to light these, and throw them where they will do the most good. And you have to do exactly what I tell you, do you understand? No matter what it is, do you agree?" At Jack's nod, Lucius reached into his pocket and pulled out the gemstone. Even in the dim light it glittered brilliantly. He held it up between them with his thumb and forefinger.

"I want you to have this. It is a very special thing, and it will help keep you safe."

The beauty of the gem alone made it a wondrous gift, but Lucius placed it in Jack's open hand, and explained, "This is the God-stone. Put it in your mouth."

"In my mouth?" Jack asked reflexively.

"I will explain, but for now, just trust me."

"I trust you with my life," Jack said with a small rueful smile.

Lucius grinned back, "And I trust you with mine. Go on now…"

Jack slipped the polished stone into his mouth, feeling it clack as his tongue trapped it against his teeth. Then his perception of the world around him changed. He looked around in amazement, the darkness lifting, until it seemed like an early dusk instead of the stygian blackness of a few seconds ago. Looking around, he saw the forest was filled with glowing lights. Thousands of tiny, pale-amber points, as small as the head of a pin, were scattered everywhere, on trees, in the soil and leaf litter. Other larger lights glowed from various spots around them; in the bole of a tree, drifting in the water.

Lucius smiled, and Jack watched as he spoke in slow-motion, "Now… take… it… out…"

Jack took the stone out of his mouth, and the world went

black again.

"Wh...What was that?!" he exclaimed, breathing hard. "It was beautiful!"

"That is the power of the God-stone. With it, you can see all the life around you, no matter where it is hiding. Natural things are this gold color," he said, pointing at a champagne-colored sparkle, "while faerie creatures are blue. If something dangerous is around, you will know. It can protect you while you sleep too."

Lucius smiled at the stunned look on Jack's face, "Did you notice how slow everything moved? The God-stone doesn't slow the world down, it makes you faster. You can't move as fast as you *think* you can move, but it will be fast enough. That may help keep you safe tonight. Now, when we leave out of here, I want you to use this. Keep a lookout around us, and make sure you tell me if anything is getting too close."

Lucius picked up the lantern and turned to start back up the path. Jack was two steps behind him as he slipped the God-stone back into his mouth. Once again, the darkness lifted until the whole forest was visible in the grey-blue hues of twilight, and various golden dots surrounded them as they pushed along. Up ahead, Lucius appeared to be trapped in syrup, ponderously lifting one foot, swinging it forward, and finally stamping it down with a thud before hauling the next foot forward. It was all Jack could do to resist zipping past him to lead the way.

Jack spotted two blue dots, one very small, and the other larger, perhaps as big as a squirrel, and he tapped

Lucius. It seemed to take at least three seconds before he came to a halt and looked at Jack, who pointed to the blue lights. Both were probably thirty to forty yards away, but even as he pointed, the larger one winked out, and Lucius smiled, "Yes..., I... saw... them, nothing... to... worry...about!" He turned and resumed his slow stomp up the trail.

Jack knew they were close from the rounded boulders he recognized in the stream, and momentarily he heard the sound of the waterfall. They were closing in on the wight.

44

TRACKING JACK

AN HOUR AFTER Emma Baker had left the office, Mr. French returned, but had no good news to report. He had returned to inform Thomas one of his deputies had failed to return to conduct his assigned patrol. It was Hank, their supply wagoneer, and when Mr. French had sent some men out to check his home, they found it aflame. They couldn't say whether or not Hank was inside the house, but the circumstances were suspicious indeed.

Thomas didn't know what to make of Hank's disappearance however, because right now he was distracted by the thought that he hadn't seen Jack since last evening. Abigail's disappearance had already been hard enough on Elizabeth, Thomas needed to at least know Jack was safe.

"I am headed to the miner's camp, ride with me will you?"

The two men mounted horses and turned their heads south. Trotting down Main Street got them plenty of sullen stares, but no one dared speak their mind. Thomas kept his head and eyes straight forward and kept riding.

A few minutes and the lights of the mining camp came into view. Although the rain wasn't falling very hard, it was enough to cause drops of water to hang from the brim of his hat, occasionally merging to form one fat enough to drop. Both men trotted along mutely as they came within hailing distance of the camp.

"I want to see if Jack is with Eli before I try the house," he explained. They walked their horses into the camp proper, and made their way through the shanties and tents to the one in which Eli and his father lived. It was a modest little slat-shack, with a stove pipe sticking up from the short roof, and smoke puffing out of it.

"Hullo Donovan!" Mr. French called out as he dismounted. The door to the little cabin swung open and Eli's father stuck his head out, wild, unkempt hair blowing around his face.

"Hullo gents," he answered with a grin and a nod. His face sobered as he saw Thomas, "Mr. Rutherford, I'm real sorry to hear about your little girl. Any news?"

Thomas swallowed, "No, not yet, but I was hoping Jack was with Eli. Have you seen him?"

By way of response, Donovan turned back into the cabin and called Eli out. The boy stepped out of the door, heedless of the rain, concern on his face.

"No sir, I haven't seen Jack since yesterday," he said, "but he was on horseback and moving fast."

"Any idea where he was headed?"

"No sir."

"Mr. Rutherford?" a voice queried. Thomas turned in his saddle to see a bristly-bearded miner standing near the mouth of a sodden tent. The scrawny man was in a long-handle undershirt, with the suspender straps of his trousers off his shoulders.

"Yes?"

"I saw your boy just a few minutes ago, passed by this camp in fact."

"You don't say, where is he then?"

"I can't say for sure, he was with that Lucius fellow, and they was walking that way," he said, pointing west.

"West?" Thomas said quizzically, raising an eyebrow, and looking at Mr. French, "There's nothing to the west but forest, correct?"

"That's right sir."

"Sir, me and Jack have a fishing spot up that way," said Eli, "I can show you the way if you want." Eli looked at his father who nodded, and he ducked back into the cabin to reappear a second later with a lantern and his hat in hand.

Eli was on foot, and led them out of the camp following the streambank. It was less than one-hundred-and-fifty yards to the treeline, and Thomas felt a sense of foreboding as the dark mass loomed before him. The rays of Eli's lantern barely seemed to penetrate the shadows around them as they dismounted. He and Mr. French wrapped the reins of their horses around some low-hanging branches, and the three of them stepped under the eaves of the trees. The light patter of the rain was significantly less under the forest canopy, which made the forest suddenly seem much quieter.

Eli started into the forest along a footpath that looked more worn by animals than by humans. Narrow, with trees and thorn-thickets on either side, they were obliged to walk single file.

Something is wrong, Thomas thought. *I can barely see my hand in front of my face, how could they be searching for Abigail out here?* A suspicion began forming in his brain – perhaps he hadn't heard from the kidnappers yet because they wanted both of his children. Maybe Lucius was involved.

"Jack!" he called out, cupping his hands around his mouth. "Jack!"

Both Eli and Mr. French took up the call, yelling into the darkness as they walked.

45

NAI'AH

THE RASPY THRUM of the goblin's chant filled the chamber, as Bael's hands flashed in an intricate weave, preparing the arcane spells he was about to unleash. His companions were likewise posted on their daises, standing erect, heads back, arms outstretched, lending their energy to the grid as well. He smiled to himself as another wave of pure eldritch power surged into his body. Little did they know that once a part of the spell, they could not simply walk away.

He couldn't escape the small inner dialogue going on within him, his future plans ripe to bursting. With Mother his obedient captive, he would use her powers to decimate the humans. He would magnify every natural disaster in the world ten-fold, a hundred-fold! He would scour the coasts of every human, letting the birds and the denizens of the deep feed on their carcasses. When they fled from the chaos into the hills to hide in holes and caves, then he would bring down an ice age, one that would rob the humans of their food sources, and the warmth they needed to live. He would freeze them all to death. Well, not all. The point was to bring the humans back under control, back into the order the Creator surely wanted them to achieve. Once they were under control and recognized Bael's ultimate authority, then he would relent and allow them to return to a peaceful way of life, subject to his instructions. In the end, this was for their own good, and the Ba'ath's as well. Bael was convinced that once the world was returned to the Ba'ath's dominance, the Creator would reveal himself to them again. Then he would reap the rewards of his bravery, his courage, and his dedication. Their ancient powers would be restored to them, and the past three millennia will have been one long nightmare, soon to be forgotten.

Once more, the golden bowl had been filled with water, and left at the base of the tree. Once more, Bael intoned the summoning spell, *"Il nath tor da braukin fer!"*

The steam rose from the bowl, quicker now that so much energy was being put into the spell. Roiling dark smoke covered the island, and the tree began to shiver and sway. The shaking became more violent, and several leaves fell, drifting down to land on the pool's surface. The bole of the tree began to warp and smooth, depressions appearing to create eyes and a mouth. A mouth which was stretched open in a fury.

Bael almost smiled to himself, and pushed more energy into the spell, dragging Mother to the chamber against her will.

A pair of eyes suddenly sprang open on the bole,

glaring with rage directly at Bael, but also taking in the rest of the scene. The branches of the tree were swinging wildly now, becoming lithe and pliable. The muffled sound of Mother's voice gained volume, and Bael glanced to either side, watching as his companions blanched at their own audacity in summoning Mother. It was time for the coup' de gras. He drew all the power he could summon, and spit the words of the binding spell, the very one that had captured Samael, "*Il nazim!*"

Instantly, the tree froze, a few final leaves quietly floating down to the ground. Mother's eyes were wide and unbelieving. He heard whimpers of dismay from the other Ba'ath, and saw them struggling to break free from the grid, disengage themselves from this deed and flee, but they were his captives as well.

"Mother!" he called, "I have a task for you."

46

SETTLING IN

THE GOD-STONE'S AMAZING properties aside, it made both movement and communication agonizingly slow, so Jack popped it out of his mouth as they neared the waterfall. A black curtain of darkness instantly fell over his vision, and for a moment he was disoriented before the pitiful light cast by the lantern anchored his view of the world. The forest had opened up around the pool of the waterfall's terminus, and everything was colored in deep shades of blue or black. The sound of the waterfall pounding down into the water and onto rocks created another point of reference for him.

Lucius came to a halt a dozen yards from the boulder Eli had been fishing from and surveyed the waterfall.

"I've been past here a time or two over the years, but I never thought to look behind the falls," he whispered, shaking his head. "Now listen, I'll go in first, and you give me a chance to get down in there before you follow, okay?"

At Jack's nod he continued, "I've never seen one of

these things before. When I find it and get it bound, you light the dynamite, throw it, then get out of there, you understand boy?" Jack nodded again.

Lucius searched the trees surrounding them until he located a cedar tree.

"This will be safe for you. Remember where this tree is, and when you come out of that cave, you run straight here and claim sanctuary."

"I understand Lucius. This is too dangerous, why can't we wait until daylight?" Jack asked.

Lucius looked down at him, his goblin eye seeming to flare, "I can't, I've been hunting this thing my whole life, every since they took Isreal. If it's there in that cave, I'm not taking any chances on it getting away. If you can't help, I understand. No shame in being afraid."

"I am afraid, but that's not what I meant. Of course I'm coming. Let's go."

Lucius smiled and made an eating motion to indicate Jack should replace the God-stone, then turned to walk toward the waterfall.

Jack popped the God-stone back into his mouth, picked up the lantern and the oil-wrapped dynamite and caught up to Lucius easily. In his perception, they slow-motion stomped their way over to the corner of the bank that gave easiest access to the cliff down which the waterfall tumbled. Lucius eased out onto the broken and irregular ledges and began sidling along towards the torrent of thundering water. Impatiently, Jack waited as Lucius disappeared behind the ghostly pale curtain of water.

Jack counted to twenty to himself before following in Lucius' steps, careful to hold the lantern and dynamite under his body to protect it as much as possible from the spray. There was a slight gap between the cliff and the waterfall that allowed him to angle underneath without getting too wet. He kept moving until the feeble glow of the lantern showed him the opening of the cave.

He saw Lucius standing with his back to him, chain in his left hand, looking down into a maw of darkness, like the throat of some great beast from legend. It terrified him to imagine what waited in the darkness, but he stepped to Lucius' side and held the lantern up.

"Jack," he whispered looking down, "take...out... the dynamite... and... open... the... lantern... so... you... can light... it."

Jack did as he was told, and stood watching as Lucius took Hank's knife from his waist with his goblin hand and began to make his way into the darkness. As Lucius' form faded into the darkness, Jack took a step forward with the lantern to keep him in view.

The tunnel ran about fifty feet in before it widened out to a small cavern, not quite as big as Lucius' cabin. Shadows flew and danced in every direction as the lantern light played over stalactite and stalagmite formations throughout the space.

The air inside the cave was cool and moist, and as he moved the light around the cavern, a bat lazily broke away from the wall and butterfly-flitted past Jack and towards the entrance. It seemed he could have simply plucked it out of the air.

The cavern appeared to be a dead-end, and Jack was about to conclude their quarry wasn't there, when something caught his eye.

Lucius made his way across the cavern to a deep shadow, which lay in a crevice in the southern wall. Suddenly, he stopped, and with his left fist still gripping the chain, motioned for Jack to freeze. Looking past Lucius and into the crevice, Jack saw what had alerted him; a slowly boiling dark mist was barely visible in the scattered light of the lantern. The wight was home.

Lucius took one step backward and turned, his eyes wide, "Light... the... dynamite... " he started, but before Jack could move to obey, the most fearsome monster he had ever imagined burst out of the crevice. He screamed as the fetid figure of the wight erupted from its hiding place and lunged at Lucius. The skin was mottled purple and green, and its' long moldering hair flew about the head like a medusa. It hissed its' hatred and anger and the horror of the black mouth with the long jagged teeth almost caused Jack's heart to seize.

Lucius tried to whip back to meet the wight's attack, but it had been too fast, and it wrapped long black arms around him as it sank its' teeth deep into his goblin shoulder.

"Aaaaahh!" Lucius yelled, the attack carrying them downward, pulverizing a long, thin stalagmite as they crashed to the ground. The wight held him tight and began worrying the flesh of his shoulder ferociously, like a dog with a rat. Lucius was able to turn Hank's knife into the wight however, and began thrusting it viciously into the creature's guts. The first few thrusts seemed to have no effect, but then the wight lifted its' head and hissed into his face as it tried to grab his goblin hand. It snapped and bit at Lucius as he thrust the knife again, this time into the wight's back. It arched up scrabbling with a hand for the knife, and that allowed Lucius to bring his other hand up to grab the monster's throat.

Jack could only yell in short exclamations as he fumbled with the lantern cover. He considered trying to strike with his chain, but was afraid he would hit Lucius.

The two wrestled across the floor, hissing and grunting. Although the knife remained stuck in its' back, the wight had managed to gain control of Lucius' goblin arm, pinning his wrist to the ground. It easily broke his left-hand grip on its' throat, and with a hard upward thrust, lifted its' body, then used the powerful downward momentum to slam a hammer-fist into Lucius' chest. His breath was expelled by the blow, and he seemed to fold in on himself in pain. The wight reared up again, and slammed another fist down, this time striking him in the head, a loud smack sounding through the cave. Jack saw a spray of blood arc from Lucius' scalp, and his head wobbled like jelly. He tried feebly to defend himself with his left arm, but it was obvious the blow had hurt him severely.

"Light... the... dynamite...! RUN...!" Lucius roared. It was simply impossible. Jack would not leave him. If they both had to die in this chamber, then so be it.

With the power of the God-stone lending unnatural speed to his movements, Jack rushed over to the combatants, swinging his chain into the side of the wight's face, and reaching for Hank's knife. The wight flinched as the knife was withdrawn, but Jack struck it six quick times between the neck and shoulder blades, driving it as deep as he could each time. The ghoul turned toward Jack, trying to sweep him away with his arm, but Jack had already danced out of the way. He darted back in again, stabbing and slashing the creatures' back to ribbons.

The wight released its' hold on Lucius, and whirled to face Jack. His speed was incredible though, and he charged in again, this time aiming to spear the knife into the monster's throat, but before he could finish the move, he saw the wight's fist coming up to meet him. He watched as it drove toward his abdomen, and even with his God-stone quickness, he was unable to avoid the rib-crushing blow.

It thundered into his stomach, driving the air from his body and blowing him back across the room. He crashed into the lantern, breaking it into pieces and spilling flaming oil everywhere. Jack writhed on the ground, struggling to regain his breath while his body tried to retch. With his expelled breath, the God-stone had flown out of his mouth and now lay in the dirt of the cave, glinting in the dying light.

The ghoul stood and shambled over to Jack, heedlessly stepping through the throbbing pool of burning oil. Jack sucked in a great gasp of air as his lungs re-inflated, and he scuttled backwards, even while his stomach tried to vomit its' contents. Jack whimpered as the wight knelt down and grabbed him by the hair. It gnashed its' teeth a few times before reaching its' other hand to grasp his jaw and force his mouth open. Jack's feet kicked and scratched at the dirt floor, while he tried to push the beast away from him. Then, terror of terrors, a long, thick black tongue slid out of the creature's mouth like a serpent, its' face bending toward his. He was about to die.

"Jack!" Jack's eyes cut to see his father holding a torch in one hand and a pistol in the other.

Jack screamed for help, and Thomas rushed over, jamming the torch into the wight's face and firing a shot directly into its' breast, but the wight swatted the torch away, and with a hiss, stood to face Thomas.

"Oh my God...!" Thomas began as he saw the corrupt thing he was facing. He fired twice more at the lich, with no visible effect.

Then, even as he stared into the creature's eyes, a loop of chain swung around the monster's neck, and it was pulled away from him.

Lucius had slung his chain around the wight's neck from behind, and now he jerked and lunged backwards, pulling the wight off its feet. He quickly brought one end of the chain over and around a thick stalagmite and pulled with all his might, crushing the beast's neck and head against the formation. If the wight had been a living thing, this alone would have killed it.

"Light the damned dynamite!" Lucius shouted, gasping with effort.

Still doubled over, Jack reached for the sticks of dynamite, but his father beat him to it, and he lit the fuse in one of the pools of burning oil.

"Jack, get out of here!" he yelled, training his pistol on the wight. The ghoul hissed violently, swinging its' taloned hands, trying to catch someone, anyone. Lucius had his feet braced against the stalagmite, and threw the ends of the chains together in a hitch to hold the creature.

Jack scrabbled for the faintly glinting God-stone, locked his fingers around it and lurched to his feet.

"Run boy, I'll be right behind you!" Lucius yelled.

"Go!" his father yelled, pushing Jack down the tunnel.

With one last look back, Jack began scrambling down the tunnel toward the waterfall. He stopped at the curtain of thundering water and turned back toward the chamber in time to see his father throw the dynamite at the wight's feet. Lucius jumped up and circled around the creature towards the tunnel. The wight redoubled its' efforts to free itself, and his father began firing into the wight's body, but Lucius pushed him into the tunnel. They were heading toward Jack, his father moving at a quick jog, Lucius stumbling along behind.

The wight struggled and thrashed, and Jack stared with horror as it suddenly writhed out from under the chain and stood up, baleful eyes staring toward the retreating men. They were still a good twenty feet away from Jack when it hissed and ran after them. Jack screamed incoherently, pointing toward the wight, and the two men quickened their trot into a sprint. They were still ten feet from Jack when the entire world disappeared in a monstrous explosion.

Orange flame filled Jack's vision as the concussive blast wave picked him off his feet, and spit him out of the cave through the waterfall. His body splashed into the water, cool darkness settling over him as he drifted, suspended in the medium of the stream, and then he knew no more.

47

DEFEAT

"MOTHER!" BAEL CALLED, I HAVE a task for you."
The words were barely out of his mouth when the
unthinkable happened. The vast bank of magical energy
supporting his spell just...evaporated.

He stood shocked for a second, as Mother wavered,
then began to move independently again. Silence reigned,
and his goblins were lying on the ground, curled up and
shaking. Of almost two-score goblins, there couldn't have
been more than five remaining upright, and those fled
screaming, terrified, from the chamber.

In the space of a single heartbeat, his fellow Ba'ath had
regained their freedom, and with curses and cries, they
were popping out of existence as quickly as possible. The
charcoal vapor of their departure wafted through the
chamber. In two more heartbeats, the goblins had been
returned to their original forms as human children. They
stood or sat in their holes, stunned and ragged, staring
around open-mouthed at each other and the scene being
played out in front of them.

He had failed, and he barely had time to contemplate his fate before Mother rushed toward him with a roar of fury that made him quail with fear. At the last instant her taloned hands slashed through the smoke where he had just stood. Bael had escaped.

48

THE WATCHER

THE STEADY AMBER LIGHT of Lumis colored everything as Blixt sat with his feet dangling over the edge of a precipice. He was in no danger of course, but the remote location would make it difficult to be found, and right now, he was in no mood to be found.

Bael was set upon his course to break the Compact, and all Blixt could do was watch. The Compact stated no Ba'ath could actively oppose another, nor directly aid any human in opposing one of their brethren. He had probably gone too far already by helping Lucius and Jack. The hiding of the girl wasn't the violation, it was the message he had sent the boy. A simple flick of his hand, just a little suggestion, and he had planted the seed of inspiration in finding the wight's lair. Strictly speaking, he hadn't helped Jack oppose another Bael, merely pointed him in the direction of the creature he sought. A fine line to be sure.

He sensed the approach of the Watcher, and he sat motionless as it delivered its' report.

"Master, the Grendl is destroyed, and the Loki are returned."

Blixt arched one eyebrow, "I see." He looked out over the desolate valley below. "Very good Lucius. You and this...Jack." He shifted, reappearing on earth in a puff of smoke in the chamber the Watcher had been surveilling.

It was a scene of stunned chaos. The living tree in the center of the chamber still shivered slightly since, unbeknownst to Blixt, Mother had just left. Two score children now shuffled around the chamber, scared and pitiful. Some of them were starting to cry.

Blixt began to whistle a soft tune, a happy little melody, while he flashed his fingers, weaving the spell...of forgetfulness.

The smell of a spring flowering washed over them, their panic and fear subsided, and several of them made their way out of the cavern.

Blixt watched for a moment, before walking over to kneel down on the central dais. Six fingers still wriggled on the stone, and he scooped them into a pocket. *These will come in handy now*, he thought.

Taking one last look around, Blixt was pleased. *Only one more piece of business to take care of*, he thought, vanishing in a hazy puff of smoke.

49

FAREWELL

JACK FIRST BECAME AWARE of a muffled splashing noise, before he felt hands grab him, and pull him to the surface.

"Jack! Jack!" panted Eli, "Oy, hey, wake up now!"

He fluttered his hand and choked, even as Eli waded back toward the bank, tugging Jack along by his shirt. He pulled Jack most of the way out of the water, turned him on his side and knelt down next to him. Jack choked and coughed water up as Eli pounded him on the back, until he raised his hand for relief.

"I'm alright," he said weakly. He lay there for a moment just trying to catch his breath, but then his mind came back to the present, and he pushed himself into a sitting position, looking around frantically. The waterfall was no longer falling with its' normal pounding rhythm, due to the collapse of the tunnel. The entire face of the cliff had crumbled in on itself, and the water was now making new paths down to rejoin the stream. Eli had a lantern, and Jack could see Mr. French nearby with a torch stuck in the ground. He worried over the body of a man, and Jack pushed himself up to crawl towards him on all fours.

Eli grabbed him under the arms and hauled him to his feet, throwing Jack's arm around his neck and walking him over to Mr. French.

As they drew closer, Jack saw his father, lying on his back a few yards away, groaning, but he did not appear to be seriously injured. The man Mr. French was seeing to was Lucius, and he wasn't moving at all.

Jack slid to the ground next to Lucius, and Mr. French sat back on his heels. Lucius' chest was still, and either blood or water darkened the ground under his body. His goblin arm rested on his chest, and his clothing had been ripped to shreds in the blast; it appeared he had taken the brunt of the explosion.

His father crawled over to kneel next to him, and put his hand on Jack's shoulder.

"He saved me Jack, maybe both of us. He shielded my body with his own. I owe him a great debt."

Jack nodded, his face flushing and hot tears forming in his eyes. They rolled down his face, but he did nothing to stop them. He did not sob, but merely stared down at Lucius, so still and small in death. His eyes were open, staring at a point in the night sky. Mr. French reached down and gently closed his eyelids. They all sat in silence, contemplating the remains of a brave man.

Several minutes went by before their reverie was interrupted by sounds of people shouting, and a line of lights appeared, moving up the path toward them.

Miners in the camp had heard the explosion, and a number of them had come to see what had happened. As they gathered around, Mr. French directed several of them to help put Lucius' body onto his horse to be taken back to town. Jack listened numbly before suddenly remembering the God-stone, and frantically checked his clothing for the precious relic. He had lost it. It was still in his hand when the dynamite exploded, and now it must be somewhere at the bottom of the stream. He peered into the dark water, torch and lantern light flitting over the surface, but no telltale glimmers appeared. The shock of the loss flitted through his mind, *It was his gift to me.*

That brought to mind the wooden box in Lucius' cabin and...*Abby!* Jack caught himself and quickly walked over to his father. Thomas had somewhat recovered, and stood near Lucius' body, speaking to the miners. Jack grabbed his shirt-sleeve and tugged insistently, pulling Thomas away from the crowd.

"Yes Jack, what is it?" he asked.

Jack held a finger to his lips, and whispered, "I know where Abby is."

50

REUNITED

THE YELLOW LIGHT of the lamp was now the only light in the room, as full dark had fallen outside. John sat spellbound as Grandpa Jack continued...

"I didn't know in what sort of circumstances we would find Abigail, so my father and I went alone to Lucius' cabin, but when we got there, she sat on the edge of the bed, her dress torn and bedraggled, swinging her crossed feet under her. She hummed a little song, and when she saw us, her face broke into a dreamy kind of smile. That was the first time I ever saw my father cry. I'll never forget it.

Of course, we rushed Abigail home to mother, and after all the tears, our home and family was whole again. It was both one of the saddest, and happiest days of my life."

"What about the rest of them? The children, I mean," asked John.

"They wandered out of the forest that day, and the next, and for a few days after that in ones and twos. The ones Lucius hid in the pool found their way to town on the fourth day, filthy and hungry. It was a miracle.

The people of Cobbs were overwhelmed – children who had gone missing ten, twenty, thirty years ago were now returned! It was hard for many people to understand, particularly because the children appeared to be the same age as they were when they were taken, no matter how long ago. Emma James' daughter was returned, as was Hank's son, and dozens of others. None of them though, remembered anything about where they had been, or *what* they had been. Several were true orphans now, their parents or family having passed away in their absence. Some were obvious immigrants, speaking only German, or maybe Dutch, but every single child was taken in by the townsfolk.

We buried Lucius next to his cabin. That was a very hard day for me, but Father ordered a specially-cut marble headstone, and we held a nice ceremony in his honor. I explained what I knew at the time to Father, and although my story must have stretched the very limits of his imagination, he believed me. He also realized that without Lucius, we never would have recovered Abigail.

Of course, that wasn't common knowledge, most folks just assumed father was showing his appreciation for Lucius having saved his life in an accidental explosion.

The repatriation of the children wasn't something we talked about either. It was too strange a situation, and that sort of story would have invited outsiders to come in and start asking questions. There was plenty of guilt about the lottery to keep people from wanting to talk about it. They had their children back, and that was enough. Now they just wanted to get back to living their lives.

"Did you move back to Philadelphia?"

"Surprisingly, no. The townsfolk connected father's actions with the recovery of their children, and after that, he could do no wrong. All he had to do was wish a thing to be done, and it was done. Abigail and I were treated like royalty, and it turned out to be a wonderful place to spend a childhood."

Grandpa Jack sighed, and squinted at John, "Now, do you believe my story?"

John nodded – because he truly did believe. As incredible as it was, the evidence he had been shown, together with Grandpa Jack's demeanor convinced him he was absolutely sincere.

"Good. Because like I told you, I need you to do something for me; for us, this family."

His heart pounding, John gulped and asked, "Sure, Grandpa, what do you want me to do?"

Grandpa Jack leaned in, "I need you to find Lucius."

"What? You mean his grave? Where he's buried?" John asked confused.

"His grave?" Grandpa Jack asked, "Of course not! Lucius isn't dead."